"I see that you have a reckless flirtation with ruination," Tristan remarked

"So it would seem," Annica replied. "Or could it be that you have a talent for catching me at my worst?"

"Are you ever at anything else?" he parried.

"If that is what you think, I wonder that you bother with me, m'lord." She felt the cut to her slowly awakening heart.

"Were it not for our contract, I wonder if I would."

"I release you from your obligation. Destroy our contract."

"You would like that, would you not? Then you could avoid the issue at hand."

"I do not know what you mean," she faltered, knowing full well what he was suggesting.

He stopped mere inches from her, and his eyes met hers directly, forbidding her the escape of looking away. "I think you are very aware of what is happening here, Annica...!"

**Harlequin Historicals is delighted
to introduce Gail Ranstrom
and her intriguing debut title,**

A Wild Justice
Harlequin Historical #617—July 2002

GAIL RANSTROM

A Wild Justice

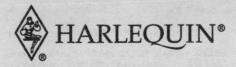

HARLEQUIN®

TORONTO • NEW YORK • LONDON
AMSTERDAM • PARIS • SYDNEY • HAMBURG
STOCKHOLM • ATHENS • TOKYO • MILAN • MADRID
PRAGUE • WARSAW • BUDAPEST • AUCKLAND

ISBN 0-373-29217-1

A WILD JUSTICE

Copyright © 2002 by Gail Ranstrom

Visit us at www.eHarlequin.com

Printed in U.S.A.

Please address questions and book requests to:
Harlequin Reader Service
U.S.: 3010 Walden Ave., P.O. Box 1325, Buffalo, NY 14269
Canadian: P.O. Box 609, Fort Erie, Ont. L2A 5X3

For Jerry, who taught me that love heals.
Always in all ways, my love.

With special acknowledgment to the original
Wednesday League. Rosanne, Margaret and Donna,
who kept me encouraged, focused and laughing.
Ladies, you're the best. Let's do this again.

Prologue

London, 1816

The library doors were locked and a copy of Miss Jane Austen's *Sense and Sensibility* lay open on the low table. Lady Annica Saylcs took her place on the forest-green sofa and nodded at the other four women. "I hereby call this meeting of the Wednesday League to order. Shall we proceed to the business at hand?"

Charity Wardlow put her teacup aside and sat forward, her blue eyes twinkling as they swept over Lady Sarah, Grace, and Constance. "'Nica and I followed Mr. Farmingdale last night. He went to the bordello again. We followed him inside this time."

"What did you see?" Constance Bennington asked, ignoring the gasps of the others, her dark eyes wide with admiration for their daring.

"Mr. Bouldin arranged for the...abbess, a woman named Naughty Alice, to take us to a secret room behind the paneling of one of the rooms. There were peepholes, and we could see and hear everything that transpired. Everything!"

Annica nodded. "Mr. Farmingdale sat at a desk, pen in hand and staring at an open ledger. A woman, clad in...well, bows in the most interesting places, lounged on a settee. He told her to fetch him sherry, and she cringed when he spoke to her. The cad actually laughed! He *relished* her fear.''

Constance sighed, trying to smooth her wiry red hair into the ribbon it had escaped. ''Many men frequent brothels and are cruel. Though it is in poor taste, society turns a blind eye as long as they are discreet. How does this help us, 'Nica?''

'''Twas what he said, Constance. He said, 'I own this place, and that means I own you. Do as I say, or suffer the consequences.''' She waited for the import of her words to register.

Grace Forbush, an elegant widow in her early-thirties, was the first to respond. ''Good heavens! Do you mean to say that Farmingdale is engaged in trade? How…déclassé!''

Annica smoothed the folds of her lavender gown. ''More than mere 'trade,' Grace. Farmingdale is a flesh peddler. Naughty Alice said he had done something that even she could not ignore, and that is why she agreed to help us. I urged, but she would not tell me what he'd done. I think we must assume it was every bit as wicked as what he and the others did to you, Sarah.''

Constance drew a long breath. ''Should this be whispered abroad, Farmingdale would be quite beyond redemption. His entrée to polite society would be withdrawn. Invitations would be withheld, and he would be fortunate not to be challenged for even addressing a female in our circle.''

Lady Sarah Hunter frowned and tucked an unruly chestnut curl behind one ear. Her violet eyes deepened as she recalled the incident. ''I hate what he did to me, and I hate that I cannot leave my house without fearing that I will encounter him, but…''

Annica leaned forward in earnest. ''If it were possible for any of us to obtain justice through the courts, we really would be discussing *Sense and Sensibility* this afternoon.

But you know what society would do with the knowledge that you were attacked. *You* would be the social outcast. *You* would be the one to suffer for it.''

"Farmingdale is the third man of four who assaulted you last autumn," Constance reminded her. "You did not balk at punishing the first two."

"But you must decide, Sarah," Charity Wardlow offered. "'Tis your vengeance and, therefore, your wishes we obey."

"Use the information," Sarah said with a brave tilt of her chin and a voice choked with emotion. "Once it is out, Mr. Farmingdale will surely have to leave London."

"And you will be able to breathe again." Annica smiled. "We shall begin tonight, at the Worthingdon soiree."

Constance looked over the rim of her cup with an air of drama. "Before we adjourn, I must put another matter before you. While reading the *Times* this morning, I stumbled upon a story that reports a woman has gone missing."

"What sort of woman?" Grace asked.

"I believe she is governess to a family in the Kensington district. And she is the third woman to go missing this month."

"Hmm, I wonder where she has gone?" Charity mused.

"Puzzling," Annica agreed. "Who reported her absence? Her employer?"

"Yes. It would appear she is without family. Just the sort we are sworn to champion. As we are nearly done with Sarah's cause, I thought we might take on a new project. Shall we look into the matter?"

"Aye!" The vote was unanimous.

"Oh, this *wild justice* is everything, is it not?" Annica exclaimed. "Richard Farmingdale is about to pay for what he did to our Sarah."

Chapter One

"You asked which of the women present tonight has a reputation for intelligence, capability and loyalty," Julius Lingate said, nodding toward a woman at the far end of the Worthingdons' ballroom. "Lady Annica Sayles fits that description to the letter."

"Go on," Tristan Sinclair, eighth earl of Auberville, interjected, studying the slender line of the woman's back, the dark hair with red glints secured in a tidy chignon at her nape, and the graceful sway of peacock-blue satin as she strolled beside a fair-haired young lady.

"Not much is known about her life in Sussex before coming to live in London. By all accounts her father—"

"The earl?"

Julius nodded and continued, "—was a souse and a particularly unpleasant man. He was in his cups when he insisted on driving the family carriage home from a visit to the vicar's. He came round a bend too fast and tipped the fool thing over. Killed himself and his wife. The valet, who was riding inside when the earl took his place on the box, threw Lady Annica clear, but 'tis said she was never the same afterward. The valet still limps. Lady Annica steadfastly refuses to discuss the event."

"Interesting. And then?"

"The title and ancestral estate went to her uncle Thomas, who is her guardian. She has her mother's estates and property, and has even controlled them for the past three years."

"How long ago was the accident?"

"She was not quite sixteen, so…nine years ago."

"Young for such hurts," Tristan mused, remembering his experiences with betrayal and loss at the hands of his mother. He'd promised himself then that he'd never trust or need a woman again. He'd marry—that much was inescapable for a man in his position—but he wouldn't *need* a woman.

"She buried herself in her art, her books and politics, acquired a reputation as a bluestocking, took up a variety of causes and reforms," Julius droned on. "That's where the problems come in. She has barely managed to stay on the right side of scandal."

Tristan smiled and relaxed. A woman with her own commitments would have little time to demand a depth of commitment he was not willing to give. "I owe you my gratitude, Jules. You have confirmed my own information." He watched the object of their conversation shake her head and send a young man away with a wave of her hand.

"It couldn't have been easy—orphaned, alone, humiliated by the scandal over her father's behavior," Julius continued.

"According to my sources, she was bloody magnificent! She neither confirmed nor denied the rumors." His quarry turned to acknowledge an acquaintance, and he was momentarily dazzled. Even at this distance, he could see the exact color of her wide, sparkling eyes—brownish evergreen, the precise shade of pine trees and wooded glens. In them was a solitary gleam that could not be disguised—the look of a soul who did not believe in love, who did not expect it. The look only a fellow cynic would recognize. Bloody magnificent, indeed!

A delicate pink stained her cheeks and her full mouth curved in a delicious smile that begged ravishment. He drew in a sharp breath. Had he known Lady Annica Sayles was so stunning, he'd not have wasted time making further inquiries. Oh yes, she'd do nicely. "She hasn't had suitors? That is difficult to believe."

"To the contrary, she's had suitors coming out of the woodwork. She smiles sweetly and then makes quick work of them. You saw what happened to that young man—and I'd wager all he asked for was a dance."

Tristan's hands tightened on the balustrade of the staircase landing. "She is rude?"

"Nay! Her manners are impeccable. One would have to experience the chill to comprehend my meaning." Julius grinned.

"Have you?"

"Indeed! Yet we've been cordial since. Now confess. What's behind your fascination with Lady Annica Sayles?"

"I've been busy settling my father's estate in Devon since resigning my commission. Now that all is running smoothly, I am ready to turn my attention to acquiring a wife and begetting an heir. The lady would appear to meet my requirements."

Julius coughed, spraying a mouthful of wine over the landing's Oriental carpet. "*Wife?* Good God, Auberville! You'd do better to court the queen! You cannot be serious."

Tristan thumped him on the back. "If I did not need an heir, I would not marry at all. Women are risky, at best. I want one who will offer the least amount of trouble and not require supervision. In short, I want a capable woman."

"Least amount of trouble? Have you heard a single word I've said?" Julius was incredulous. "Lady Annica isn't suitable at all. She's no biddable miss. With no parents to set her limits, she sets her own. She is beyond capable—she is headstrong. Good God, Tris—she gambles at cards! I believe James Stanford saw her 'blow a cloud' in Bennington's game room. She is considered a *bluestocking*. 'Tis whispered she has been known to wear trousers. She has political views and speaks them. She is engaged in social reform and is not received in certain circles as a result.''

"That will change when she is Lady Auberville. And if one must be bound to a woman for life, she should at least be able to function adequately without constant instruction or supervision, and carry on a conversation regarding subjects other than gowns and social events. A woman I can talk to, Jules. Is that too much to ask?''

Julius raised his eyebrows heavenward. "Lady Annica is unmarried by choice, not lack of offers. If you are set on her, you had better prepare for a fight.''

Lady Annica and her companion paused just beneath their position on the landing. Two other women joined them and they all bent their heads together, their voices dropping to whispers—exchanging some piece of feminine confidence, no doubt. Lady Annica was so lovely and delicate that he could scarcely envision her engaging in the activities Julius described. She laughed at something her companion said, and the delightfully wicked sound sent shivers up his spine.

He had been undecided until a few moments ago. But now, having heard her laugh, he was certain that, if he did not marry her, he would at least know how to provoke that sound. He had some interesting ideas even now.

"Once she learns your intentions, you are not likely to gain entry to her salon," Julius whispered.

Tristan smiled. Diplomacy, strategic planning and expediency were his forte. "Do you think I should give her a sporting chance?''

"That would be quite decent of you, Tris.'' His friend shot him a wry grin. "'Tis more than she'd give you, and I've never known you to give an edge away. Egad! The wagers that will be laid on this. I can't wait to see the carnage. Lady Annica and Auberville! Shall I introduce you now?''

Tristan smiled, the excitement of the game rising in him. ''No. I'd wager the indirect approach would be best. I know her uncle, Lord Thomas Sayles. He may be of some use to me.''

Tristan's lips curved in what his enemies called his ''predatory smile'' when he caught sight of Thomas Sayles, seventh earl of Lakehurst, reading the *Times* in the lounge of White's Club for Gentlemen the following afternoon. This was like the old days in Tunis—diplomacy and negotiations, cat and mouse. Not the bloody covert activities he engaged in now.

''Ah, there you are, Thomas. Hendricks said I might find you here,'' he said in greeting.

His target, a middle-aged man with a gray mustache and balding head, looked up and gave him a distracted smile. ''Auberville. Haven't seen you for a good long while, lad. Is there something I can do for you?''

''No. Just came to pay my respects and say goodbye.''

Lord Sayles perked up and gestured to the deep club chair across from him. He waved for a silent waiter to bring a glass of claret for his guest. ''Going somewhere?''

''I shall be removing to Devon before long.''

''Can't retreat this early in the season, lad. What will the ladies say if you do not give them a fair chance at you? Lucy mentioned your name as one of the season's most eligible.''

''Your wife flatters me, Thomas, but for now I have other things on my mind.''

''What might that be?''

He gave a lazy shrug, leading the conversation. ''Deuced nuisance, really. I've been trying to find an illustrator for a publication on flowering shrubs indigenous to the Cornish coast. All the best artists are contracted. Perhaps I'll have better luck in Devon.''

"Have you tried Beetleson?''

Evidently Thomas was going to need some guiding. "I was hoping to find an original approach. So many of these books have been done that I fear mine will be lost in the stacks unless I have a fresh presentation." Tristan sighed. "I tell you, Thomas, I'd be willing to accept a dilettante at this point.''

"Dilettante, eh? The Ladies Art Society awarded my niece, Annica, a First in oils and watercolors two years running. The watercolor in the foyer here is one of hers.''

"Your niece?" Tristan appeared to consider this for a moment. "Would she engage in such an undertaking? Most women do not want to enter a business arrangement.''

"This is the very thing that would appeal to 'Nica. She has become a most unusual woman.''

"Would her husband allow her to accompany me—chaperoned, of course—to the sites of several specimens?''

"Annica is not married, Auberville. As her guardian, I would not object at all. She could use some outings in male company. She is with her bluestocking friends too much.''

"I would be interested in talking to her, Thomas. I shall send her a note requesting an interview.''

"No!" Thomas raised one hand in a gesture of interdiction. "I wouldn't warn her, were I you. Drop in tomorrow afternoon. Use my name. She will see you as a courtesy to me.''

Tristan assumed an air of deep thought. "If you are certain, Thomas. I wouldn't want to put the lady out.''

"She'd relish the opportunity to prove herself as capable as a man. Be warned, though—she is an unconventional female. She can be quite curt. Doesn't mean anything by it, but doesn't like to waste her time, she says. Good thing you're not a timid man.''

Tristan raised his glass again. "I have dealt with brusque people ere now, Thomas, but thank you for the warning."

Annica set her watering can aside and lifted the gilt-edged calling card from the silver tray. "Tristan Sinclair, Lord Auberville." She flipped the card over to read the scrawled message, "Referred by Lord Thomas Sayles."

She'd heard of the man who was taking London by storm. She raised her eyebrows. What could society's darling want with her? Still, his credentials were impeccable, and she knew her uncle Thomas would be appalled if she declined to receive him.

"Show him to me, Hodgeson," she said in a resigned tone. The greenhouse was an unlikely place to receive callers, but he had not made an appointment, after all.

Her manservant cleared his throat and flushed. "Will you require half an hour to change, milady?"

"Whatever for?" Annica looked down at her trousers, smudged with dirt and grime. Her conscience tweaked her, but only for a moment. "His lordship was not expected. I refuse to set my day in a dither because of an unexpected caller."

"But it is Lord Auberville—"

"Why, so it is." She smiled evenly. "Then I suppose I must be polite. Thank you for the reminder, Hodgeson." She halted further discussion with an airy wave of her hand.

She allowed Hodgeson to act as her social conscience due to her deep affection for him, finding it more difficult to dismiss his pained expressions than her aunt's and uncle's frequent laments. Indeed, Hodgeson's raised eyebrow was the closest thing to a reproach that she ever felt, and his occasional limp was all the reminder she needed of all she owed him.

Glancing about for a place to put her trowel and gloves, she caught sight of a weed beneath her potting bench and bent to remove it. Though she yanked and pulled, the plant was more deeply rooted than she'd thought. She tugged sharply to dislodge it and, when the roots gave way, was unprepared. Her bottom landed with a plop on the hard-packed earth of the greenhouse floor. Dirt sprayed her face. Her braid loosened from its coil and slipped down her back.

"Phooey!" She spat dirt off the tip of her tongue.

From behind, strong hands cupped her elbows and lifted her to her feet. "Are you injured?" a husky voice asked.

She turned to face the new arrival. Disconcerted by what she found, she stood docilely while the man removed a snowy linen handkerchief from his waistcoat pocket and wiped at the dirt across her nose. When she tried to back away, he held her immobile by catching her chin, then tilting her face up to him again.

Warmth crept into her cheeks and she watched a half smile play across sensual lips, causing a rogue dimple to deepen in the man's chin. Clear cool blue eyes that would shame a winter sky twinkled at her, and a cap of dark blond hair streaked golden by the sun topped a face with enough mystery to be interesting. A fading jagged scar ran across his left cheekbone, and she was not aware of touching it until the man smiled again. As he did, a little thrill raced from her fingertips to the back of her neck.

"From a d-duel?" she asked, feeling like a schoolgirl.

"I scarcely know what to say. I'm tempted to answer whatever would most please you."

"The truth pleases me."

"Shell fragment. Trafalgar."

She winced, feeling a sharp stab of pain in her own cheek. Oddly, the mark saved this man from the stigma of masculine beauty and placed him in a far more intriguing category. And, just as odd, she thought she read danger in the smile.

"Lady Annica, I presume?" he murmured, releasing her chin.

She cleared her throat, broke eye contact and stepped back, gathering her wits. "Yes. And you must be Lord Auberville." She waved at the card on the potting bench.

"Have I come at a bad time?"

"Not to be rude, Auberville, but did we have an appointment? I cannot for the life of me remember having met you, let alone having invited you to call upon me."

"We have not met. I came at your uncle's suggestion."

Annica felt a twinge of disappointment and annoyance that this man was going to be just like all the others. For a moment she had wondered if… "I must admit, he came very close this time. You may go now."

"I beg your pardon?"

"Uncle Thomas never tires of throwing fresh meat to the lioness. It has been nearly a year since the last time, though, and I thought he had finally given up."

"I do not…" Auberville lowered his dark blond eyebrows.

"I am unmarried by choice, Auberville. I do not entertain suitors. I am not interested in making any alliances, no matter how sensible or beneficial to both families. I cannot be persuaded by false flattery nor pretty speeches. I am, in short, a hard nut to crack. Take my advice—we shall both be happier if you do not waste your time in the effort."

He spread his arms wide, a picture of innocent confusion. "You have me at a disadvantage, Lady Annica," he said. "I haven't the faintest notion of what you are talking about."

"Did Uncle Thomas not send you to see if we might be what he calls 'a fit'?"

"Good Lord! Is that what you thought?"

Annica frowned when the handsome young earl began laughing. "Is that not the case, Lord Auberville?"

"Not at all, dear woman."

"Then what are you doing here?"

"Botany."

Her mind went blank. "I fear you have *me* at a loss."

"I mentioned to your uncle that I am preparing for publication a treatise on flowering shrubs indigenous to the Cornish coast. My editor has requested a folio of approximately fifteen illustrations. Thomas said you are a talented illustrator, and pointed out an example of your work. I'd pay handsomely, of course."

"Your tea, milady," Hodgeson announced. Unperturbed by the scene before him, he placed the silver tray on a table by a cushioned garden bench and turned to regard her with an impassive face. "Will I be showing his lordship out now, milady?"

"Another cup, Hodgeson."

He lifted one eyebrow slightly before he nodded and left to fetch the cup.

"My apologies, Auberville," Annica murmured, squirming with embarrassment. She must seem like an egotistical chit to the handsome lord. She turned away and slapped the dirt from her trousers. She bent over to put the weed in a basket and rinse her hands in a bucket of water. "I'm apt to assume the worst where Uncle Thomas is concerned. He means well, but I cannot make him understand that I really have no wish to marry. 'Tisn't as if the family line will die with me. Heaven knows, his own children promise to be a prolific lot," she said, glancing over her shoulder. She was surprised to find Lord Auberville watching her with a cryptic expression on his handsome face. The corners of his mouth twitched as if he found something amusing.

"But I must say I am intrigued by your offer." She straightened and turned to face him. "Would I be likely to have the specimens here, in my own collection?"

"There's the rub," he admitted. "The specimens are sufficiently rare as to be generally unavailable. I have located twelve of the fifteen in various conservatories or green-houses in or near London. Three others—the most rare, and therefore the most important—do not thrive under cultiva-tion. They bloom only in mid-August, for a fortnight, on the western coast. They are a variety of phlox, but quite unlike any growing elsewhere.''

"Interesting," Annica conceded. She motioned her caller to the garden bench and took a seat beside him. The extra cup arrived, and she poured for them both. "'Tis mid-May. That will delay your submission until autumn, will it not? Sugar? Milk?"

"Lemon," he requested. "We are not in a hurry. My editor and I would prefer to wait and have the illustrations done properly than rush into publication without them."

"I admire your patience, milord." She dropped a lemon wedge into his cup and handed it to him before adding a drop of milk to her own. "My own experience has indicated that most men are wanting in that regard."

"I assure you, I'm a very patient man." He favored her with an enigmatic smile.

Unaccountably unnerved by that comment, Annica turned back to her duties as hostess. Using the silver tongs to place a slice of sponge cake on a small plate, she arranged several strawberries and a dollop of whipped cream on top. A sprig of mint leaf finished her artful arrangement. She placed a fork on the side and presented him with the dish.

"Thank you, Lady Annica," he said, his voice nearly a purr.

She nodded and took a sip of her tea. "Will you be giving me a list of the plants and conservatories where the speci-mens are to be found?"

"Unfortunately, no. I'd prefer that, of course, but the owners of the conservatories have agreed to allow me access only upon appointment. Wretched inconvenience, but there it is. I suppose we could arrange to go together.''

Annica shrugged, as if indifferent. ''When did you want to begin, milord?'' she asked. ''I do have a few other commitments.''

''Oh, ah, I should think immediately. If we can have the rest done before we have to leave for Cornwall, we could be ready for submission by the end of August.''

''Has your publisher set you a deadline?''

''September 5.''

She frowned and pushed her cake around on her plate with a fork. The thought of taking on such a project was surprisingly appealing, though she couldn't say why. ''I shall put some of my other projects aside in order to accommodate you, Lord Auberville. Give me a day or two to tidy up loose ends.''

''There you are 'Nica! I've looked all over the house. Are you—oh!'' The plump, gray-haired woman stopped short. ''Hodgeson did not tell me we had a guest, dear.''

''I suppose he thought it was of little consequence.''

''Oh, I am certain you do not mean that, Annica.'' The woman smiled apologetically at their guest.

Annica bit her lip, realizing her glaring faux pas. ''Sorry, Auberville. I meant that Hodgeson must have thought my having a caller…not that *you* were of…well.'' She stammered to a halt, then took a deep breath and changed direction. ''Aunt Lucy, may I present Tristan Sinclair, Lord Auberville? My lord, please to meet my aunt, Lady Lucille Sayles.''

Having already come to his feet, he took her aunt's offered hand and bowed over it. ''Lady Sayles, I am charmed.''

Aunt Lucy inclined her head in acknowledgment. ''Do sit down, and please accept my apologies for the interruption.''

''Join us, Aunt Lucy. We have concluded our business.''

"Oh." Her face fell. "I see."

Annica knew what her aunt thought, and laughed. "No, Aunt Lucy, I have not given him 'short shrift.' Auberville came to me with a business proposition at Uncle Thomas's suggestion. I am going to illustrate his treatise on Cornish flowering plants."

"But you've never done that sort of thing."

"Uncle has shown him one of my pieces, and he says my work is acceptable."

"More than acceptable, Lady Annica. Quite charming," Auberville offered.

"You and my husband are acquainted?" Lucy asked.

"We belong to the same club," he explained.

"I see. How fortunate for 'Nica. She has always said she would like to do something of importance. To have her work published in a quality book will be quite an achievement."

Achievement! "Oh, good heavens! I forgot this is Wednesday. The ladies will be waiting at the Book Emporium." Annica sprang to her feet, set her cup aside, kissed her aunt's cheek and backed toward the greenhouse door. "Auberville—my apologies. Aunt Lucy will keep you company while you finish your tea. So good meeting you and all that. See you soon—next week latest."

"Bluestocking society, you know—call themselves the Wednesday League," she heard her aunt lament as she hurried across the lawn. "Spinsters and one widow. So disappointing."

"Psst! Over here, yer ladyship!"

Annica kept her head down and slowly circled the table in one aisle of the bookseller's shop, examining titles as she went. When she came shoulder to shoulder with a short, powerfully built man, she stopped and picked up a copy of *Pride and Prejudice*. "I did not notice you without your red waistcoat, Mr. Bouldin,'' she whispered, referring to the Bow Street Runner's mark of identification.

''You said as 'ow you didn't want to be noticed, yer ladyship.''

''Quite right. It would never do to have society know that I conduct investigations. I fear such a thing would put me far beyond the pale. Now, did you bring information regarding Farmingdale?'' she whispered.

''Aye. 'E's leavin' tomorrow night, just after midnight.'' He passed her a piece of paper. ''That's where an' when.''

''Well done, Mr. Bouldin. My group has another job for you.''

''I gathered as much, yer ladyship.'' The man nodded. ''I already started lookin' for the fourth bloke. What else d'ye 'ave for me?''

She glanced around to be certain she was not observed, then took a piece of paper and several banknotes from her reticule. She slipped them between the pages of the book and returned it to the table, selecting another for examination.

The man scratched his dark head and retrieved the book Annica had just put down. He read the paper and pocketed the banknotes.

''What's this about, Lady A.?''

''Precisely what *we* want to know, Mr. Bouldin.'' Annica glanced toward the door, struggling with unease. ''These women have disappeared without a trace. They must be somewhere. And this morning I received word that Constance Bennington's abigail, Frederika Ballard, did not return from her day off.''

''I've 'eard rumors about this, yer ladyship. I'd leave it alone, was I you.''

Annica lifted her eyebrows slightly. ''I cannot ignore the issue, Mr. Bouldin, because next time it could be one of my friends.''

Chapter Two

Tristan attempted to hide his impatience with the older man across from him. He had more important things to be about this evening than listening to Lord Kilgrew.

"...so you see why I have asked you here, my boy."

"Actually, no," he answered. "Could you speak more plainly, m'lord?"

"We want you to nose about, use your sources and see if there's anything to the rumors, eh? Use your connections, lad. If Mustafa el-Daibul has concocted a white slavery scheme, you'll know it—and know how to deal with it. You've got a singleness of mind that makes you both ruthless and successful. You are unparalleled as a strategist."

Tristan ran his fingers through his hair. He stood and went to look out the dingy office window at the darkened street below. "I resigned when my father died, sir."

"One never resigns from the Foreign Office, Auberville. Nor retires. You knew that going in. And we knew the appeal to you was in the danger and the risks you'd take."

Yes, he'd known. He was painfully aware of his reputation as a dangerous man when he was on assignment. Furthermore, it was no secret that he'd been overruled last year when he'd wanted to put an end to Mustafa el-Daibul after the disastrous Algerian affair, his last mission.

He had been sent to Tunis covertly, along with another unit working independently, in an attempt to locate British hostages held for ransom by the Barbary pirates. But there had been a traitor in their midst during that fiasco, a man they came to call The Turk. They'd had to close the operation down quickly to prevent further damage and deaths. Perhaps Tristan's superiors thought he'd like a chance to even the score now.

Perhaps they were right.

Another assignment would complicate his life somewhat, and complicate his personal plans. But he could not turn away from a chance to even the score and discover the identity of The Turk. "I shall look into the matter, sir," he said, turning from the window.

"Keep it confidential, Auberville. Can't have this business of missing women whispered abroad. Cause a panic and all that."

"Report to you, sir?"

Kilgrew handed him a piece of paper with a name scrawled across it. "Send word to him. He's been put on the problem as well. He has hired a room in Whitechapel for your meetings. He will report to you and act as our liaison. We shall arrange a meeting if circumstances require."

Tristan glanced at the paper. The Sheikh! He knew the code name quite well, one chosen in jest for the man's popularity with women. He counted the man as one of his few friends—one who knew the best and worst of him. He felt the same anger over The Turk's betrayal as Tristan. They would make a good team. The man was as single-minded as he.

"Done," he said, impatient to end the interview. He retrieved his hat, cane and gloves from the table near the door.

"Hear you've set out to find yourself a wife, my boy. About time. Man in your position needs heirs—someone to keep the home fires burning whilst he's off on business."

"So I've heard, sir. Loyalty, someone you can count on, is everything, is it not?" Tristan lifted one eyebrow, neither confirming nor denying the rumor.

Annica Sayles was definitely going to be a worthy opponent, Tristan knew. She'd instructed him to call for her at quarter past one and take her to the first specimen. He'd received royal summonses with less authority than this short missive held.

Once he'd recovered from the shock of finding her in trousers, he'd grown rather fond of the sight. The lady's derrière had looked quite charming as she bobbed and strained, trying to pull the weed. Perhaps he ought to have made his arrival known, but the scene was so amusing he could scarcely move.

And when she bent again, to rinse her hands in the water bucket, he found himself wondering if she had any idea how appealing a woman's bottom in men's trousers could look. He'd concluded she couldn't possibly know. She'd never give him that much pleasure. At least not deliberately. Still, for some unaccountable reason, his heart felt lighter today.

The contrast between Lady Annica's looks and her manners was surprising. Her dark hair and sparkling eyes were sultry and exotic, promising a deeply sensual nature. Her throaty, delicious laugh hinted at a wicked sense of humor. Oh, but her manners! She was all brusque business—at once imperative and self-confident. He found himself wondering which was the real Lady Annica Sayles—the exotic, sensuous woman, or the autocratic little termagant. He was intrigued by the prospect of having either in his bed.

* * *

"Gads! How could I have been so rash?" Annica turned in a wide circle in the center of her little studio, a wide portfolio open on her drafting table.

"I'm certain I could not say, milady," Hodgeson replied. He stood patiently, his hands clasped behind his back, his jutting chin tilted upward. "Lord Auberville is waiting, milady. Perhaps you could inquire of him?"

Annica stopped her frantic rummaging and turned to face the man. What an impish sense of humor he had! "Waiting, Hodgeson? Why did you not tell me?"

"Begging your pardon, milady, I just did."

"Oh. Well, please offer my apologies and tell him I shall be down in a moment." She began stuffing tablets, a palette, brushes, rags and paints into the portfolio. When she glanced up to find Hodgeson still standing inside the door, she took it as a sure sign the man had something to say. "What is it, Hodgeson?"

"Lord Auberville, milady."

"Yes?"

"He has the eyes of a hunter, milady."

Annica blinked, recalling the penetrating blue gaze. She was certain very little escaped Tristan Sinclair's "hunter eyes." "I agree, Hodgeson. I'm certain it served him well in the military and diplomatic corp. By all reports, he was accounted a hero at Trafalgar and several times since. Is that all?"

The servant shifted his weight uncomfortably. "For the present, milady."

"Thank you, Hodgeson." She inclined her head.

Finished with packing her portfolio, she tied the lavender ribbon of her ivory bonnet beneath her chin and took a final glance in the looking glass. A pattern of small lavender flowers danced across the ivory muslin dress, which was tied in back with a lavender bow. Lavender slippers peeked beneath her narrow hem. Annica smiled at her reflection, pleased with the result. In the next moment she frowned, wondering why she had taken such care with her costume.

"Just to show him I'm not always dirt splattered and disheveled," she said to her reflection.

Portfolio under one arm and easel under the other, she started down the stairs. She was almost to the foyer when the easel slipped from under her arm and clattered to the bottom of the steps. Instinct made her lunge to catch it, but the toe of her slipper caught in the narrow hem of her gown.

"Drat!" she exclaimed as she toppled forward.

Tristan caught her by the shoulders before she tumbled to the floor. "God's eyes, madam! Did you not have sense enough to ask for help? Did you think you could carry all this yourself?"

Annica could feel the heat rise in her cheeks even as an indignant reply formed on her tongue. "I am quite capable, milord. I seldom require help."

"Disaster does not require a helping hand. You tempted fate by attempting too much."

Annica looked up into his handsome, outraged face, surprised to see a flash of true concern. Somewhat mollified, she allowed him to straighten her bonnet as she watched the play of other, not-so-easy-to-read emotions cross his face.

"Are you reckless, Annica Sayles, or merely stubborn?" he asked when she stood her ground.

"Perhaps a little of both," she admitted, trying not to think of the warm glow in her middle at hearing him speak her name so intimately.

"Ahem." Hodgeson held out her lavender shawl.

Tristan stepped back and faced the servant with a cool smile.

"Do not forget, milady. You are expected at the Parson affair this evening," Hodgeson reminded her. "Lady Ellen and Lord Gilbert will be accompanying you."

Annica knit her brow at this. Hodgeson was behaving quite strangely. "Yes, Hodgeson. Thank you. I shall be prompt."

Tristan retrieved the easel and portfolio from the floor and followed her out the door. Settled in the carriage, he made himself comfortable across from her as the horses started off at a brisk trot.

Annica noted the strange light in his eyes again when he took a folded sheet of paper from an inside pocket of his jacket and presented it to her.

"What is this?"

"A contract."

"For what?"

"For you, Lady Annica. Have we not reached an agreement regarding the illustrations? This document spells out the terms—how much is to be paid, to whom, how many illustrations are to be provided, the deadline for delivery. It's a standard contract to protect both of us from any misunderstandings. You do not object to that, do you?"

"I suppose not." She read it carefully, agreeing with the terms until she came to a default clause. "What is this, my lord? It reads as if, once I begin the first sketch, I forfeit my right to cancel, save for a death in my immediate family."

"That is correct," Tristan admitted.

"While you, on the other hand, retain the right to terminate our contract at any time?"

"Upon payment in full to St. Anne's Orphanage for fifteen sketches, whether delivered or not," he explained.

"What if *I* choose not to complete the illustrations?"

"You do not have that option. Sorry, Lady Annica, but as time is of the essence, I must have a guarantee that I'll be delivered of fifteen sketches on time. All the sketches must be from the same artist, to preserve the integrity of the work. Once you have begun, I need an assurance that you will carry through. Even if you change your mind or grow bored with the project.''

''I am not a fickle person, Auberville. If I give my word, you may be assured that I will carry through.''

''Then you'll have no objection to signing the contract.''

Neatly maneuvered, she could only nod and do so. Auberville was well within his rights, and only asking what was reasonable—what he'd ask of a man in the same situation. She should be flattered, she supposed, that he was treating her as he would any male artist. Then why was she feeling trapped?

Arriving at Kensington Gardens, Tristan led her down a path to a small groundskeeper's potting shed. He set up her easel and opened her portfolio while she experimented with the best angle and light for a small potted shrub with soft pink blossoms.

He paced the confines of the shed while she applied herself to her task. Her concentration was not so complete that she was unaware of her companion. He reminded her of a restless beast, and the little shed was teeming with his animal presence. But when he stood behind her to watch her work, his absolute stillness was even more disconcerting.

''Do you have any comments, milord?'' she asked after an hour.

There was a soft sound behind her as Tristan shifted his weight and leaned closer. She could feel his warm breath along her cheek, and the intimacy unnerved her.

''I am not disappointed, Lady Annica. Your work is not only accurate, it has a wistful charm,'' he said.

''Is it satisfactory, then?'' She cleared her throat, hoping her voice would hold steady.

''Ah, yes. I'm very pleased,'' he purred.

''Just a quarter of an hour more,'' she told him, changing brushes. ''I shall apply the finishing touches at home.''

''You have a deft stroke, Lady Annica. Your feeling for

depth and shadow is startling. You do not merely record, you define.''

His voice was an intangible embrace. Heat washed over her, and she wondered if she were blushing. She hadn't done that in a very long time. How did he manage to keep her off balance?

''Have you ever done portraiture?''

''Just simple sketches of my cousins, Gilbert and Ellen.''

''I'd be curious to see the world through your eyes, Lady Annica,'' Auberville said in a low voice. ''I comprehend that your vision is quite beyond the ordinary.''

She faltered. Her hand began to tremble and her heartbeat accelerated. Distance! She needed distance! ''Lord Auberville, could you stand away? You...you are affecting my light.''

Tristan moved around her to lean against the potting bench, her canvas between them and his arms crossed over his chest. ''Is my conversation distracting as well?''

''No, my lord. I often find silence more distracting than noise. Perhaps because I am not accustomed to it.''

He cast her a thoughtful smile. ''A result of your family?''

''They are a noisy lot,'' she admitted.

''I've missed that,'' he said. ''The ticking of a clock was my only companion as a lad. I escaped that suffocating environment at the first opportunity. I envy you your family, Lady Annica.''

''You do? I've always craved enough peace and quiet to even *hear* a clock tick. As fond as I am of them, I find it difficult not to be driven to distraction by Uncle Thomas's vagueness, Ellen's complete docility, Gilbert's adolescent masculine superiority and Aunt Lucy's constant attempts to 'polish' me.''

''Polishing, eh? You appear to be quite polished, Lady

Annica. 'Tis I who lack that particular refinement. My father did not concern himself with such things.''

"Mothers are the usual polishers, Auberville,'' Annica murmured, warm from his praise. She applied a yellow-green variegation to the underside of a leaf.

"I scarcely remember my mother. She left when I was very young.'' His tone was flat and dull, forbidding further questions.

She sighed and wondered what hurts he must be harboring. "Hmm. While I do not know you well, I would guess that you are polished to a high luster. But if you wish for more, allow me to offer Aunt Lucy. She adores polishing. She'd be glad of the chance to redeem her reputation after her dreadful failure with me. Despite that, I give her my highest recommendation. Ellen and Gilbert are turning out rather well.'' Annica wiped her brush on a rag and selected a smaller brush.

"Why do you do that, Lady Annica?''

The lowered voice caressed her, surrounded her. "W-what?''

"You are unkind to yourself. I gather you do not like Lady Annica Sayles much.''

She was astonished at his perception, then angry at his presumption. "Whatever I think of myself, Auberville, is my own affair. Shall we talk about you instead?''

He grinned, watching her face. "Was that so close to the truth that it caused you discomfort?''

"Did you enjoy your service in the Royal Navy, Auberville?''

He laughed, not in the least contrite, that she could tell. "Mostly.'' He picked up a small potted plant, examined it and placed it back on the potting bench.

His male energy was unsettling and she sought for a subject to distract him—for her sake more than his. "In what way did you serve?''

"I was a lieutenant with Vice Admiral Collingwood aboard the *Royal Sovereign*. After Trafalgar, my superiors discovered that I had a natural bent for strategy and diplomacy. Before I knew it, and likely because my father interceded to remove me from combat duty, I'd been assigned elsewhere."

"Where?"

Tristan's lips twitched as if he were enjoying a private joke. "The Diplomatic Corps in the Mediterranean. The Barbary Coast has always been a pain in the…Royal Treasury. Though the fact was kept fairly quiet, our government engaged in negotiations with a group of pashas. Paying tribute was not an option any longer, and having our ships attacked regularly did not improve the king's temper. We needed to reach a mutually beneficial agreement. Negotiations were long and arduous. *That,* my superior officers felt, was my true talent—I never give up, Lady Annica, and I know how to obtain my objective."

She experienced a shiver of excitement up her spine. Being the focus of Tristan Sinclair's attention would be a very interesting position, indeed. "Were you successful?"

"Mostly." A darkness settled over his expression.

"What satisfaction it must have given you to have had such a far-reaching effect on world events. Lives were altered because of what you accomplished, my lord—for the better."

Tristan stepped forward to look over the top of her canvas. His voice lowered again to a soft purr. "I suspected the world would look different through evergreen eyes, Lady Annica. Thank you for redeeming what I have thus considered a mediocre life."

She realized that her innocent comment had revealed more of her own feelings than was wise. She busied herself with putting her brushes and rags away and carefully placing a cover sheet over her work.

Tristan collapsed her easel and followed her down the path past the orangerie. "I have worked you too long, Lady Annica. May I make amends by taking you to tea at Vauxhall Gardens?"

She glanced at the sun, low in the sky. "Thank you, Auberville, but I must hurry on home. Hodgeson will be quite put out if I am any later than I am now."

"Ah, yes, the Parson rout, is it not? I am invited there also. But tell me, do you always do your servant's bidding?"

"I do no one's bidding," she snapped. "And, for all his prickishness, I am quite fond of Hodgeson. He is more than my manservant. He saved my life many years ago, and that has given him certain privileges. After my parents...well, Hodgeson agreed to stay on. He has always looked after me. He feels responsible for me now, I suppose."

Tristan nodded as he helped her into his carriage. "Well, Lady Annica, that is one sketch finished, and fourteen to go. Do you still think you are equal to the task?"

She favored him with an angelic smile. "I never give up either, Lord Auberville."

Indeed, giving up was the last thing on Annica's mind as she prepared for the Parsons' rout that evening. She chose a marine-blue silk gown dotted with a tiny pattern of golden fleurs-de-lis. Gold satin slippers peeked beneath the narrow hem, and gold ribbons were woven through her dark hair like a molten stream. The low cut of her décolletage barely saved her modesty—some were bound to say it had not saved it at all—but it showed her curves to excellent advantage. The silk folds caressed and skimmed her body as she moved, enticing the viewer with hints of the supple, willowy figure beneath.

Annica glanced in her looking glass, pleased with the results. The bright jewel tones complemented her dark coloring, and she knew she would turn heads tonight. In the next moment she frowned, wondering why that prospect suddenly pleased her when it had never mattered before. She had taken pains with her costume twice in the same day! Could this have something to do with—

"Ahem." A voice spoke from her doorway.

She turned to find Hodgeson regarding her with his usual wooden expression. "Yes, Hodgeson?"

"The carriage has been brought around, milady. Your cousins and Miss Wardlow are in the foyer. I'm certain they will not mind waiting while you put on your chemisette."

Annica turned back to her looking glass. The cut of her gown was admittedly low, but if she filled it in with a chemisette, she would lose the effect she had so carefully created. Perhaps a necklace? No, Hodgeson was just being a nursemaid again. She smiled and shook her head. "I rather like it this way."

"Hmm," Hodgeson said. "Will you be seeing his lordship this evening?"

"Oh. I believe he mentioned that he has been invited to the Parsons', too, but we made no plans to meet there."

"I see, milady. Will you be needing a wrap?"

"My silk shawl, please. Where is my abigail, Hodgeson? She seems to disappear of late just before I am ready to leave. You should not have to do these silly little things for me."

Hodgeson went to her wardrobe and found her shawl as she applied a few drops of rose oil behind her ears. "I shall speak with her, milady. When do you plan to return?"

"Not until well after midnight. Gilbert and Ellen will be home sooner, but Charity and I may go on to other entertainments. Tell Mary she need not wait up. I am capable of removing my clothing without help."

"Since there is so little of it," Hodgeson muttered under his breath.

"Pardon me?"

"I was commenting upon the fine weather, milady."

"Yes, well, thank you, Hodgeson. You are correct. 'Tis a fine evening, and I will not be needing anything heavier than my shawl," she said.

And the pocket pistol in my reticule.

Chapter Three

Toying with the knob of his gold-crowned sword cane, Tristan stood in the doorway of the Parsons' ballroom, watching Geoffrey Morgan waltz with Lady Annica. She laughed at something he said and her head tilted prettily to one side. The light silk of her gown clung to the curves of her hips and legs, clearly revealing her lithe figure and easy grace. Her dark curls tumbled in a riot around a coronet of gold, studded with sapphires, that matched her blue-and-gold gown.

The dance ended and Morgan halted abruptly, forcing Annica to cling to his arm when he released her. They turned to leave the dance floor, and Tristan caught his breath. The low sweep of her neckline threatened to reveal all, and he found that he had mixed emotions regarding that possibility. He would kill to have Annica naked to his eyes, but he'd kill to prevent her being seen thus by any other man.

Good Lord! What was this odd possessiveness? It was only natural to have such feelings. She was, after all, in his employ, and he was considering making an offer for her. Yes, that was it. Proprietorship. That was all.

Grace Forbush joined Annica's small group near the French doors leading to the gardens. Tristan smiled when

she caught sight of him and signaled him over. He'd known
her since childhood and had a great respect for her intelligence and integrity. If Annica was Grace's friend, that was
high praise.

"Tristan Sinclair!" she greeted him. "How good to see
you again. Or should I say Lord Auberville? I was sorry to
hear about your father, my dear."

"Thank you, Mrs. Forbush. You are looking well." He
smiled and took her offered hand as he leaned down to
accept a formal kiss on his cheek. "And you may call me
whatever pleases you. Old friends should not stand on cer-
emony."

"I understand you have become acquainted with my dear
friend Annica." Grace turned to nod toward Charity and
asked, "Have you met Miss Wardlow?"

"Charmed, Miss Wardlow," he said with a slight bow.

Charity bobbed a quick curtsy. "Lord Auberville. I am
pleased to meet you. 'Nica has told me how very amusing
you—*ouch!*" She turned to Annica with a puzzled frown.

Annica's eyes sparked as she snapped her fan open and
fluttered it nervously. "M'lord." She acknowledged him
with a nod. "How are you this evening?"

"Well enough, Lady Annica." He bowed and lifted her
hand to his lips, fighting the urge to turn it up and kiss the
more sensitive palm. No doubt such an action would shock
the little bluestocking. There would be time for that later.
Instead, he lingered over her hand just a fraction of a moment too long to be decent, but not quite long enough to be
scandalous.

A deep fringe of dark lashes lowered in a shyness he had
not expected of her. Her fingers trembled and a soft intake
of breath portended well for her sensuality. If Lady Annica
could ignite from such an innocent kiss, he dared not even
dream what she would do in his bed.

But should he ask her to dance? No. Too soon. He dare

not give his game away too early. She needed to anticipate him a little longer. *Patience,* he admonished himself. He turned to Grace. "Would you, Grace? We have years to catch up on."

"I'd be delighted." She offered Tristan her hand again. Before he could lead her onto the dance floor, she paused and turned back to her friends. "Remember—quarter before twelve outside Parliament. I'll bring Constance."

Annica closed her fan with a sharp slap across her palm and turned away, a haughty set to her aristocratic features.

Tristan held back a chortle as he led Grace onto the dance floor, pleased at the peeved expression on Lady Annica's lovely face. Subtlety was not her strong suit.

"I perceive you are not pleased about this, 'Nica, but do not overset yourself. Half an hour and 'twill be over." Surprisingly, Sarah was steady and composed. The sweet, haunted face was more relaxed as Grace's torn coach crossed London Bridge than it had been since the night Annica had found the girl cowering where Farmingdale and the others had discarded her when they were finished with her.

"Sarah, I am not..." Annica stopped. She *was* uncomfortable. Men who had nothing to lose were the most dangerous, thus making Farmingdale positively lethal. She tried again. "We have taken risks before."

The coach drew up at the berth of the *Fair Isles* at the Surrey docks. The footman hopped down and opened the door. "'Ere we are, Mrs. Forbush. Looks as if they're ready to leave."

"Thank you, William. Wait here. We shan't be long," Grace instructed the man as he gave the five women a hand down.

The ship's lanterns illuminated the darkness, casting an eerie glow in the fog. The last of the cargo and supplies were being hoisted in nets on pulleys. One tall, slender man stood apart from the rest, waiting for the order to board.

Sarah took a deep breath, and her hands tightened into little fists as she went forward alone. Annica and the others followed at a discreet distance, and stopped when she did.

"Mr. Farmingdale?" Sarah said, her voice muffled by the clang of the ship's bell.

The solitary man turned. Surprise registered on his angular face and he took a step forward. "Lady Sarah? Good God—is it you?"

"Yes. I've come to see you off. You see, I have gone to a great deal of trouble to arrange this whole thing, and I wouldn't want to miss the best part."

"You? *You* arranged…what?"

"Your fall, Mr. Farmingdale. The ruin of your reputation. The need for you to leave England."

"*You* did it?" His voice raised in outrage.

"Yes, 'twas me," Sarah admitted softly.

"We should have killed you when we were done with you!" he snarled. "Taylor said you'd be too ashamed to tell any—"

"And where *is* Mr. Taylor?"

"In prison. He made a few bad investments and his debts were all called in at once."

"Ah, yes. That was rather clever, was it not? I must give 'Nica Sayles the credit, though. 'Twas her idea to buy his debts—and my money that clinched the purchase."

"And Harris?" At her nod, he sneered. "'Twould serve you right if I told everyone what we did to you. Who'd have you then, Lady Sarah Hunter? Yes—I will expose *you.*"

Sarah's smile was chilling. "Do so, and your admission will damn you more than me. What do I care if you leave London under a cloud, or hang for rape? Either way, you are removed from polite society."

Farmingdale's face turned dark red and his hands clenched into fists. "What do you want from me?"

"The name of the last man in your group that night. I never saw his face."

Farmingdale sneered again as he moved closer. "You must be insane to think I'd give you his name. But I'll see that he knows who is behind this odd run of bad luck for us."

"I survived what you did, Mr. Farmingdale—courting me, luring me down that path in Vauxhall Gardens to your friends, the attack—and I'm still quite sane. But never mind. We will discover the identity of the other man. He cannot hide forever.

"In the meantime, I wanted you to know who ruined *you*. You will carry that knowledge with you for the rest of your life, just as I will carry the memory of what you did to me. Do you begin to understand, sir, the depth of my contempt?"

He advanced, his hands out to grasp her, and an ugly smirk curling his lips. "You'll pay for this, you little—"

A fierce protectiveness seized Annica, and she stepped forward to flank Sarah. She opened her reticule and reached inside. "Not another inch, Mr. Farmingdale."

"I'd listen to 'Nica," Charity warned, appearing out of the fog on Sarah's left. "She just acquired a new pocket pistol, and she is eager to try it out."

"You wouldn't dare," Farmingdale scoffed. "You'd never get away with it."

"With what, Mr. Farmingdale?" Constance smiled sweetly when she and Grace completed the semicircle at Sarah's back. "Why, we just came to see a friend off. How could we possibly suspect a madman would attack us, and that Annica would be forced to defend us? Unfortunate, but there it is."

"There are five witnesses to that fact," Grace explained

in a bored tone. "Do you care to go against us? Would you like to explain in a court of law about your business practices should you survive? That is your only other choice, sir."

Farmingdale's jaw clenched, and he ran his fingers through his sandy hair. "You are the devil's whelp," he cursed. "All of you! You have ruined me—forced me to leave the country!"

"Yes, we have," Sarah agreed happily.

The ship's bell rang the final call for passengers to board. Richard Farmingdale glanced over his shoulder to the gangway, then back to the small group of women. His eyes had an angry glitter and he looked for a moment as if he would do something foolish. Pulleys squeaked and the anchor chain rattled as the slack was taken up.

"Damn you!" he shouted above the sudden din. "I will even this score, Lady Sarah. Do not doubt it." He turned abruptly and ran for the gangway, which a sailor was ready to hoist away from the dock.

The women moved closer together, forming a tight group as they watched the *Fair Isles* being towed from her moorings into the river current.

Annica shivered and turned in a slow circle, searching the fog-shrouded shadows. Foreboding raised the fine hairs on her arms and neck. She could feel the weight of watching eyes.

"'Nica?" Charity whispered.

"'Tis nothing," she murmured. Just the same, someone was out there—someone dangerous.

Annica tossed and turned in her bed later that night, her skin clammy and her stomach burning with anxiety. On some level, she knew it was just the old dream, the memory, back to haunt her, but she could not stop it from coming, nor could she reason away the panic.

"*Goddamn her, Eunice! The chit took the silver! Annie! Where are you?*" Her father's slurred, drunken voice echoed through the house. "*Where can she be at midnight? I'll break all her thievin' fingers when I lay han's on her.*"

"*She's but twelve. You cannot—*" her mother began.

Little Annica glanced over her shoulder as she pushed the pillowslip filled with odd pieces of silver toward the maid her father had just dismissed. She winced as the candelabra clanked against a teapot. "*Hurry, Judith! Run! Papa's coming!*"

The maid paused with her hand on the latch of the kitchen door. "*He'll send after me for thieving!*"

"*He will not.*" She fought to keep her voice steady. "*He'd look a fool, Judith. He will stand the loss before he will report it. Besides, Mama said it will all be mine one day. And you'll need it when the baby comes.*"

"*God bless ye.*" Judith backed out the kitchen door.

"*Where is the wicked chit?*" Papa's voice came again.

Panicked, Annica threw the bolt on the outside door, whirled toward the servants' stairs and ran. She had to escape!

The kitchen door flew open and candlelight reached as far as the fourth step to the second floor, where she had stopped, frozen. Her father staggered toward her, hellfire in his eyes.

"*C'mon, Annie. Come to Papa.*"

Oh, he was deep in his cups tonight! She backed slowly up the stairs, fearing sudden movement might provoke a lunge.

His slur changed to a ridiculous wheedle. "*Annie? Papa just wants to ask a question. C'mon, now. Don't run away.*"

This was bad…very bad. Worse than she had feared.

"*Please, Edward. She's only a child,*" her mother begged.

"*I warned ye! 'Tis no wonder no one loves you or the*

chit! Ye're both contentious bitches!" Edward snarled, and turned on her mother. He struck her with a backhanded blow, and when she began to cry, Annica's eyes filled with tears, too.

She rounded a corner on the first floor and dashed down the hallway, stumbling as her toes caught in the hem of her nightgown. The library! Yes! The huge hollow beneath Papa's desk made a perfect hiding place. She made straight for it, scrambled beneath the desk and curled herself into a ball, hugging her knees and trying to disappear in a corner of the recess. Cold tendrils of fear crept up from the soles of her bare feet and made her shiver.

Footsteps on the staircase echoed in her breast, tolling doom. "Edward, put your riding crop away. She is terrified of you. Leave her be."

"Terrified? She's fearless! She's got a reckless streak to defy me so!" The whoosh and crack of the crop on the reception table outside the library followed this denouncement.

Little Annica pressed her cheek to the floor, peering beneath the narrow gap at the front of her father's desk. Muddy boots entered the room and made straight for the liquor cupboard.

"Ahem," a voice interrupted. Annica squinted toward the door again to see the worn but highly polished shoes of her father's valet, Mr. Hodgeson. "Begging your pardon, milord, but will you require the coach again tonight?"

Horrified, Annica watched the valet's feet approach in their usual even gait. Papers shuffled and tapped against the surface of the desk, as if he were putting things to rights.

"Get the hell outta here, Hodgeson. Me and my wife have business to settle."

"As you wish, milord." The polished toe inched forward to push a telltale edge of Annica's nightdress under the desk. She caught her breath. Hodgeson knew. She heard his *soft whisper. "Do not move, milady, for everyone's sake. You know you cannot help when he is in this mood."*

"Out, I said!" *her father shouted.* "An' shut the door! C'mere, Eunice. Like I said, you an' I have business."

The door closed behind Hodgeson, and her mother's crying resumed.

Annica bit her lower lip and swallowed her sobs, reminding herself why she had risked this terror. Because Mama said that's what made one civilized—that the strong must stand up for the weak, and that those with courage should act. Even if it meant another beating.

Mama wept and Annica covered her ears. When she tried to make her papa stop hurting her mother, he only yelled louder. Always, when she tried to stop the abuse, it only made things worse. She felt so powerless, so helpless. So angry.

A scream rent the air, then the ripping of cloth. Nausea gurgled low in Annica's belly. Her father panted and made an ugly grunting sound that warned her not to look—to cover her ears and squeeze her eyes shut.

But she learned her lesson. She'd never marry. She'd never submit to such a fate, never become mere chattel subject to a man's whims and ill temper. Or, like poor, pregnant Judith, now fleeing in the night, a man's betrayal and indifference.

Annica held her breath and didn't even move to wipe her tears on her sleeve. Never. Never. Never.

"Never! No, never…" Sitting bolt upright in bed, Annica gasped for breath.

When her head cleared, she raised her knees and lay her cheek against them, just as she'd done as a child hiding beneath that desk. She breathed evenly, waiting for the panic to fade and her heartbeat to slow. A breeze drifted through her open window, ruffling the lace panel curtains and cooling her panic-fevered cheeks. "You're safe, 'Nica," she whispered into the night. "You're safe."

Why had the old dream come again? What had happened to reawaken her fears and call forth that memory, that vow? She could not think of any threat to her freedom, nor to the emotionally flat tranquility of her life. Indeed, her only new acquaintance was...Auberville?

She sighed as Tristan's devilishly handsome face and clear blue "hunter's eyes" filled her mind. Since his return to England, he had earned a reputation as a formidable adversary, a shrewd businessman, a desirable lover and a dangerous man to trifle with. If she had any sense at all, she'd finish his infernal illustrations and never see him again.

The soft night breeze wafted across her cheek again, reminding her of Tristan's gentle touch. She turned her face to the open window, craving more of that sensation.

Oh, her papa had been right—she did have a reckless streak!

Chapter Four

When, the following afternoon, an unmarked private coach careened around a corner and bore down on Annica's curricle with complete disregard for danger, she had no prickle of misgiving, no sense of foreboding. As she watched it approach, she was certain that it would stop or veer aside at the last minute.

Then memories of her last coaching accident rose to her mind—her mother's screams and her father's drunken curses—and turned her limbs to ice. Her feet seemed mired in quicksand, unable to respond to the approaching danger. The rattle of the harness and roaring wheels of the oncoming coach drew ominously near, and still it did not alter its course as it bore down on her open carriage with singular purpose.

Her driver bailed out and landed on the curb, rolling aside as he did. Unable to advance or retreat due to the crowded lanes, the horses neighed and reared. Annica stood, but the jolting of the carriage threw her back on the seat.

"Lady Annica!" her driver yelled. "Jump!"

Standing again, eyes riveted to the oncoming coach, she was only vaguely aware of an iron grip on her arms from behind as she was swung out of the curricle to the ground from behind.

There followed a crash, the snapping of wood, the jangle of metal fittings and the scream of women in the distance. Annica could hear the offending coach break through the intersection and recede into the distance. It had run her curricle down and kept on going!

The cacophony died, and she became aware of her own labored breathing. The weight on top of her squeezed the air from her lungs and pressed her to the ground. The solid thumping of another heart beat against her back. The weight was not oppressive, but comforting and protective.

"M-mumf," she mumbled—all she could manage with the little air and space afforded her.

Warm breath tickled her ear. "An interesting position, is it not?"

She recognized the voice at once, and Tristan's strong, gentle hands lifted her into a sitting position. Relief flooded her, leaving her weak and trembling.

"Are you injured, Lady Annica?" he asked.

"I be-believe I am whole, Auberville." She was dismayed when her voice broke. "Have you seen my driver?"

"He was well away from the carriage. I am certain he is around here somewhere. Shall we concentrate on you?"

She glanced down at herself and noted a rip in her bottle-green gown and a streak of dirt down one sleeve. Her bonnet lay on the cobblestones and her hair fell loose, tangling down her back. She must look dreadful, but was so grateful to be alive that she could not care. "I seem to be all in one piece."

A finger crooked under her chin and lifted her face upward. "I cannot tell you how relieved I am," Tristan said, a smile curving the sensuous lips.

"I...I feel like a witless child," she murmured. "I could not move."

"There was very little time, Lady Annica, and I suspect you would have escaped on your own had the horses not reared and thrown you off balance."

She nodded, grateful for an assessment that salvaged her pride. Her gaze fell upon her bonnet, flattened in the lane. She shivered. *She* could have been crushed on the cobblestones.

Tristan stood and leaned over to help her to her feet. "Do you think you can stand?"

She stared up, amazed at how tall he seemed. The scar beneath his left eye was livid in contrast to his white face, and she began to understand that he had actually feared for her.

When she did not give an immediate reply, he held out his hand. "Allow me to assist you."

She placed her hand in his, noting the strength in his simple gesture. A tingle went up her arm, causing a shiver of delight.

Self-consciously she turned to survey the wreckage of her curricle, overturned in the opposing lane of traffic. The twisted frame and bent wheels were unrecognizable, and the shaft broken at the axle. The horses, still harnessed to the shaft, were uninjured. The driver of another coach was murmuring soothing sounds to them.

"Lady Annica! Lady Annica!" her driver shouted, pushing through the gathered crowd. "Where are you?"

"Here, Thompson," she called.

"Blimey!" Thompson exclaimed, coming to her side. "What'll yer uncle say, milady? 'E'll 'ave me 'ead."

"He will not dismiss you, Thompson," Annica reassured him. "This was not your fault. Had traffic not backed up into the intersection—"

Tristan cut the man short with a frosty glance. "Thompson, I will see her ladyship home. Can you handle things here?"

"Aye, sir," the driver said, never even questioning Tristan's right to make decisions.

Annica's knees buckled, a reaction to the last few minutes. Over her feeble protests, Tristan scooped her into his arms and held her against the hard wall of his chest as he carried her away from the crowd. She was struck with the certain knowledge that nothing bad could possibly happen to her while she was held thus by this man. She fought a twinge of disappointment when he placed her in a black barouche bearing the Auberville crest.

"Traffic is at a standstill. We can go nowhere," he said when she was settled against the rich leather cushions. He took a seat beside her. "The drivers will have the wreckage cleared in no time, and I want you safely out of the street before someone tries to run you down again."

"Run me down? You make it sound deliberate."

"It certainly looked that way to me, Lady Annica. Do you have enemies who would like to see you dead?"

"No!" Just the same, she had a quick flash of misgiving. Richard Farmingdale might wish her harm—but he had left the country. "My opinions and activities make me unpopular in some circles, but I can think of no one who would want me dead. And how could anyone know that I would be stuck in an intersection?"

Tristan nodded, a grim look settling across his features.

She set the problem aside. She could not think while he was studying her so intently. He would be bound to suspect the direction of her thoughts. She pushed the hair out of her eyes. "I...I must look a fright."

"You have never looked lovelier, Lady Annica." He took her hand and gazed down at it in consternation. "You are trembling again. You are injured. I shall summon a coach from the next street to take you to a physician."

"No! No, 'tis just that I am overset by events.... I cannot help thinking of what might have happened. You see, my mother..." Tristan's coach lurched and started forward, covering her awkward pause.

"How insensitive of me," he muttered.

"Please do not trouble yourself, Auberville. It was a very long time ago." She felt the old panic returning and hastened to change the subject. "Can we talk of something else, please?"

He shrugged. "If you wish."

"Where did you come from just now, Auberville?" she asked. "Can it be mere coincidence that placed you here?"

"I was following you, Lady Annica."

"You were? Why?"

"I went to St. Anne's Orphanage to make payment for your illustrations, as you requested. The sisters told me Thursday is your usual day, and that you had just departed. I wanted to give you the receipt and inquire if you might be able to accompany me to another specimen on the morrow. We had all but caught up with you when traffic stopped and I saw the coach bear down on you."

She sighed. "It would appear I owe you my life. Lord, how I loathe that."

The corners of Tristan's mouth twitched, as if he were fighting a smile. "I swear I shall not ask anything in return for your soul, if that is what has you worried, Lady Annica."

"I was not worried on my account, but yours. It is a great burden to carry—the responsibility for another's life. Just ask Hodgeson. I know there must be days when he wishes he hadn't saved mine."

"Ah, yes. I had forgotten how that went. Let me see if I can remember." He assumed a thoughtful air. "I will give you advice, and you will feel as if you must take it. I shall have to accept responsibility for all your actions, and if you come to no good, I will conclude that I should have left you on that carriage. Indeed, you shall have to name your first-born 'Auberville'—even if it is a girl—and send extravagant gifts on the birth of each of mine. I shall have to be named godfather to your children, as well. Soon you will be unable to make a single move without my assistance.''

Annica laughed. ''You may set your mind at ease regarding my naming a girl child 'Auberville.'''

''I am encouraged to hear that you will *have* a child.''

''Mere figure of speech, Auberville. Simple supposition.''

''Ah, I begin to see! It is because I am a *man* that you do not want to owe me your life, is it not?''

''Why do you say that?''

''Because you are a notorious man-hater. I can see how it would rankle you to owe your life to one.''

''That is the second absurd statement you have made today.'' Annica frowned. ''I do not hate men at all. Why do you say so?''

''You refuse to entertain them. You have never consented for one to call upon you. You have dismissed all offers for your hand as beyond consideration.''

''*Au contraire.* I am overweeningly fond of Uncle Thomas, Gilbert and Hodgeson,'' she said in her defense. ''And, since I do not intend to marry, entertaining suitors, allowing young men to call and considering offers would be a complete waste of time, not to mention an unkindness to the gentlemen involved. I would not wish to give hope where there is none, Auberville.''

''Then you *do* like men?'' he asked, arching one eyebrow as if in disbelief.

''Yes. I like them very much. In their place. 'Tis what they eventually become that I do not like.''

''And what is that?''

''Husbands.''

He laughed. Loud and long. ''I suppose you excuse that particular shortcoming so long as the man is someone else's husband,'' he finally managed to murmur.

"Precisely." She smiled.

"I shall have to remember that." He leaned close to her, reclaimed her hand and lowered his voice, forcing her to tilt her head back to look into his eyes. "Will I have to marry before I can move past your defenses?"

"If…if you *do* marry, Auberville," she whispered, surprised by her own words, "'twill be too late."

"And there is my dilemma, Lady Annica. What would you suggest I do?"

The coach slowed and stopped outside her door. She could not have moved had lightning struck. Still holding her hand, Tristan leaned ever closer, lowering his mouth toward hers.

She could hear his driver hop down from the box and come around the side of the coach. Briefly, she wished him a broken leg. A moment! she prayed. Just one more moment!

She wanted to taste Tristan's mouth, to feel for herself if his lips were as soft as they looked—as delicious—and to know if the hollow, hard thumping in her chest would cause it to explode with excitement.

"'Ere we are, yer lordship," the driver announced as he threw the coach door open. "All safe an' sound."

Mr. Bouldin looked over his shoulder with a nervous glance. "What's the emergency, milady?"

Annica watched her abigail select a length of Belgian lace from the vendor several stalls down the arcade. She had only a moment to relay the details of yesterday's "accident" before Mary returned.

"Lordy!" the Bow Street Runner exclaimed.

She shivered, remembering her close call, and then how she had felt with Tristan's arms around her. "Lord Auberville snatched me from my curricle in the nick of time. But

I have grown uneasy. Indeed, I have begun to wonder if someone made an attempt upon my life.''

''We've always been careful that no one know who—''

''Yes, of course.'' Annica waved airily. She was in a rush and had no patience to repeat things they both knew. ''But we went to see Farmingdale off. *He* knows, and he made certain threats, Mr. Bouldin. I have begun to wonder if he managed to leave word for Lady Sarah's last assailant.''

''There was no time to send a message, milady. You watched the ship leave yourselves.''

Annica remembered her feeling of unease that night. Had it been Farmingdale's cohort hiding in the shadows? ''That is correct, Mr. Bouldin, but is there any way to be certain?''

''Until we know who the fourth man is…'' He shrugged.

She had suspected as much. ''Then Sarah is still in danger. I will have a word with her, Mr. Bouldin, and see to it that she goes nowhere alone and that she takes great care in all things.''

Mr. Bouldin frowned. ''You are the one in danger, milady. 'Tis your carriage that was run down.''

She shivered. ''Do not worry about me, Mr. Bouldin. I can take care of myself. Lady Sarah, however, is quite vulnerable.''

He gave her a doubtful glance. ''Ye mustn't discount the danger to yerself, Lady Annica.''

''Auberville could be wrong. Accidents happen, even to the most wary.''

''I take yer meaning. I had a near call of me own yesterday. Man in my business has to have eyes in the back of his head.''

Annica felt a prickle of misgiving. ''Do you think it may have had something to do with our investigations or with one of your other clients?''

''Who can say, milady?'' The Bow Street Runner gave another eloquent shrug, spreading both arms wide.

"If you suspect someone is after you, you must cease at once. I will not have you incur injury on my account."

He regarded her with a veiled expression that Annica read as stubbornness, and she knew he would tell her anything, then do as he saw fit. She took a wad of banknotes from her reticule and put them in his hand.

"I want Sarah's last assailant found as quickly as possible—and his weakness determined. The sooner he is dealt with, the less we will have to worry about accidents."

"Aye, Lady Annica. I'll bring m' partner, Renquist, in on this one."

"I'd appreciate that, sir." She glanced again toward Mary. The maid was offering a coin to the merchant with one hand and taking her purchase in the other. "Meet me at the Book Emporium day after tomorrow at half past noon. If I am able to discover anything new, I shall tell you then."

"Aye, milady. We'll find the degenerate or my name ain't Bouldin."

Chapter Five

The moment had arrived.

Chandeliers sparkled in the Grays' ballroom as the orchestra struck a tune. Annica swallowed her nervousness, adjusted the off-the-shoulder sleeves of her violet peau de soie gown, and gave what she hoped was a regal nod. Somehow, she suspected, Auberville was not fooled.

She placed her hand in his and felt a tingle travel up her arm, to catch in her throat as a small muffled gasp. When his arm went around her and his hand settled at her waist, she suddenly understood why the waltz was a dangerous dance. Face-to-face, so close together, the position bordered on an embrace and was scant inches from a kiss.

A kiss! Just the thought made the heat rise in her cheeks and her heart lurch like a ship at sea. She missed a step and scuffed his shoe. "Sorry," she murmured. "I am still a little unsteady from the coaching accident yesterday."

He smiled, his devastating blue eyes crinkling at the corners, but he made no comment.

What was it about Auberville that made her so acutely conscious of herself—of being a woman? What stranger inside her reveled in that fact? And who was this Annica she had become?

She must have waltzed several hundred times since the dance had become popular, but she'd never been aware of the heat of a hand resting on her waist, nor the contrast of gentleness and power as he led. He actually shortened the length of his stride to accommodate her. She was positive she had never noticed how intimate a whisper was until he leaned over to whisper in her ear.

"You are so concentrated, my lady. You need not count your steps. That is my job. Follow my lead, and you will do well."

Follow his lead? But she always had difficulty following a man's lead. She swallowed hard. "I have waltzed before, Auberville."

"I have seen you do it," he told her with an amused smile. "Yet you seem somewhat distracted this evening. Is there anything I can help you with?"

Annica knew she should not, but she tilted her head back and looked up into the captivating eyes. *You could kiss me,* she thought, and was so panicked that it took her a full minute before she could speak. Seizing on the first thing that came to mind, she said, "My uncle discharged Thompson this morning, m'lord. Would you know anything about that?"

"Who?"

"Thompson. My driver. The one who—"

"Ah, yes. The one who drove your coach into an intersection and then abandoned you? He is not deserving of your concern. When you were most in need, he thought only of himself."

"Did you have anything to do with his dismissal, Lord Auberville?" she persisted.

He gave a curt nod. "I recommended it when I spoke to Lord Thomas yesterday. As I expected, he was appalled by Thompson's behavior. The man betrayed your uncle's trust.

'Tis as simple as that. Your uncle will find you a more diligent driver.''

''I promised Thompson he would not be fired. Surely you cannot fault him for wanting to survive?''

''His first duty was to keep *you* from harm's way,'' Tristan murmured, leaning close to her ear. ''He saved himself at your expense, Lady Annica. That was inexcusable.''

Her heart skipped and she glanced away, uncomfortable with the intensity of his gaze. She wondered if he had this effect on all women, and if he flirted so outrageously with them, too.

''I hope you will save me another dance, Lady Annica,'' he told her when the dance ended and he returned her to her friends.

''Ah, Lady Annica!'' Julius grinned happily, releasing Charity's hand. ''Here you are. I believe this is my dance.''

She allowed Julius Lingate to lead her onto the dance floor, but then the orchestra struck a reel. ''I do not think I am up to this,'' she said, laughing, then crossed to the opposite side of the room to avoid being swept into a set.

''May I fetch you a cup of punch?'' Julius offered.

Annica took his arm companionably as they strolled toward a long table set with a fountain bubbling pink citrus punch. ''Thank you for being so understanding, Mr. Lingate.'' She smiled and cocked her head to one side. Here was an opportunity she dare not waste. It might never come again. ''Actually, there is something I would like to discuss with you.''

''I am at your service,'' he said with a bow.

''I would like to ask you a few questions about your friend, Lord Auberville.''

''This is most unusual, Lady Annica.''

''Because I am a woman?'' she asked.

''Er, well, yes.''

She straightened and assumed her most businesslike manner. Her voice deepened as she mimicked her uncle Thomas, linked arms with Julius Lingate and led him toward the Grays' library, deciding to have a little fun while setting him straight. "Now, now, my boy. A few simple questions. Nothing very complicated."

"I really do not think—"

"Nonsense!" Annica cut off his protest. "There's no problem a little brandy and a cigar cannot solve. We are civilized English, after all. Call me Nick, old boy."

Julius gazed at her in disbelief as she crossed to the humidor on Mr. Gray's desk and extracted two pungent cigars. She gave them to him to trim while she went to a side table to pour brandy into two snifters. She handed one snifter to him and took a cigar, which Julius, looking at a loss, lit for her.

She puffed until a gray-blue cloud hovered over their heads. Holding the smoking missile in one hand and sipping from the snifter in the other, Annica assumed a crafty smile. She sat down behind Mr. Gray's desk and leaned back in his chair. "Now, lad—Auberville. How well do you know him?"

"Since school. Eton."

"Ah, yes. Well, has he always been so…persistent?"

"Indeed," Julius said.

Relishing her role now that she was underway, she took a healthy swig of the brandy, gathering courage. "I see. And is he given to light flirtations?"

Julius squirmed in his chair. "There's nothing light about Auberville. All his affairs have been long-lived and discreet."

"All of them?" She frowned. "How many would that be?"

"Oh, ah, I wouldn't…know."

"Could you guess? Two? Ten? Twenty?"

"Not so many as that," he muttered.

"So Auberville takes his comforts where he finds them, eh?" she asked. An unfamiliar emotion tweaked her as she realized she could gladly scratch out the eyes of those nameless women.

"But it's been years since he had—" Julius stopped in midsentence. "That is, Auberville has not—"

"Not what?" a deeply masculine voice asked.

Annica turned toward the library door to find Auberville standing there. Thank heavens he had not heard the topic of their discussion. Her masquerade with brandy and cigar seemed a little extreme when she saw him lift one eyebrow just slightly, indicating not surprise, but disapproval.

"Did you have some business to be about, Lingate?" he asked.

Julius cleared his throat and set his brandy snifter down on the polished surface of the desk. "I believe I do. See you later, Auberville. Lady Annica."

Julius shot her a nervous smile and waved one hand as he passed Tristan on his way to the door.

"So?" Tristan said in a low voice when the door closed.

Annica tapped her cigar out in a small dish. She tossed back the rest of her brandy in a gesture of defiance and set the snifter down with a bang. "So."

"Once again, I see that you have a reckless flirtation with ruination, Annica Sayles."

"So it would seem. Or could it be that you have a talent for catching me at my worst?" she challenged.

"Are you ever at anything else?" he parried.

"If that is what you think, I wonder that you bother with me, m'lord." She felt the cut to her slowly awakening heart.

"Were it not for our contract, I wonder if I would."

"I release you from your obligation. Destroy our contract."

"You would like that, would you not? That would allow you to flee to the countryside, counting yourself lucky at escaping another close call. Then you could avoid the issue at hand.''

''I…I do not know what you mean,'' she faltered, good in a ruse but never good in a direct lie. She knew full well what he was suggesting. He was going to call her bluff!

He sauntered closer to the desk and smiled as he leaned across the smooth expanse, bracing himself by placing his hands flat on the surface. His head stopped mere inches from hers, and his eyes met hers directly, forbidding her the escape of looking away. ''I think you do. I think you are very aware of what is happening here, Annica.''

The sound of her given name alone, without the artifice of title or formality, caused her to blink. *Odd,* she thought, *how you can hear a name spoken every day of your life, and suddenly it is spoken in a way that gives it new meaning.*

Tristan straightened and came around the side of the desk in a swift, fluid movement. He lifted her out of the chair and swept her into arms so strong she could not even think of resisting. His lips came down to hers, barely touching as he whispered an invitation. ''If you must flirt with disaster, madam, allow me to show you a far more interesting way.''

His mouth claimed hers hungrily, as if he were starving for it. Indeed, Annica felt as if she were being devoured, and she relished the way his mouth moved on hers—nibbling, worshipping, demanding as his right more than any man had ever had the temerity to demand. So caught up was she in this new and exciting emotion, her response was to surrender to a force stronger than pride, stronger than fear, stronger than reason.

Her arms went up to cling to the powerful shoulders and her fingers fondled the silken curls at the back of his neck. A moan found its way to her throat when he lifted his lips from hers.

''Annica, Annica…'' His voice was a hoarse whisper. ''I

cannot believe the effect you have on me." He kissed her again, in a series of insistent nibbles that urged her to open to him. When her lips parted, his tongue slipped through in an intimate invasion.

Was it the brandy that made her head spin, made rational thought impossible? Or was it Tristan's consuming lips? Oh, he was right—this was a far more interesting way to flirt with disaster! Every instinct she possessed warned her to run—and quickly—before running was impossible.

Too late, a mocking little voice taunted as her heated blood flowed thick and sweet through her veins. She wanted more of Tristan's mouth, and was ready to ask for it—for anything that would prolong the delicious burning in her belly and the delicate trembling of her limbs.

He gripped her waist and put her firmly away from him. "This is a first for me, Annica. It goes against my nature to deny myself something I want as badly as I want you, but this is neither the time nor the place for this pursuit."

Denied the support of his arms, she sagged and caught her balance by gripping the edge of the desk. Bewildered, she glanced up at him and murmured, "The brandy…"

"No doubt." He gave her a satisfied smile.

"I…I must return to the ballroom. Charity and the others will wonder what has become of me."

"What *has* become of you, Annica?"

You! You have become of me! she wanted to cry. "I fear we have crossed a line in our arrangement, Lord Auberville. I wonder if it will be possible, now, to go back."

"No, nor would I want to. Shall we begin to call it a friendship, Annica? And do you think you could learn to use my given name?"

"I'm not certain what you are asking…Tristan."

"Neither am I. Believe me, I am as surprised as you by the nature of what happened here. I never expected you to have such a powerful effect on me. Go now, before I change my mind.''

Feeling like a child, she hurried to the door. She paused and turned to see him looking after her with a strange light in his eyes. Was she about to lose her heart? *Never! Oh, never!*

Shaken but amused, Tristan watched the library door close. Annica! She was everything he had ever wanted...*to avoid.*

He enjoyed her wit, her unique view of the world and her sense of humor. He adored the sweetly confused look on her face when he forced her to acknowledge the attraction between them, and he felt his body respond in the most primal way when he looked into eyes deepened with desire.

But Annica was unconventional. She was frank and forthright, intelligent and decisive. His instinct warned him that she would claim a greater depth of emotional commitment than he was prepared to give. But that simply was not possible. He had no more to give.

The distance he kept from others was his mother's legacy. She had been flighty and frivolous, bestowing her affections where her whims led her. And her whims had led her to run away with a ship's captain in search of...what? Adventure? Excitement? Or escape from the dull grind of life as a wife and mother? Her disloyalty and desertion had left him inconsolable. What a bitter lesson for a boy barely out of the nursery.

Women, unless they were as sensible and capable as a man, were a disloyal, self-indulgent lot. And that is why he needed to keep a part of himself separate, untouched and unmoved by that untrustworthy gender.

To complicate matters, Annica's only instinct when faced with romance was to flee. Perhaps it was that very vulnerability that drew him. Something of her hidden past reached him and communed with his own pain.

The thought of Annica in pain caused a twitch in the scarred muscle beneath his left eye. Her father must have done extensive damage to mold her in such a manner. Tristan's hands tightened into fists as he wished the man was alive—if only so he could kill him. He poured himself a stiff brandy instead and warmed it between his palms as he gazed into the amber depths.

He was faced with a difficult decision. Should he abandon his pursuit of Annica and resume his search for a suitable wife? Or redefine his requirements? The mere thought of replacing her with another woman caused him to sneer with disdain. The decision had been made before he'd posed the question.

Chapter Six

"It is not suitable for you to be associating with men of his ilk, Lady Annica." Hodgeson's concern could not be ignored. Annica sighed as he helped her down from the carriage in front of the Book Emporium.

"I am not having him over for tea, Hodgeson, and there is nothing wrong with his 'ilk.'" Annica closed her rose-bud-embroidered parasol and tucked a stray wisp of dark hair into her pink bonnet. "Mr. Bouldin and I have a business arrangement."

"That is what you have said regarding your relationship with Lord Auberville, milady."

Annica tilted her chin upward. "It is not the same thing at all."

"My point precisely, milady. Which?"

"Which what?"

Hodgeson look confused. "Which is a business relationship, and which is the other?"

"Other what?" Annica frowned.

Hodgeson closed his eyes and cleared his throat. "Never mind, milady."

Relieved that her ploy of confusing him had worked again, Annica nodded. "I shall not be long, Hodgeson."

She smoothed her ivory muslin dress, dotted like her parasol with pink rosebuds, and left Hodgeson standing by the carriage.

She caught sight of her friend near a stack of books in the reference section. "Good morning, Charity."

Charity smiled and closed the book she had been examining to show Annica the title. "Medical books are so very…educational, are they not?"

"Have you been studying the diagrams again?"

Charity winked.

"Is Mr. Bouldin here yet?"

"Behind the history shelves."

They browsed in that direction, looking for all the world as if they had nothing on their minds but finding a book of poetry. At last they flanked a rough-looking man in dark, nondescript clothing.

"What do you have for us, Mr. Bouldin?" Annica whispered.

"I'm 'avin' a bit o' trouble, milady. That last bloke—Wilkes—I cannot pin the goods on him. Ain't no one left what can tattle on 'im, if ye catch my drift."

Annica nodded. "I do, indeed. It was an unavoidable complication, Mr. Bouldin. Keep at it. Someone knows something and, sooner or later, they will tell. Roger Wilkes was the last friend Farmingdale had."

"'E's the likely villain, milady," Bouldin agreed. "'E ain't got the same 'abits that Farmingdale 'ad, but 'e 'angs out at the right places. Gambling 'ells, brothels, opium dens."

"Faith!" Charity exclaimed.

Bouldin shifted his weight uneasily. He glanced behind him and then peeked over the books on the shelf to the other side. Satisfied that they were private, he met Annica's eyes. "That other name you gave me, milady? Mr. Geoffrey Morgan? There's something afoot there, and it ain't good. If it don't concern you, leave it alone.''

''Is it dangerous, or merely unpleasant?''

''Both, milady. And illegal besides. I 'aven't got all the particulars. I did as I told ye—hired more runners an' put my partner on it.''

''If he is a danger to others, we must be forewarned. Continue your investigation until your findings are conclusive.''

''If you say so, milady. Me and Renquist will follow this one an' Wilkes full-time.''

Annica fished in her reticule and brought forth several sovereigns. ''You will be needing this for the extra runners. Thank you, Mr. Bouldin. I knew I could count on you. Shall we meet here Friday next? Same time?''

''Aye, milady.'' Bouldin tipped his hat and moved away.

''Now, suppose you tell me what you are up to, 'Nica Sayles,'' Charity said when they were alone.

''I have simply observed someone giving our Constance the eye. I thought we should be aware of any potential problems.''

''Who?''

''Geoffrey Morgan. If I recall correctly, he was in town when Sarah was attacked, and left town shortly after. Perhaps that is coincidence, perhaps not. The point is that he is so deucedly secretive. One does not become secretive unless one has something to hide. I hope Mr. Bouldin will be able to discover what Mr. Morgan's game is before Constance's heart is broken.''

''I have seen her dance with Roger Wilkes and Lord Tristan, as well, though it's obvious she favors Mr. Morgan. Even though she has been caught up tracking down Frederika, she makes time for him. They are becoming quite an item, you know. The on dit has it that he will offer for her soon. I think it is better if she favors Mr. Morgan—'' Char-

ity smiled ''—because I think Tristan Sinclair favors someone else.''

''Oh? Who?''

''A dark, sultry beauty. Names are not being mentioned,
of course. It is still too soon.''

''How long has this been whispered?''

''Since you were seen leaving the Grays' library a bit
flustered last night, and Lord Tristan a little while later.''

''Lord!'' Annica sighed. ''How will I ever hush this up?''

''I am not certain you should. After all, it isn't as if Auberville is déclassé.'' Charity paused dramatically. ''In fact,
I think your reputation could benefit from the hint of a
thaw.''

''I am puzzled at how society can lose interest in something so quickly and yet retain it in their memory until hell
freezes. But never mind. We have other business to be
about.''

''Ah, yes. Where are we to meet with the others?''

''St. James's Street—the bastion of English manhood.''

''Gads! There must be a more receptive route.''

''The unreceptiveness of the route is what makes it so
desirable,'' Annica said.

Charity squared her shoulders and lifted her chin. ''Once
more into the breach, dear friend!'' she paraphrased the
Bard.

Annica opened her reticule and took out two wide red
ribbons. Bold white lettering proclaimed Enfranchisement
For Women on one and Social Reform on the other. ''Which
do you want, Charity?''

''I shall take Social Reform.''

They slipped the sashes over their heads to wear diago-
nally across their chests. With a reassuring smile at one
another, they stepped out of the bookstore and onto the
street.

Hodgeson was nearly apoplectic when he saw them. "Milady," he said, gesturing at the banners, "what is this?"

Annica looked him straight in his rheumy blue eyes. "What is what, Hodgeson?"

A long moment passed while the man tried to speak and no sounds came forth. Annica read the emotions flickering across his face and knew he was debating the wisdom of argument.

Finally he asked, "Will Miss Wardlow be riding with us, milady?"

Disgruntled-looking men came to stand at the entrances to the clubs lining the fashionable street. Women and children paused to watch while tradesmen called taunts and threw rotten vegetables.

Annica ducked a tomato that whizzed past her left ear and splattered on Hodgeson's black jacket. His usually stoic expression gave way to an outraged snarl.

"Impertinent pup!" Hodgeson shouted at the miscreant, using his placard stating Women Are People, Too to swat the moldy onion that followed.

"Are you not glad we armed you, Hodgeson?" Annica smiled. "Would you like me to tell you what your advertisement says?"

The servant turned back to her, fighting to regain his composure. "No, milady. I very much fear this may be one of those times that ignorance is bliss."

"I told you to wait at Hyde Park—"

"I could never allow you and Miss Wardlow to be seen in such a place unescorted."

A commotion from the front line of marching women drew their attention. Several men on horseback broke through the line and scattered the protesters. Outraged screams met this tactic, and the marchers fought back using their signs and placards.

Shouting grew louder and the press of the crowd closed around them. Anger and fear spiraled to hysteria. Annica reached out to lay hold of Charity's arm, but the surge of retreating people separated them. Limping, Hodgeson, too, was swept away in Charity's direction.

Annica called to them but her voice was lost in the cacophony of neighing horses and frightened shouts. A rough hand at the small of her back pushed her deeper into the crowd. She tripped over a fallen sign and fought to keep her balance.

Bloody hell! She is bent on self-destruction! How she has managed thus far to keep from teetering over the brink into ruination, I cannot imagine. Do I want to spend the rest of my life snatching her away from the yawning jaws of disaster?

Tristan applied his elbow to the rib cage of a bully boy engaged in purse-snatching in the confusion. Using the butt of his cane, he made steady progress toward the pretty pink bonnet.

Annica's parasol came up to swing at a dark, bearded man who appeared intent on dragging her away. Alarm was quickly followed by an urgency Tristan hadn't felt since standing on the deck of the *Royal Sovereign* at Trafalgar. Ah, but he had to credit Annica with courage. She was not afraid to fight for her convictions, and she stood ready to pay them more than mere lip service.

A second man, as deliberate as the first, pushed her from behind, forcing her to fall toward the bearded man. She staggered, regained her balance and swung her parasol again, catching both men across the midsection. The abuse proved too much for the substitute cudgel and it snapped in the middle. The pink fabric held it together, but the end dangled uselessly as she swung it again.

"Misogynists!" she cursed over the melee.

Her bonnet fell back, dangling by the ribbons. Indignation burned bright spots on her cheeks and the fire of battle lit her evergreen eyes. She was stunning! Tristan could almost pity the man who had provoked such a response from the formidable Lady Annica.

"Annica!" he shouted. "Over here!"

She turned toward his voice and was bumped again. The bearded man was rather too single-minded in his targeting of Annica, Tristan thought. He applied his elbow to a few more rib cages and a ruthless iron backhand swept several men out of his way.

"Keep 'er off the streets and at 'ome, guv'nor," one tradesman yelled from the curb. Tristan wondered if he'd just heard for the first time what he would be hearing the rest of his life.

Royal guardsmen rode into the free-for-all, adding to the chaos. Knowing he had scant seconds before all hell broke loose, Tristan closed the gap separating him from Annica. Bending and throwing her over his shoulder, he made his way to the curb and ducked down a side street, where his coach was waiting.

"Tristan!" Her voice was muffled against his back. "Put me down! Charity and Hodgeson! I cannot leave them!"

"They were on the other side of the street, out of the fray," he told her. "Hodgeson saw me coming after you. They were heading for your carriage."

"I must go back—"

The thunder of a pistol shot reverberated off the buildings to either side of them.

"We are not going back, Annica." He threw the door to his coach open and propelled her onto the cushioned seat. Following fast behind, he tapped the roof with his cane and called, "Away, Davis! Go 'round the long way. Keep off of St. James's Street."

The coach lurched as the driver cracked his whip. Annica fell off balance and gasped as Tristan gripped her shoulders.

"Before we begin the argument, Annica, I want you to know that I do not object to your sentiment, only your method."

"I have no idea what you mean."

"Do you not?"

She blushed and dropped her gaze to her lap. "I cannot think this is any of your business, Lord Auberville."

"Tristan," he instructed. "And I've made you my business."

"I will not countenance your interference."

"Interference? Should I have turned my back when I saw you in the street under attack and about to be trampled?"

"No! Indeed, I appreciate your assistance, but not the assumption that you have the right to dictate my activities."

"Shall we say *monitor* your activities? Your safety and well-being are my chief concern. That does not mean I wish to schedule your activities, or to edit them." Her bonnet still hung down her back on tangled ribbons. He set the bonnet to rights and untangled the ribbons. "I only want you to be more careful."

"I am not accustomed to accounting for my whereabouts and interests. I do not think I like it. Furthermore, the issue of rights for females is quite dear to my heart. I—"

"I will not permit you to divert me from my original topic—your *method* of pursuing female enfranchisement."

"Your *objection* to my method, you mean." Annica tilted her chin in a defiant gesture.

"As you will," he conceded.

"But you have absolutely no right to interfere with anything I may or may not choose to do."

"We are not discussing rights, nor are we discussing political or social issues. We are discussing risks. Can you stick to that subject, please, and not try to confuse the issue, nor try to divert me from the topic? It will never work, Annica. I have far too much experience in negotiations.''

She gave him a grudging look of respect and settled back against the cushions. "What *of* the risks, m'lord?''

"They are unacceptable.''

"I weighed them beforehand and found them unavoidable and, therefore, acceptable.''

"You were nearly a casualty, Annica, and that would not have been acceptable.''

"There may be casualties. No cause worth winning ever came easily—or cheaply.'' She leaned toward him in earnest. "My only recourse would have been to stay at home and allow the cause to go unheard. What progress would ever be made if those with courage enough did not speak out?''

Tristan considered her argument. He agreed that only courageous people could change the course of history, but he could not allow Annica to be a casualty. "That's a bloody good defense, madam. Very well. You've convinced me of the necessity to wage your war, but you must be more prudent in choosing your battles. The march may have been necessary, but to carry it down St. James's Street was ill-advised. I shall expect you to use better judgment in the future.''

She stared at him, a stunned look on her dirt-smudged face. He smoothed the dark tangles of hair away from her cheeks to tuck into her bonnet, and removed a handkerchief from his pocket to wipe at the soiled spots. "What is it, Annica?''

"I am confounded if I know what just happened here.''

"We have discussed your political activities.''

"Are you not going to try to stop me? Are you not going to shout and threaten? Are you not going to dismiss my opinions and convictions as mere twaddle?''

"That would be a foolish mistake.''

"Yes. It would."

"And I am no fool."

"No, you are not." She tilted her head to one side and studied him closely. "I perceive, in fact, that you are a different sort of man than I have ever known."

"Ah, you've noticed."

The brilliant smile she bestowed on him caused a quickening of his pulse and an ominous firming in his loins. He leaned down and nibbled lightly on her full lower lip. She sighed and gave herself over to him in a surrender so tenuous that he scarcely dared move. With no more tutelage than the previous evening, she brought her arms up to circle his neck, her eyes half closed with sensual delight.

"How is it you do this so well?" she whispered.

"Practice," he murmured against her lips.

The sweet petals parted, inviting more intimate contact. He accepted, and tightened his arms about her, light-headed at her response. He'd taken bawds and virgins, courtesans and noblewomen, and he'd found many who could stir his blood, but he'd never encountered one who could touch his heart. He hadn't believed himself capable of such bittersweet yearning.

"Mmm," Annica breathed when he lifted his mouth from hers. "Then I must practice, too."

"Allow me to assist you," he said, intently aware of the softness of Annica's breasts against his chest. He longed to lay her bare to his touch, press his lips to the sweet-scented flesh, taste the dew of her warmth and hear her chant his name in a litany of passion.

"Tristan, Tristan…teach me more," she whispered as if in answer to his prayers.

The appeal took him by surprise. Obediently, he turned his attention to one delicate earlobe. When she shivered with delight, his body sprang to full readiness. His hand found its way to her soft bosom. The taut flesh firmed and pressed enticing little dots into his sensitive palm, arousing him more, inviting his mouth to taste that flesh, too.

"Annica, dear God…" he groaned, unable to hear his own voice over the thundering of blood through his veins.

Had she been anyone else, he'd have taken her that moment. But she was Annica Sayles, and he realized with fatal certainty that she was the woman he would marry. Capable or not, she amused him, challenged him and aroused him like no other woman had. And she deserved better than a hasty, uncomfortable coupling in a coach. But, God help him, he could take no more right now without taking it all.

Getting a firm grip on his emotions, he steadied his breathing and put her clothing to rights, trying to ignore the look of confusion on her pretty face. "Hodgeson and Miss Wardlow will be waiting."

"Yes," she whispered.

Tristan met the deep liquid green of her eyes and his heart soared. He'd risk betrayal for that heady sensation. *Yes…* that was the word he wanted most to hear from her. A long moment passed while her embarrassed glance gave silent acknowledgment of what both were thinking.

"You've narrowly missed becoming another sort of casualty, Annica." He dropped a yearning kiss on her swollen lips and smiled. "We shall have to be more careful in the future."

"Or quicker." She smiled, charming him completely.

Stripped to her chemise, Annica stood on a stool with her arms extended while Madame Marie draped a muslin pattern over her form. Immediately upon rejoining Charity and Hodgeson, she had decided that she needed a new gown. One Tristan had not seen.

Charity fingered a length of fine ivory silk shot with subtle stripes of gold metallic thread. "This is lovely stuff,

'Nica. 'Tis heavy enough to wear alone, yet light enough to cling. Auberville's eyes will pop when he sees you in this!''

Annica worried her lower lip. ''D'you think so, Charity? He is not easy to impress.''

''Yes, definitely. In case you had not noticed, *you* impress him. Have you been flirting with him?''

Gazing at her reflection in the wide mirror in Madame Marie's fitting room, Annica was horrified to see a crimson blush spread from the low cut of her chemise up to the roots of her hair. ''I am not certain, but I think so. At least, that has been my intention, but I am sorely ignorant.''

Charity laughed. ''Though you have had precious little experience in that feminine art, I am certain you have mastered it as quickly as everything you set your mind to doing.''

Annica acknowledged the compliment with a wince. ''I wonder if I am not in over my head, Charity. The last thing I want is to be shackled, anyway. I cannot think of a logical reason to entertain his interest, if, indeed, he is interested.''

''He would be utterly unsuitable for *me,* 'Nica, because he would intimidate me. There is something dangerous about him that puts one in mind of an animal about to pounce. As if he watches and waits for just the right moment, and then—*poof!* But you are his equal. He is the man for you if you want one who can make your heart pound and—''

''Charity! That's enough! You know I shall never marry.''

Madame Marie, kneeling at Annica's feet, spat a mouthful of pins into a dish and contributed, ''Not every romance must end in marriage, eh? Pleasure does not depend upon a ring. Eet can be more…exciting weethout, eef you take my meaning.''

Annica pondered Marie's words. Could the modiste be suggesting…surely not! But the notion was intriguing. She already knew that Auberville had indulged in discreet liaisons. If one intended never to marry, what was the harm in—no, that did not bear thinking about. Such thoughts made Annica's limbs go weak. To the contrary, she resolved to avoid Auberville except in the performance of her contract with him. Once that was completed, she would finish with him entirely. Then, perhaps, her persistent unsettling dreams would end.

Chapter Seven

"Why have you been avoiding me, m'lady?" Tristan asked as he set her easel up on the riverbank. Finishing his task, he turned to her. "I could have sworn you actually ran when you caught sight of me last night at the Abbington ball."

"How odd," she hedged, glancing over her shoulder toward their chaperons, Julius and Charity. She laid out her paint box and brushes and unfolded a small stool with a canvas seat. "I am not the sort to run away, m'lord."

"Are you not?" He lowered his voice intimately. "I suspect you have spent the past several years running from anything that comes a little too close to your heart, Lady Annica. And the past several days running from me."

A flash of fear passed over her face. "That is absurd."

"Not absurd in the least."

"I…I have been distracted of late. Very busy."

"You are making excuses. If you have reservations regarding our relationship, you must say so." He crossed his arms over his chest and tilted his head to one side.

"To be honest, I am a little confused by what has happened between us. Had I known what lay ahead… But how could we possibly have known what lay ahead for us?"

Tristan smiled. *He* had known. With the exception of Annica's "accidents," he had planned it all. He'd been patient, allowing her the luxury of time, if not escape. Her propensity to run from the possibility of being hurt troubled him most. He understood the instinct, but he could not yet risk trusting her to stay with him through good times and bad.

He watched the dusky-pink mouth move in a faltering attempt at explanation, and felt himself being intensely drawn to it. When her tongue slipped nervously over her lips to moisten them, he felt a thickening in his groin. He fought the impulse to press her back against the soft bed of moss and wildflowers and lay her bare to his gaze. He wanted to crush her against him and plunder that innocent mouth with his own.

"I had not thought to ever have such a friendship," Annica was saying. "To the contrary, I have done my best to avoid it. I have filled my life with matters of greater importance. Social reform. The Seamen's Widows and Orphans Trust. St. Anne's Orphanage. Women's suffrage. Literature. My art…"

He leaned closer, forcing her to tilt her head upward to meet his gaze. "Those things are commitments, Annica— duties and convictions. They relate to your beliefs, not your needs."

"I…I have obligations."

"As do I," he said, trying not to think of the fact that he should be engaged in important international business today, and not in wooing a beguiling little sprite.

"I fear how my life would change if I allowed…if I made a different sort of commitment."

He smiled, vastly encouraged to hear that she had at least entertained the notion. "Do you fear you will not be able to find time for all the things in your life? That you will have to make difficult choices?"

She took her seat on the little stool and busied herself

with laying out her paints and brushes. "I am not afraid of *difficult* choices, Auberville. I have made them ere now. I am afraid I will not have *any* choices—that they will be taken from me and made for me without my consent. I am certain I needn't explain a married woman's status in the eyes of the law. Any woman with common sense would have reservations about that."

"Is it so very difficult for you to trust, Annica?"

"Life has taught me an opposite lesson. If it were not difficult for me to trust, I would be a very silly woman."

"What is your secret, Annica?" he murmured. "Who hurt you?"

She seemed on the verge of giving him an answer, knitting her brow in fretful lines and pressing her lips together as if to speak. But she shook her head instead. "I do not know what you mean, m'lord."

He would swear it was tears that made her eyes sparkle in the sunlight. "I think you do, but I will not press."

She sighed and turned her gaze to the flowering plant she had come to paint. "I would appreciate that, Auberville."

He raised an eyebrow and watched her for a long moment. He had thought that exposing her self-delusions would break through the walls she had built, but he could not bear to see her pain. Perhaps a strategic retreat was in order. Given enough freedom, enough rope, she'd come around. Meanwhile, he could use a little time to pursue his business for the Foreign Office.

"Mayhap you are correct, m'lady," he said, backing away. "We took a wrong turning. Thank God it has not gone so far that we cannot be friends. We *can* remain friends, can we not?"

"Y-yes." Annica's reply was so soft he barely heard it. Her look of sweet confusion was more promising than her words. "I...I hope we shall always be friends."

"Quite. We are agreed, then." He placed her canvas on

the easel and stepped away. "I shall go sit with Lingate and Miss Wardlow. Call if you have need of anything."

He gained some satisfaction from the fact that Annica kept glancing in his direction throughout the remainder of the afternoon. Ah yes, she would miss him. She would miss the excitement of their kisses and the challenge of flying close to the flame without being burned. Soon. She'd be ready soon.

That night, at the Sunderlands' soiree, Annica found the opportunity she had been awaiting. She straightened her back, assumed as sweet a smile as she was capable of, and advanced on the hapless man. Geoffrey Morgan, his long slender form draped in elegant black and silver, was leaning one shoulder against the doorjamb and jingling the coins in his pocket as he studied the Sunderlands' gaming room and its occupants.

"Ah, Mr. Morgan! How fortuitous. I have been hoping to find you. A friend told me you are somewhat of an expert at *vingt et un,* and that if I wished to learn the game, I must learn it from you. Please? 'Twill only take a few moments. I am a quick study. I've already learned faro and whist."

He turned and gave her a small bow. If he was dismayed, he did a good job of hiding it. That was a sign in his favor. "I shall be happy to oblige, Lady Annica. I wonder, though, why you need to learn *vingt et un.*"

"I foolishly promised to accommodate my cousin in a friendly game with favors as the wager. If I know Gilbert, he will have me fetching and polishing his boots, grooming his horse, writing his correspondence and doing his lessons. He gave me a week to learn, but I forgot until tonight. Our game is tomorrow."

Mr. Morgan swept one arm toward an empty table and inclined his head, his hazel eyes glittering with amusement.

"At least you have chosen a fairly uncomplicated game. If you can count cards and keep track, you should do well."

He held a chair for her, then took the one opposite. He picked up the deck of cards from the center of the table and began shuffling.

"I ought to have asked if you have other obligations, Mr. Morgan," Annica said after a short pause. "I did not mean to take you away from anything of import."

"What could be more important than saving a lady from a conniving cousin?" He grinned.

He dealt two hands, faceup, and explained the rudiments of the game, the odds and the rules. "D'you think you have it?"

"I believe so, Mr. Morgan."

"I shall be happy to oblige you in a few practice hands," he offered.

She smiled and inclined her head as a servant brought Morgan a glass of brandy. He did not appear to be the least bit nervous or uncomfortable with her attention, and that was another sign in his favor. She took her time deliberating over her cards to allow him ample opportunity to drink, fidget or otherwise betray himself.

"How kind of you to help me, sir. Considering the company you keep, I almost expected you to leave me to my own devices."

"What company is that?"

"Harris, Taylor, Farmingdale, Wilkes…"

Mr. Morgan straightened and his smile faded. "You are behind the times. I have ceased keeping their company."

"Oh? I had not noticed."

"I was never really one of that crowd." Morgan dealt another hand, looking uncomfortable for the first time.

His terse reply did not give her much to work with. Sarah had been assaulted last All Hallows Eve. When had Mr. Morgan broken his association with the others? Annica sighed, not liking the necessity of being a bully, but persisted for Sarah's sake. "I'd have sworn I saw you arrive with Mr. Wilkes and Mr. Farmingdale at the Worthingdon ball but a few weeks past."

"Not I, my lady. 'Twas early October when I last sallied forth with them."

That was telling. Had he ceased association when the others began planning their perfidy? She tried a different tack. "Oh, well—no matter. I have not seen Mr. Taylor or Mr. Harris around of late, nor Mr. Farmingdale. I danced with Mr. Wilkes recently, and he has asked permission to keep my company."

"Believe me when I say that Roger Wilkes is not your sort."

"Why do you say so?"

"You have a reputation for being sensible as well as intelligent, Lady Annica. Wilkes is neither. I cannot imagine what you would have in common."

Suppressing a smile, Annica lifted a corner to peek at her card and tapped the back. "Another, please."

"I beg your pardon, but that would be ill-advised."

"Trust me, sir, I need the extra card."

"Not that. Keeping company with Wilkes would be ill-advised."

"Why? For the crime of being a little dimwitted?"

"Trust *me,* Lady Annica—keep clear of Roger Wilkes. You must listen to me in this."

"I cannot doubt your sincerity, sir, but I have given my consent to his offer to escort me tomorrow evening. I would require a compelling reason to reconsider." She shrugged one shoulder in an attempt at nonchalance. "Were there such a reason, I would certainly acquiesce."

A hard look settled over his features. "Suffice it to say that you must not go with Mr. Wilkes." He glanced over her shoulder. "Auberville," he acknowledged.

Auberville! Annica turned in her chair and looked up to find Tristan standing behind her. She felt her heart leap and her mouth went dry. How much had he heard?

"Morgan." He nodded to the other man.

"Lady Annica was just telling me that she has decided to entertain Roger Wilkes."

Tristan's chin went up as if he'd been slapped. "Is that true, Lady Annica?"

"I...I was considering it." She glanced away at the look of utter disbelief on Tristan's face.

"If you are considering such a thing to spite me, I assure you it will not be necessary."

"Why would I want to spite you, Lord Auberville?"

His intense eyes narrowed. "Because I teased you about not entertaining men? Because you want to prove that you are 'as whole as any woman'?"

Mr. Morgan lifted his eyebrows. He stood and bowed. "I must be going, Lady Annica. Auberville."

Tristan nodded to him and took the chair across from her. When they were alone, he swept the cards together and began shuffling, his attention never leaving her. "What stakes were you and Morgan wagering?"

"None," she said. His unwavering study made her feel as if she had a smudge on her cheek or something caught between her teeth. His focus, his intensity, fascinated her as completely as flame fascinates a moth.

"I'd have taught you the game, Annica." Tristan's voice was low and deceptively soft, masking an underlying steel that told more of his true nature than his easy charm suggested. "I will teach you whatever you choose."

"V-vingt et un," she stuttered, thinking of another game entirely.

He dealt the cards, a hard glint in his eyes. "If you allow Roger Wilkes to call, you will be inviting trouble."

"I appreciate the warning, Auberville, but I have always chosen my own friends."

His expression darkened. "My feelings of chivalry for the fairer sex do not extend to choosing their friends. If I warn you of something, you may be sure there is a need."

"Very well, then. I shall consider what you have said."

Tristan leaned forward, his whole manner giving credence to his words. "He is a dolt, and undeserving of one as intelligent as you."

"Are you protecting my delicate sensibilities? How very diverting." She regretted her sarcasm almost immediately.

"Someone must, Lady Annica, though it would appear to be a thankless task."

She glanced down, and the sound of Tristan's chair scraping back as he stood caused her to sigh. She had made him angry. She was startled by the flash of pain that thought caused her.

He leaned over her shoulder on his way by and reached across the table to flip his cards faceup—revealing a king and the ace of spades. She smelled the clean woodsy scent of his cologne and felt his breath tickle her ear. "*Vingt et un,* Lady Annica," he whispered, sending shivers up her spine. "This is a game of concentration and strategy. You are outmatched."

Breathless, Annica rushed into the parlor the following afternoon and gasped, "Ellen! Say it isn't so!"

"I'm afraid it is true, 'Nica. Every word," her pretty blond cousin announced with a cheerful smile.

"So nice of you to join us, my dear," Aunt Lucy said, patting the sofa beside her.

"I will support Ellen in anything she decides. For herself." Annica glanced askance at her cousin, wondering why the demure twenty-year-old had agreed to marry a wealthy earl twice her years. Merely following her parents' advice, no doubt.

"We can always count on you, dear." Aunt Lucy smiled. "We have decided to make the announcement at a masquerade ball Friday next. I could use your help with the guest list and addressing the invitations."

"You shall have it all afternoon and into the night."

"Thank you, 'Nica." Ellen sighed and put her cup aside. She folded her hands in her lap, a distant look in her eyes.

"Ellen, I had no idea you had fallen in love. It must have been sudden. *Coup de foudre,* I believe the French call it—the thunderbolt." Annica paused with her teacup halfway to her lips. Her memory slipped back to her first glance of Tristan Sinclair and how the sight of him had left her speechless and bemused. She gave herself a mental shake and cleared her throat.

Ellen blinked. "I suppose I shall learn to love him. The match is eminently suitable. He is an earl, after all."

"You are marrying Lord Dennison because it is *suitable?*"

"Annica, please," Aunt Lucy sighed.

"Why, even Miss Jane Austen has said she would not marry without affection," Annica persisted.

"And Miss Austen is *not* married, is she, my dear? *That* is what comes of being a bluestocking," Aunt Lucy pronounced. "Please do not cause trouble for Ellen. You must not plant doubt where there ought not to be any."

She ignored her aunt to go straight to the heart of the matter. "Ellen, are you pleased to be marrying Lord Dennison?"

"I…yes." Ellen gave her an uncertain smile. "It pleases me. Mother and Father are pleased. Even Gilbert has said that Lord Dennison will make an excellent brother-in-law."

"Because he keeps an excellent *stable.*" Annica sat back

and took a sip of tea. "I can see how suitable Dennison is. Suitable for everyone but you, Ellen."

"Nevertheless…"

"Nevertheless, if that is your decision, I shall support it. Lead me to the invitations, then." She heard a distant knock at the front door and wondered if it was too much to hope for some interruption to rescue her from the tedious task.

"Thank you, 'Nica. I know how busy you have been," Aunt Lucy said. "Lord Auberville's sketches, your blue-stocking league, the ladies' marches. You really must be more careful, dear. Another disaster like that last one in St. James's Street could see an end to Auberville's interest."

"He is not interested, Aunt Lucy."

"Poppycock! I know the signs when I see them. 'Tis in his eyes when he looks at you. I have observed him across a room from you, and he is most attentive to your activities."

The sudden image of Aunt Lucy as a social frigate, cruising through hostile drawing rooms, gathering information, assessing, forming strategies, made Annica smile, despite the fact that she was about to deliver a bitter blow to her aunt. "I believe he has decided I am more trouble than I am worth. We have vowed to remain friends, though."

Aunt Lucy's face dropped. Her plump hand came up to wave airily at the annoying little fact. "'Tis not too late to repair the damage, m'dear."

"Repair?" Annica's interest peaked but she was careful to conceal it. After all, she had *meant* to discourage him, hadn't she? "How might such a thing be accomplished?"

"I should be pleased to assist you, dear child. If you follow my advice, your reputation will improve overnight and Auberville will be back at the door."

"How do you know what Auberville wants, Aunt Lucy?"

"Auberville wants what all men want—a biddable

woman of pleasing temperament and unchallenging demeanor.''

"Biddable? Pleasing temperament? Unchallenging? I do not think I could feign that.''

"I'm certain if you ended your campaign for social reform—''

"*Lie?* Aunt Lucy, he'd be bound to discover my deceit.''

"No, dear. I propose you actually sever your ties with that radical group.''

"Ah." Annica arched one eyebrow in the intimidating manner she had seen Auberville employ. "Then you are saying I should compromise my principles?''

"Could you not just put such indelicate issues aside—''

"No, Aunt Lucy, I could not. What interested me—what made Auberville different—was that he challenged me and was not intimidated. In fact, it was his complete lack of outrage regarding such matters that allowed me to think that we might—''

"*Ahem...*''

Annica turned to find Hodgeson standing at the parlor door. "Yes, Hodgeson?''

"Begging your pardon, milady, but a message has just arrived. I have put it on your writing desk in the library.''

Annica nodded. This was likely from Charity regarding the night's festivities. She would have to send a note by messenger begging off in order to accommodate Aunt Lucy and Ellen. "Thank you, Hodgeson. I shall attend to it straightaway.'' She stood and hurried to the door. "This should not take long, Aunt. Ready the invitations to the masquerade, and I shall be back presently.''

Hodgeson led the way down the corridor and held the library door open for her, then stood just inside, chin up, hands behind his back, and as stiff as a board. His stance and manner told her, as mere words could not, that he did not approve of the message or the messenger. The letter must be from Mr. Bouldin.

She sat and broke the seal. The writing was Mr. Bouldin's. She scanned the spidery script.

Lady A.,
I have urgent news of an unexpected nature. Meet me half past midnight at the Bear and Bull Tavern in Whitefriars.

Yrs, B.

Ignoring the unspoken question in Hodgeson's eyes, she went to the fireplace and dropped the parchment on the flames.

"You are distressed, milady?"

Annica sighed and closed her eyes, feeling quite unsettled. "Ellen has made a 'suitable' match, and all I can think of is how thoroughly I would adore making an utterly *unsuitable* match. The urge will pass, but pray there are no unsuitable men lurking about in the meanwhile."

Chapter Eight

Raucous laughter preceded a group of men out the door of the Bear and Bull Tavern. Drunken shouting and good-natured back-slapping marked their farewells to one another. Annica shrank into the fog-shrouded alley, afraid she would be noticed.

She was uncertain how to proceed. Would Mr. Bouldin expect her to walk brazenly into the tavern and ask for him? Glad she had resorted to the artifice of the trousers that had been delivered earlier from Madame Marie's, she tucked a stray curl, damp from the light drizzle, beneath her workman's cap and pulled it down closer about her ears. There was nothing for it but to go inside. Keeping her head bowed and her hands hidden in her pockets, she pushed the tavern door open with one shoulder.

The dimly lit interior smelled of flat ale and unwashed bodies. This was not Mr. Bouldin's usual sort of place, she was certain. No one paid attention as she ambled to the far side of the room and sat in the corner, where she could watch the door. She laid a shilling on the small wooden table in front of her and, when a haggard-looking woman came for her order, answered, ''A pint,'' in as deep a voice as she could manage.

Glancing cautiously around, she was dismayed that Mr. Bouldin was nowhere to be seen. Patrons came and went over the next half hour, but none were familiar.

Discouraged, she finally stood, convinced that Mr. Bouldin had forgotten their appointment. A stranger who had glanced her way once or twice came to her table, his eyes narrowed in the gloom.

"You waitin' to see Harry?" he asked.

Annica hesitated. The man appeared clean enough, and handsome in a short dark sort of way, but she'd never seen him before. She sat again, resigning herself to this new problem. "I'm waiting for Bouldin," she admitted in a low voice.

A small smile curved the stranger's lips. He sat down. "I've been watching you, but it's so dark in here that I couldn't tell. My name's Renquist." His cockney accent disappeared.

Renquist. Mr. Bouldin's partner. "I'm Nick."

Renquist nodded. "Sure you are." A gloomy look settled across his features and he took a long drink from his tankard before wiping his mouth on his sleeve. "'Fraid I've got some bad news, Nick."

Annica's heart skipped a beat. "Urgent news of an unexpected nature" was the way Mr. Bouldin had phrased it. He must have sent word by Renquist. "Well?" she asked, sitting forward and lowering her voice to a whisper.

"Harry's dead."

"Harry?" she repeated.

"Bouldin."

Annica blinked. Surely she hadn't heard correctly. "Mr. Bouldin is dead? Are you certain?"

There was no joy in the short muffled laugh. "Oh, 'tis certain. Throat cut ear to ear. Blood everywhere. Damn me, but Bouldin was a cautious man. I do not know how—"

"Dead?" Annica repeated dumbly. A lump formed in her

throat and tears sprang to her eyes. She could not comprehend the single word. "Mr. Bouldin is *dead?*"

"Look, Nick, we've been working on a few of your 'projects.' We'd trade off now and again so the blokes wouldn't catch on. I've no way of knowing which of your 'projects' got him, but I'd wager good money 'twas one of 'em."

Her heartbeat, racing a moment ago, stilled to an occasional dull thud. "My projects?" Her brain felt like molasses, thick and slow. She could not comprehend the simplest sentence. Instead she remembered Mr. Bouldin telling her that he'd had a few "near calls" lately.

"That's our job, Nick," Renquist added. "No sense blaming yourself."

Harry. His name had been Harry. She'd known him four years, since the Wednesday League had formed, and she'd never known his name was Harry. "Did he have a family, Mr. Renquist?"

"Two grown sons. A wife. They're a good lot. He had money put away, thanks to your commissions."

Annica looked up, meeting smoky dark eyes filled with concern. "What is *your* given name, Mr. Renquist?"

The man hesitated and gave her an odd look. "Francis."

"Do you have a family?"

"Never had time."

The dampness from the fog and drizzle seeped through her cape. She shivered, feeling cold and dazed. "When did it happen?"

"Two hours ago. He found something and was going to tell you. He asked me to meet him this side of London Bridge beforehand so he could tell me what was afoot. By the time I arrived, he was dead. There was a note pinned to his coat. For you, I think." Renquist pulled out a small scrap of paper from inside his jacket and slid it across the table.

She unfolded the paper and winced when she saw a ragged blotch of blood on one corner. "Stop hiding behind your hirelings. I'll kill them all just like I killed this one. Show yourself, coward, or escape while you can.'' She covered her mouth to stifle a horrified cry.

''I'm no coward, Nick, but this has me nervous. Drop it. Let this one get away.''

She nodded her agreement. ''You must, of course. The threat is quite explicit about my hirelings. If the killer found Mr. Bouldin out, he will find you. But,'' she said, her eyes wide, ''if this is the result of one of my projects, Mr. Renquist, it is all the worse for that. Murder cannot go unanswered. My group and I must go on. We are committed.''

''Bouldin was my partner, Nick. Count me in. But I need a few days to put my affairs in order, if you know what I mean.''

She knew very well what he meant. Putting her own affairs in order was suddenly uppermost in her mind, too. ''Of course, Mr. Renquist. Do you know how to reach me?''

The man nodded. ''Harry told me a couple of days ago. He must have known he'd got himself into a snake pit.''

''Are you certain he gave you no information? A name? Which of the men he was following? Anything?''

''Harry played it close to the vest. All I know is that it must have been something big, and he must have got proof.''

''Thank you, Mr. Renquist. I am sorry about…Harry. I shall miss him. He was a good, honest man.'' She brushed impatiently at the tears that kept rolling down her cheeks. ''If there is anything I can do for his family, you must tell me.''

Renquist stood and gave her an anxious smile. ''Have your driver take you home, Nick. You've had a bad shock. A hot toddy by the fire would stop that shivering.''

''Yes.'' Annica nodded, aware of her trembling hands for the first time. How could she tell him she had no driver? That, in a fit of reckless impatience, she'd sneaked away alone, sublimely confident of her ability to take care of herself?

Had Harry Bouldin felt that same confidence until just a few hours ago?

"Bloody goddamned hell!" She was the last person Tristan expected to encounter. But that *was* Annica. Oh yes, the dark curls escaping a soft workman's cap, the slight frame and easy gait, the determined set of shoulders and—had that not been enough—the familiar, firmly rounded bottom revealed by the damp clinging fabric, could belong to no one else. He'd committed that particular sight to memory and now would recognize it anywhere.

And what in the name of all that was holy was she doing in Whitefriars in the dead of night? After an hour of watching his quarry hide in an alley to watch the tavern, the quarry was about to escape. Tristan turned to see the man disappear around a corner. The Sheikh, meanwhile, was off chasing another suspect, so Tristan had to make a quick decision. Annica or his target? A glance around revealed that Annica was quite alone. Not even a coach.

"Bloody goddamned hell," he muttered again. He started down the darkened street after her. As if to annoy him further, the rain that had been threatening all night began to fall—heavily. Despite the pressing nature of his business, he could not allow his future wife to roam the London streets alone after midnight. Knowing Annica, some disaster would be close behind.

And there, in front of his eyes, the next disaster loomed. A pickpocket slipped from the shadows and fell into step behind her. His hand emerged from the folds of his coat, and Tristan saw the glint of a sharpened blade. His annoyance vanished, and he launched himself toward them with grim purpose, praying he could reach her in time.

The pickpocket seized Annica around the neck from behind. But ere he could bring the knife to her throat, Annica swung her elbow back sharply, delivering a pointed blow to the pickpocket's diaphragm. As he doubled over, she smashed her heel down on his instep. The knife flashed as the villain slashed a semicircle in an effort to clear an escape route. Annica yelped and leaped back, but the blade caught in the fabric of her short cape.

Tristan closed the distance to land one solid upward blow and lay the pickpocket out unconscious on the cobblestones. He barely spared a glance for the man as he stepped over his prostrate body to seize Annica by the shoulders.

The frantic look in her eyes warned him that she was still confused and did not recognize him. She tried to pull away, beating her fists against his chest and kicking at him.

"Annica! Stop! It's me," he whispered, trying to contain the small dervish.

"Auberville?" She peered through the rain and gloom.

"Are you hurt?"

She sagged against him, panting. "I think not."

He stepped back to look her over. A streak of blood slashed across the vest and white shirt along her rib cage, visible beneath the cape. A tightness in Tristan's chest portended panic. "Dear Lord! How bad is it?"

She looked down. "It stings."

Tristan had seen mortally wounded men ignore their injuries and continue to fight in the heat of battle. The mere thought that she could be seriously wounded brought emotion welling up in his chest. He removed his cravat and pressed it against her wound. "Hold this tight!"

Thunder boomed directly overhead and rain fell in sheets. He scooped her up and hurried down a side street toward a sign proclaiming the Blue Bell Inn.

"Tristan!" she gasped. "Put me down!" But her arms encircled his neck and her cheek rested against his chest. Her relief, the way she leaned into him, evoked a strong protective surge—so fierce it astonished him. He could have slain a dragon in that moment.

"The pickpocket," she whispered. "We must notify—"

"Confound it, Annica! Do you want to report this to the authorities? Do you want to explain to *them* what you're doing alone in Whitefriars in the middle of the night?" He reached the door of the Blue Bell Inn and kicked it open.

Fifteen minutes later, with a disapproving innkeeper still deceived by her disguise and muttering about the certain fate of sodomites, Annica and Tristan were safely shut away from prying eyes. A fire sprang to life when Tristan dropped a match on the kindling, and the cold, sparse chamber was instantly more inviting. Rain beat against the panes of a mullioned window, narrowing their world to this one room.

Still disoriented, she pulled her workman's cap off and shook her head. Her hair fell over her shoulders and down her back, curling from the dampness. The flat, empty feeling of loss came back to her. Harry Bouldin—a man she had known and respected—was dead because of her investigations.

Tristan removed a small silver flask from his pocket, took one glance at her and downed a quick gulp before placing it on the table. He shrugged out of his greatcoat and threw it over a chair, then went to the washstand, got the pitcher and bowl and placed them on the hearth to warm. "Come here," he ordered.

"Tristan, I—"

He had a grim, determined look on his face. "I will not be diverted, Annica. What are you doing in Whitefriars in the middle of the night? Where is your coach? Your footman? Miss Wardlow? Hodgeson? A companion or chaperon of any kind?"

She sighed, knowing she would have to give him some

sort of answer. "I had to meet someone, and I knew Hodgeson would not approve."

"Hodgeson? What of your uncle Thomas?"

"He would not have approved, either." She tried a smile.

"Do not jolly me," he warned. "Who did you meet?"

"A Bow Street Runner," she admitted. Her mind worked quickly, trying to find a way to redirect Tristan before he got too close to the truth.

"Why? For God's sake, Annica, what business could you have with a runner? And in the middle of the night, no less?"

Thinking of Sarah and Mr. Bouldin, she blinked back fresh tears and cleared her throat. "Something was lost, Auberville."

"What loss could warrant the risks you've taken?"

"Tristan—"

"You should have come to me. I'd have handled it for you."

"We no longer have that sort of friendship, Auberville. I am quite capable, after all, and this is a private matter."

"Capable! I'm growing to loathe that word," he muttered under his breath. "What have you done? Pawned your jewelry for a gambling debt? Are you paying hush money to someone? Are you plotting some reformationist rebellion? Where have you planted the bomb, Annica?"

"Something was lost and I hired a runner to find it. He sent a message saying he had got information."

"He found your lost object?" Tristan looked doubtful.

"He…he never came," she said, looking down at her feet to hide her sudden tears.

Tristan shook his head. He came to her and cupped her shoulders, holding her immobile. "Promise me that you will never do this again."

Acutely aware of the warmth of his touch, she felt her

heart give a sudden lurch. "I cannot make such a promise, Auberville."

"You must," he insisted. "'Tis too bloody dangerous! You cannot even imagine what sort of deeds are done in this part of town in the dead of night. You could have been killed. And, damn it, Annica, this sort of stunt could ruin you forever! It is one thing to have a reputation as an eccentric or an original, and quite another to be ruined."

"I understand 'ruined' better than you, Tristan," she snapped, looking up into the handsome face etched with concern. "Every woman I know is aware of how little it would take to achieve it. Furthermore, if I decide to risk ruination, you may rest assured that the cause will be worth it, and you will not be able to stop me." She broke away and took two steps backward.

He raised one eyebrow. "Will I not?"

"Who are you to say me nay?"

"Tristan Sinclair, Lord Auberville! The one man who is man enough to do it," he told her through gritted teeth.

"Then, if you would protect me, you'd best remove yourself before we are discovered, Auberville. Being in this room as we are now is enough to ruin me, and well you know it."

"I shall cure that little ill tomorrow," he snapped.

"*That* will be a fancy trick! And whilst we're on it, what were *you* doing outside the Bear and Bull tonight? Have you been following me?"

"It would appear I should have been. 'Twas one of life's little ironies that placed me there. I recognized your charming little derrière as you came out of the tavern, lucky for you—"

"Lucky? I swear, you are rather too full of yourself. I had vanquished the pickpocket ere you interfered."

"You have a talent for disaster, madam. You are wounded! Thank God 'twas no worse. You could be dead!"

The thought sobered her, and the memory of Mr. Bouldin returned full force. Tears filled her eyes, and she wiped impatiently at them with the back of her hand.

Tristan's attitude changed in an instant from indignation to concern. "What is it? Do you hurt? Tell me, damn it."

"I thought we agreed to be friends. Would you deal with a friend as you are dealing with me now? Leave me alone, Tristan. I guarantee, you cannot help me out of this."

He regarded her unflinchingly for one long moment. Annica knew he was struggling with a difficult decision, and she was closer to being afraid in that moment than ever before—of what plan he might be hatching. His jaw tightened and a muscle jumped as he clenched his teeth. He took a deep breath and let it out, clearly mastering his temper and coming to a decision. "Leaving you alone will not be possible now," he said in a quiet voice. "Shall we see your wound? No more delays—" he held a hand up to silence her "—and no diversions."

He unfastened her short cape and let it drop to the floor, focusing his attention on her right side, where she still pressed his cravat. He took the embroidered silk from her and worked quickly to unbutton her vest and drop that, too, to the floor.

She wiped her eyes on the sleeve of her shirt and sniffed. When he tugged her white linen shirt from the waistband of her trousers, she put her hands over his to stop him. She could not expose herself with Tristan in the room. In fact, she doubted that she should expose herself with Tristan anywhere in the vicinity. She looked at him, her mouth suddenly dry.

"You must not," she whispered, fearing what his touch would do to her resolve.

"Your wound needs attention," he said in a husky voice.

"You are not a physician, Auberville."

"I have patched wounds before, Lady Annica. This needs

to be seen to *now*." He retrieved the silver flask from the table and placed it on the hearth beside the basin.

She glanced down and was surprised to see a red slash staining her shirt. Convinced, she dropped her hands to her sides. She could feel the heat rising in her cheeks, but she bit her lower lip and nodded in consent.

Kneeling, Tristan lifted the fabric just enough to bare her lower right rib cage. She was amazed to see his fingers tremble as he traced the line of her wound. She was more aware of the tingling caused by his touch than any discomfort from the cut. Feeling dizzy, she shuddered, closed her eyes and placed her hand on the top of his head to steady herself.

When he looked up from her wound, his face was pale and the scar beneath his left eye stood out in stark contrast. "'Tis no more than a deep scratch. It will not require stitching."

A guarded look shadowed his eyes as he stood and backed away from her. He turned toward the fire as if searching for an answer there, then back to her. There was a lean, hungry look about him. The heat of that steady gaze held her entranced. She could not have moved had she caught fire. Nor did she want to.

He unbuttoned his vest and then his shirt, revealing his strongly muscled chest. His gaze never left hers. Her heart leaped into her throat and her knees went weak. She prayed he would not guess the effect he was having on her rioting emotions. Still watching her, he rent his shirt into several long strips and dipped one sleeve in the washbowl. Kneeling before her, and with a touch so gentle she could barely feel it, he cleaned the cut, then nodded in satisfaction. A fresh strip of cloth was doused with brandy from the flask, and that, too, was pressed to her wound. The alcohol stung, and she gasped in surprise.

Tristan looked up at her. "That should keep you until

you are home.'' He stood, brushing the length of her as he did. The move was seductive…deliberate.

She dropped her shirttails and held his shoulders to keep her balance. She had never touched a man's naked flesh before and the heat and firmness left her short of breath. Curious, she dropped her head back to look up into the unreadable face.

His mouth lowered reluctantly, as if drawn against his will. ''We've gone too far to pretend nothing is happening here,'' he murmured against her lips.

Diversion was an absurd waste of time. In a flash of clarity, she knew she had been waiting for him to claim her since he had first smiled at her. And she knew, too, that she had been considering surrender ever since Madame Marie had told her that not every romance must end in marriage.

His arms tightened, crushing her against his bare chest, and he deepened the kiss—a kiss unlike his others. This one did not ask, it demanded, seizing control of her senses. She yielded, powerless to control whatever savage forces were raging inside her, and glad of it. When his tongue invaded her mouth, little shock waves rippled along her spine.

He blazed a trail of hot kisses down the column of her throat. Bending her backward over one steady arm, he used the other to open her shirt. One gentle hand began a breathtaking stroking of the soft flesh of her breast. His mouth stopped in its downward progress from her ear to cherish the hollow of her throat, and she gasped when her pulse leaped to meet his lips.

Tristan's responding moan vibrated along her every nerve, and she shivered at the sensation. She was tingling in the most amazing places!

He swept her up and carried her to the narrow bed, covering her face and neck with small, eager kisses. He had her boots off in two short tugs and her trousers unfastened before she could protest. Her shirt, already undone, was quickly discarded.

"Annica…Annica…you overwhelm me. I cannot even think when you sigh," he murmured against her heated flesh.

She was past dissembling, past modesty. She fumbled with the waistband of his trousers, urgent to discover this unknown territory.

He was the model of masculine beauty, like a nude statue of a Greek god she had seen in a museum. Lord! Was the rest of Tristan like that statue?

Boots, trousers and small clothes joined the pile on the floor before he turned back to the bed. She could not help staring. The rest of Tristan was *very* like the statue, but stronger, more powerful. Larger. Much larger. And erect. She took heart from the fact that she had never heard of anyone dying from what they were about to do.

When he came down beside her on the bed, he did not return to her lips but made for sweeter destinations. His mouth closed over one rosy aureole, and it became taut and exquisitely sensitive as he teased and cherished the little bud. Annica twined her fingers through his hair, drawing him closer. "Tristan! Oh…never stop!"

He shuddered and his hoarse voice pulled her out of the sensuous fog surrounding her. "What we are about to do will change you, sprite. If you would say no, say it now, and quickly, because in a moment there will be no choice left to make."

She reached out to brush back a thick shock of golden hair that had fallen over his forehead. "I feel as if I shall burst into flames at any moment. I could not bear to end it now."

"What of the risks?"

"I've weighed the risks…."

The deep vibration of his laugh against her flesh caused

a liquid fire to course through her veins. "A neat trick, madam, since you have no idea what lies ahead."

She traced the ridges of his muscles with her fingertips, fascinated by the supple firmness of his flesh and the way his muscles moved beneath his skin. She was awed by their strength.

His hand slipped past her bandaged ribs to the soft flesh of her belly and to the crisp thatch of nether hair and beyond. Her blood turned to molten lava—hot, thick, all-consuming. Though she had felt the excitement of his kisses, she'd never felt such mindless compulsion to rush onward. All she knew was that, if he stopped now, she would die.

When he parted the soft petals guarding her sheath, she bit her lip to prevent an embarrassed outcry, but her hips betrayed her by rising to his hand. That touch, that invasion, was closer to heaven than she had ever been.

"Yes, that's it," he groaned. "You are so ripe that you respond as if we are already one. Come, sprite, open for me."

She raised one knee to grant him fuller access. Dizzy with delight, she wondered if this was what it was like to swoon. Perhaps she was the swooning kind, after all. She reached for him, wanting to touch him as intimately as he touched her, to give back some of the joy she took.

His arm beside her head braced his weight, the other caught her hand on its downward path and raised it to his lips. He skimmed a kiss along the knuckles before placing it on his chest. "This will be difficult enough, Annica. Do not distract me, or we'll both regret it."

She bit her lower lip and nodded.

The hand bracing his weight laced through the tangles of her hair. "Steady, Annica. Hold on to me."

She did as he asked, feeling the strain of control in his powerful muscles, and she trusted that he would be as gentle as it was in his power to be. She began to doubt the wisdom of her decision with his first tentative probing. Then he nibbled an earlobe, and her fear went whistling down the wind. A bittersweet ache brought her knees up alongside his hips.

He pressed downward again, gaining a shallow entry. She was startled by a sudden tightness where only moments before she had felt herself opening to his coaxing. He held her gaze, an exultant look about him, and her body turned fluid as he thrust again, slowly, gently.

She closed her eyes and took a deep shuddering breath when the new and bewilderingly erotic sensation swept through her. Despite the building pressure, she desperately wanted more of that feeling. "Tristan…"

He plunged downward, tearing the fragile barrier. She gasped and stiffened in surprise. Relenting, now that the deed was done, he smoothed her hair back from her face. He kissed her and stilled his movements, allowing her time for the discomfort to ease, time for her to accustom herself to his size. He eased his weight from her by rolling over and dragging her with him, placing her above him, but still rooted within her.

He whispered an apology of sorts. "That was the worst of it, sprite. Henceforth, this will bring you only pleasure."

She nodded, growing accustomed to the tender intrusion. Her hair tumbled about them and, both hands free at last, he caught it between his fingers and pressed it to his lips.

He inhaled deeply. "You smell of juniper and moss and wildflowers. Your skin tastes as sweet as wild berries. Annica, my woodland sprite. Annica, of the evergreen eyes."

"That is quite poetical, my lord." She sighed, pleased with the comparison.

"Perhaps I have a poet's soul."

She shivered. "You are a warrior, Tristan—a hunter."

He pulled her head down by the dark tendrils to nip one tender earlobe. "You've found me out, sprite. And now that the warrior has *invaded* this particular territory—" his hands slid down her back to caress her buttocks "—what should he do next?"

"Conquer, my lord. If he can."

His laugh turned to a soft groan when he stirred within her, causing an exquisite tightening in her passage again. The feeling was irresistibly intimate. They had truly become one person, one flesh, and she felt his strength and power. Overcome with the heady sensation, she prayed it would never end.

She moved experimentally, and he gave a low rumbling groan. His arms tightened around her and he rolled over again, still buried within her.

"'Tis time to finish this, sprite. I'm at the end of my control," he told her, an apology in the deep voice.

The discomfort eased, but Annica felt urgency rising again. Tristan quickened the ancient primal rhythms. Her passion built with alarming speed and intensity, filling her to the bursting point. She matched his moves and was rewarded with praise.

"Yes...that's it, sprite. I knew from the moment I heard you laugh that you were a woman made for love," he sighed. "A woman made for me."

Waves of fire washed over her and a glorious radiance erupted at her core. It was the most amazingly joyful, most intensely pleasurable sensation she had ever experienced. The release of the unendurable tension was like the loosening of a flight of birds into an endless, deep blue sky. When it ebbed, lethargy left her weak and trembling.

"*Now* you are mine," he whispered in her ear with a deep, answering shudder.

The public coach drew up around the corner from the Sayles home, and Tristan lifted Annica down. He tossed a coin to the driver and waited until the man disappeared.

The storm had passed, and the waning night was moments

from fading to dawn. The clean, rain-washed air was bracing, clearing away the remnants of the passion they had so recently shared. Aware that they had dallied longer than was safe, he now faced a greater problem—how to get her inside without notice.

He hurried her around back to the garden wall. At the gate, he looked down into the sultry features he had learned to read so well in the last hours. The softness in her eyes pleased him best. That was a new look—the look of a well-loved woman—and he had put it there.

He pulled her short cape closer around her in a protective gesture that surprised him. "Go in, Annica. Rest. I shall come to you in late afternoon, depending upon how many favors I must call in."

She sighed, fatigue written in every line of her body. "I am numb, Tristan. I cannot even think. Did we have an appointment this afternoon? Another specimen?"

"Not another specimen, m'dear. Business of another kind."

The muffled clank of pots from the kitchen interrupted them, and Tristan shook his head. "Damn. Too late. I suppose we shall have to pay the piper now."

Annica reached up, laid a finger across his lips and smiled. "I do not use the kitchen door," she whispered.

He grimaced. "You would not walk boldly in the front door?"

"Good night, Tristan. Keep well." She slipped from his arms and ran silently across the lawn to the thick ivy vine growing against the walls and along the eaves.

He wanted to call her back when she began to climb toward an open window on the second floor. She was absurdly reckless and obviously needed a much stronger hand than that of her uncle Thomas. And as for her assessment of risks...

She was halfway up the vine when her foot slipped and

she dangled for one tense moment before she gained purchase again. He heard a soft giggle before she turned to wave at him and continue her climb. He held his breath until she disappeared through an open window.

How many times had she made that particular ascent? He made a mental note to instruct his gardener to remove any vines and trellises outside the bedchamber windows at Auberville Hall. Thank God there were none outside Clarendon Place, his London house.

Chapter Nine

Nervous chatter followed Annica into the conservatory. The members of the Wednesday League had all arrived at once, anxious to hear the reason for Annica's urgent summons.

"Heavens, 'Nica, you look at sixes and sevens! What is wrong?" Grace asked.

"Mr. Bouldin is dead!"

"What! How do you know?"

"I was supposed to meet him at a tavern in Whitefriars. He had got some information and needed to see me at once."

"What was it?" Sarah asked, her eyes wide.

Annica pulled the conservatory door closed and led the women toward a grouping of chairs by the fountain. "I do not know. He did not come. Mr. Renquist, his partner, met me instead." She sat down, her copy of Jane Austen's *Mansfield Park* in her lap.

"Well, then, what did Mr. Renquist report?" Charity asked.

"Mr. Bouldin...*Harry*—" Annica's voice broke "—was murdered just before he was to meet me."

Stunned silence met this announcement. Constance

leaned forward and took Annica's hand. "I am sorry, 'Nica. I know how much you liked him."

"The killer left this note." She took the bloodstained missive from between the pages of her little book and read it to the women. "Mr. Renquist was certain the murderer was one of the men I asked Mr. Bouldin to investigate."

"*One* of the men? I knew about Roger Wilkes, but who else did you set him on?" Grace asked.

"Geoffrey Morgan," Annica admitted in a soft voice.

"*Geoffrey Morgan?*" Constance shrilled. "Who gave you the authority to investigate Mr. Morgan? You exceed yourself."

"Come now, ladies. We must keep cool heads," Grace intervened. "'Tis done, and cannot be *undone*."

"I am sorry, Constance." Annica sighed. "Mr. Morgan was not quite what he seemed. I feared you might come to harm."

"You had no right!"

"None but my affection for you," she agreed.

"He...he is a most unusual man. Very mysterious," Charity interjected. "His family connections are unquestionable, but his past is obscure."

"In view of recent events, Constance, I, for one, am interested in the results of that investigation," Grace said, smoothing one chestnut curl into place.

Annica sniffled and sighed again, sorry for the dissension in their group. "The Morgan family is of minor nobility from Yorkshire. Geoffrey, the only son of Baron Alfred Morgan, will inherit the title and estates. He has one sister, who married some years ago and removed to Dover. There is modest wealth."

Constance buried her face in her hands. "I could have told you all this."

"Can you tell us where he has been since the completion of his studies at Cambridge ten years ago?" Charity asked.

Constance looked up, her eyes wide.

"Can you tell us where he disappeared to several months ago, and why he has shown up again?" Annica asked. She took a deep breath and plunged onward. "Can you tell us where he was last night after ten o'clock?"

"This is preposterous!" Constance sputtered. "I would stake my life upon his honesty. And…and we could even make a case against your respectable Lord Auberville! *He* was in town when Sarah was raped, and then disappeared until just recently. Where was *he* last night after ten o'clock?"

Annica dropped her gaze to her lap. Where *had* Tristan been before happening upon her?

"I do not understand what you have against Geoff. He is simply a private man. He would not rape Sarah, nor murder a Bow Street Runner! You are completely wrong about this."

"I pray you are right, Constance," Annica said.

"I will not be a party to ruining Mr. Morgan!"

"We are not asking that. Indeed, he is not our only suspect. There is still Mr. Wilkes." Annica put the bloodstained note away in the folds of her book. "But there is, now, undeniable danger in continuing our investigation. The threat in the murderer's warning applies to all of us. In the face of that threat, ladies, and bearing it in mind, we must decide if we wish to proceed—and if so, how?"

"Aye," Grace voted. "Continue."

"Continue," Charity and Sarah agreed.

"Nay." Constance shook her head. "Drop this, Annica. You can only come to grief."

"I cannot drop it." Annica's voice was firm, denying any appeal. "I must continue. If not for Sarah, then for Mr. Bouldin and his family—and I shall do so with or without the assistance of this group. I have already decided to try my hand at following Mr. Wilkes during the day so that Mr.

Renquist will be free to pursue other leads. According to Mr. Renquist, Mr. Wilkes visits his club every day at noon. I shall lay in wait for him there.''

Constance glanced away, clearly angry. ''Then go to it, 'Nica, since I shall not be a party to it at all. Instead, I shall use this interim to see if I can find Frederika.''

''In view of the seriousness of this problem, perhaps we ought to meet twice a week,'' Grace said.

''Shall we say Tuesday at the Moores' crush?'' Charity suggested. ''Ten o'clock at the folly in the garden.''

''Yes. And Friday next at Aunt Lucy's masquerade,'' Annica said. ''I've sent invitations to all our suspects. We shall have them all under one roof at the same time.''

The ring of uneven footsteps on the tile floor alerted them to an intruder. Hodgeson came around a potted palm and bowed. ''Excuse me, milady, but your uncle requests your presence in the library at once,'' he announced.

Annica sighed. ''I hope he has not got a report of me.''

''He and Lord Auberville have been closeted for the past several hours, milady. Drinking claret. No cigars that I could see,'' he informed her with an inscrutable look. ''Your aunt was summoned a few minutes ago.''

''Please tell them I will be with them momentarily. And thank you for the warning, Hodgeson.'' Annica's stomach did a flip-flop. Surely Tristan would not have been so ungentlemanly as to reveal their indiscretion? But what could he and Uncle Thomas have been discussing for so long? What would require Aunt Lucy's presence?

''Ladies, will you excuse me? It would appear there is something afoot, and I'd best face it as quickly as possible.''

''Trouble, 'Nica?''

Heat flooded Annica's cheeks as she recalled Tristan's passion—the warmth of his skin, the incredible intimacy of being physically joined, and the breathtaking delight of the sensations to which he had introduced her. "No. No trouble at all."

Tristan leaned one arm on the mantel of the fireplace and lifted his glass of claret with the other. If this was Annica's idea of "momentarily," he would be surprised.

Thomas shifted his weight in his chair behind the massive desk and cleared his throat. "I believe she had to take her leave of Miss Wardlow," he explained.

Tristan nodded, wondering at his own anxiety. His head had been whirling since leaving Annica this morning. He hadn't slept—there wasn't time. The trap was closing around the little sprite, and he was anxious to have it finished. The sooner, the better. She needed a man who could look after her properly, before she came to grief. And he needed to wrap this up so he could give his full attention to Kilgrew's assignment.

Lucille Sayles sighed and clasped her hands tighter.

The library door opened and closed, and Annica came forward dressed in a becoming confection of grass-green silk embroidered with garlands of pink roses. Her glossy dark hair had been loosely pulled back and secured at her nape with a twist of pink and green ribbons. She looked fresh and innocent and, were it not for the pale violet shadows beneath her eyes, he could almost believe he had dreamed the events of last night.

Ah, but no dream could have prepared him for the reality. He'd lost himself in her. The mere memory of her in the throes of passion caused an ominous thickening in his groin. He'd had enough women to have lost count long ago, but Annica was unique. She challenged him, engaged him, and she aroused him with the barest lift of an eyebrow. That she was not particularly capable no longer concerned him. The rest, however, was still unknown. Would she run? Was she trustworthy and steadfast?

She glanced sideways at him, a becoming blush staining her cheeks. Her eyes had the woodland sprite look—half wild, half come-hither. He knew she was remembering last night, and his own body tightened with the memory.

Thomas gestured to a chair. "Sit down, my dear. We have a matter to discuss with you. I know it is unusual, but Auberville felt this would be the best way to handle the matter."

"Ahh…" she said as she sat and smoothed her skirts.

Tristan smiled, reading her nervousness from that single gesture. She could not meet his gaze.

"We have had these discussions before, 'Nica, and your stubbornness is legendary. But now, you see, Auberville has made an offer. It is a generous one, and I hope you consider it more seriously than the others, as I believe it is time for you to quit playing coy. At your age, there will not be many more."

Annica turned in her chair to look at him, her eyes round with genuine surprise. "Offer?"

"A marriage offer," Thomas clarified.

"Good heavens! Whatever for?" she exclaimed.

Tristan coughed. This was not the response he had hoped for. Though, knowing Annica, he should not have been surprised.

"For marriage," Thomas repeated. "I must say how pleased I was, dear niece. I had hoped, when I sent him to you some time ago, that you might, well, take a shine to him."

"Yes," Lucy interjected. "Annica dear, I am relieved that you are no longer allowing what your father did to taint—"

"*Friendship!*" Annica interrupted. She turned to Tristan and blinked. "You amaze me, Auberville. Had we not agreed—"

Tristan held up one hand to cut her off. "In view of recent events, Annica, I am surprised you did not expect this."

"How could I? I thought we would continue as before."

He had to stop her before she gave them away. "Thomas, Lucille, would you be so good as to excuse us for a moment?"

The older couple stood and looked from Tristan to Annica and back again. Thomas nodded. "Needs a little urging, eh? This is where we lose 'em. Well, good luck, Auberville. You'll likely need it. We shall be outside. Come along, Lucy."

"But Annica will need our support," Lucille protested.

"Auberville will need it," Thomas corrected.

The moment the door closed behind them, Annica came to her feet. "Tristan, this is completely unnecessary. I told you—I weighed the risks and—"

"Found them acceptable," Tristan finished. He placed his glass of claret on the mantel and went to her. "But I did not find them acceptable at all."

"You? What risk did *you* take?"

He shrugged. "The risk that my child—my heir—might be born a bastard."

"Child? What child?"

"Surely I do not have to explain physiology to such a charming little bluestocking as yourself?"

Annica blushed. "Of course not, Auberville."

"And, though my intentions were good, sprite, you so enchanted me that I lost my presence of mind. I did not withdraw in time to spare you that possibility. You could be *enceinte* even now." He touched her cheek in a familiar gesture, hoping that would warm her heart with memories of last night.

"Oh!" She turned away, blushing crimson.

"So you see, I must insist upon marriage," he concluded. He caught her chin on one crooked finger, lifting her face to look directly into her eyes. "It is impossible to know everything about a potential spouse, but I know your basic character to be honest and intelligent. I admire your commitment to those less fortunate than you, though I sometimes take exception to your methods. On the few occasions when we have been at odds, you have not been given to hysterics and were open to reason. Add your propensity to heat my blood, and we have an ideal match."

"Thank you, milord." She smiled sweetly.

Tristan felt the short hairs on the back of his neck prickle—an instinctive warning that something had gone wrong in the negotiations. Though she was smiling, he detected an edge of anger in her voice. "Have you found some fault in my reasoning?"

"Just one, Auberville. It does not take into account my own wishes."

"You allowed me to make love to you."

"Yes, but I did not weigh marriage as a particular risk of that venture. I was informed recently that a romance needn't always end in marriage. I know you've had mistresses before, so I concluded that such an arrangement must be agreeable to you."

He was surprised by this statement and the fact that it rankled him. "Who told you such a thing?"

"Though it is not spoken of in polite society, it is well known that you have had mistresses in the past. You yourself told me you had practice in those arts. Since you did not wed your mistresses, I concluded such things were acceptable to you. I did not ever imagine you would insist upon marriage."

He could not think how to defend himself against such a logical argument. "You misjudged me. Did you weigh getting with child as a possible risk of our little interlude?"

Annica sat heavily, looking down at her clasped hands.

"You have not thought this out, have you? It would be best if you tell me right now what is stopping you."

"I am afraid," she said without hesitation. Her eyes, sparkling with unshed tears, lifted from her lap to meet his.

Tristan was torn between sympathy and exasperation. How could she possibly fear him? "I would never hurt you, Annica."

She hesitated and her gaze darted to the door, as if measuring her chances of escape. "I...I have grown accustomed to my life. I do not want to forfeit my friends, my beliefs, my activities. I am afraid a husband would curtail them—"

"You are bloody right, madam. No more midnight rendezvous with Bow Street Runners in Whitefriars. If you have a problem, I will expect you to come to me."

"—or...or that I'd be subjected to a husband's temper and control. Be at his mercy," she finished, as if she had not been interrupted.

"I do not have a temper, Annica, but I am accustomed to running my own household. I will not be henpecked or harangued, but neither am I inclined to be controlling. I have never struck a woman in my life, nor will I ever. And, since you mention it, there are no tenderer mercies upon which you could be thrown."

Thrown! Into marriage! Good Lord! Her worst nightmare! Annica watched Tristan as he began to pace. She realized that, unlike her father, he was nervous, not angry. Tristan Sinclair, Lord Auberville, was apprehensive! The diplomat who negotiated truces with pirates and cutthroats in the palaces of emirs was unsure of himself in her library! That endearing fact brought a cautious warmth back to her heart.

But marriage? No. Impossible. She trusted this man more than she'd trusted any man in her life, but marriage was beyond the scope of her wildest imagination. She'd seen marriage. She knew better.

Without thinking, she began a long-practiced, oft-delivered speech. "My lord, I...I thank you for the great compliment you have paid me by your proposal, but I believe I am not suited to the married state. 'Twould distress me, m'lord, to find that you, as all men do, told me lies and made promises you could not keep in order to persuade an affirmative answer. I would only feel betrayed in the end, and disappoint you as a result. And you would soon tire of—"

"Stop right there, Annica. I deserve better than that. And I deserve better than to have you make a mistress of *me*."

Annica's mouth dropped open. Was that what she had done—used Tristan the same as men used the women she avenged? Was she as guilty as they? She had not suspected for one moment that such an arrangement would not be acceptable to the discreet but somewhat licentious lord. "My lord, I value your friendship far beyond a mere convenience, but—"

Tristan ran his long fingers through his hair in a gesture of exasperation. "This is absurd! How have you managed to turn the tables on me?"

"I would not hurt you for all the world, m'lord, but neither can I allow you to hurt me."

"Hurt you? To the contrary! I have acquired a special license in the effort to protect you from gossip, ruination and public embarrassment from the early arrival of a child."

Annica clasped her hands together so tightly that her knuckles turned white. *Child!* There it was again. The most compelling reason for marriage she had heard yet. "But, what of my work with St. Anne's Orphanage? The social reform movement, my commitments to the Ladies Enfranchisement League and the Wednesday League? I could not bear to give them up."

"I would not ask that of you, Annica. I have no quarrel with your sentiments, only with your methods. I want no repeat of the riots, and I want you to keep me informed of your activities. But I would not prevent you from acting in accord with your conscience. I believe you have a good one, and I trust your heart—if not always your judgment.''

"That is very kind of you to say so, Tristan.''

"Then, will you marry me, Annica Sayles?''

"Tristan, I…'' *Never. Never. Never!* "I cannot.''

"Marriage is a convenient institution to legitimize one's heirs. I stand by that reason and appeal to you on those grounds if none other.''

She had a quick flash of herself hiding beneath a desk from her father's wrath, then an image of a small Tristan, sitting alone at a window with a ticking clock as his only companion, wondering why his mother had abandoned him. Despite her own fears, she could not abandon Tristan, too. And he appeared to want her baby—if there was one. Unlike her father, who had never wanted her.

The small child's voice repeating her firm vow came again. She pressed her temples with her fingertips to still the throbbing. "I am confused, m'lord. You make a compelling case, but I…this is so beyond me that…''

"Then we are agreed?''

It was impossible to think with Tristan so near. And so insistent. "Agreed? To what, m'lord. I cannot say the word you want to hear. The prospect is foreign to my every plan, my every wish. Must you have an answer now? This day?''

"I would prefer your unqualified acceptance and a commitment to say our vows on the morrow.''

Tears welled in her eyes. She knew her panic was showing, but she could not hide it. "I cannot bend that far, Tristan.''

"Then I will give you a fortnight to think, if you will swear to tell me if you find that you are with child. Trust me, Annica. I will not disappoint you.''

She bowed her head over her hands and gave a little nod.

Tristan did not hesitate. He crossed the library and threw the door open. "Come in, Thomas and Lucy. Annica has consented to consider my offer and give an answer within the fortnight."

Chapter Ten

By Tuesday evening at the Moores' crush, the news of Tristan's offer for Annica had spread from South Kensington to Southwark. Roger Wilkes was quite peeved regarding the news of the pending engagement, and Annica marveled at his audacity. "Really, Mr. Wilkes, I cannot imagine why you think you are entitled to any sort of explanation. If I should choose to marry Auberville, it is my own affair."

"Affair?" he laughed snidely. "Is that it, then? He has offered to make an honest woman of you?"

Annica halted in the center of the dance floor and swept Wilkes with a scathing glance. There was nothing extraordinary about the man. He was average in every way. Of an average height and build, muddy brown hair, pale blue eyes and a pale complexion. There was nothing about him to suggest his depravity. But she could not separate the man from her suspicion of what he'd done to Sarah.

She snapped her fan open and walked haughtily to the sidelines. She was in no mood to indulge the likes of Roger Wilkes in a fit of pique. She was exhausted and confused, and she was tired of answering ridiculous questions regarding Auberville. How had that news got out, anyway?

"Lady Annica! Wait! I meant no offense—"

"What else could I take from your comment? You have overstepped the boundaries of good manners and common sense." She reached the French doors to the terrace, fighting the instinct to give him the cut direct and leave him looking like the fool he was. But there was too much at stake—a rape, a murder and a threat to the entire Wednesday League.

"You must forgive me, Lady Annica," Wilkes said, following her into the cool night air. "I was distraught to think that you had fallen victim to Auberville's trap."

Annica took three deep breaths and calmed herself. "Trap? You are speaking nonsense, Mr. Wilkes."

"I think not. Word has it that he set his sights on you because he admired your competence and independence—the only things he values in a woman. He hooked you, Lady Annica, and he reeled you in. He does not want to take care of you. He wants you because you take care of yourself, and he can leave you to raise his brats while he does as he pleases."

Annica swallowed hard. Though Wilkes was not reliable, there was just enough of her own fears in his words to give her pause. "Mr. Wilkes, you must not give credence to gossip."

"Gossip is passed from ear to ear, Lady Annica. My source is close enough to have heard it firsthand. Thus it is far more reliable than gossip."

"You must promise me you will not repeat what you have told me. If you do, it will prevent any friendship between us."

"I thought you deserved a warning."

"I do not need your warnings, sir," she told him with an uncompromising shrug of one shoulder. "Certainly no one has forced you to be my friend. Nor can I see anyone holding you captive here. Feel free to go."

She prayed he would leave her alone to collect her thoughts, but when she turned back, he was watching her with an appraising eye. That look raised goose bumps on the back of her neck, and she knew that she had not discouraged Wilkes in the least. She had challenged him.

"I shall stay, Lady Annica, because I believe you are worth the effort." Wilkes seized her gloved hand and brushed a kiss across the knuckles.

The sound of footsteps interrupted him. "Here you are, Lady Annica," Auberville said over Wilkes's shoulder. He came around the man to stand beside her.

His warm hand came to rest on her waist and she smiled, pleased beyond words at his impeccable timing.

"I have been looking for you, my dear," he said. "There is a small matter I wished to discuss. Good evening, Wilkes."

"Auberville," Wilkes said, giving a stiff bow.

"I'd like to speak with my intended privately, Wilkes." A muscle jumped along his jaw.

Bowing over her hand, Wilkes murmured, "I shall see you later, Lady Annica." Then he backed away.

She turned to look up at Tristan's face in the dim light of the hanging lanterns. "Auberville?"

"Annica, for the last time, I want you to stay clear of Wilkes. He is not the sort of person you should cultivate."

Though she could not have agreed with him more, she also could not tell him why it was necessary for her to maintain a civil relationship with the man—at least for the time being. "He is harmless, Tristan."

"*Harmless* is not a word I would use for the likes of Wilkes."

"What do you know about him, Tristan?"

"That is not a matter to interest you, my dear. Simply trust that I have your welfare at heart."

"That sort of condescension does not go down well with me, Tristan. If you think this autocratic attitude is the manner in which to deal with me, perhaps you should think again. I am not a child, I am not brainless and I do not appreciate being told what sort of persons to cultivate.''

''And I am not a man accustomed to justifying his opinions and decisions,'' he countered.

Or perhaps you are afraid Wilkes will tell me about your carefully laid trap—as he has. ''Is there a middle ground, Auberville, or would you prefer we walk away while we still can?''

''You will not be rid of me so easily, Annica.''

''What *will* it take?'' She could have bitten her tongue the moment the words were out. Tristan was dead right in his assessment and unfailing in his instinct to protect her. She was being childish to challenge him in so ridiculous a manner.

He gave her the slow, easy smile that always left her slightly confused and disoriented. ''Nothing, sprite. I am determined that you will make an honest man of me. And I've never thought of you as brainless. Willful, perhaps, or determined—but never brainless. I will attempt to be less 'autocratic' if you will attempt to respect my opinions.''

''You rarely voice an opinion, Auberville.''

''That is precisely why I expect you to listen when I do. Shall we try again? Roger Wilkes is not the sort of man I wish you to traffic with, my dear.''

She heaved a long-suffering sigh. ''Very well, Tristan. I understand your concern, and I shall keep it in mind. I promise to be careful in my dealings with him, but I cannot simply cut him at this particular time.''

Tristan pulled her into his arms, bent his mouth to hers and kissed her thoroughly. ''Nicely done, m'dear. You reaffirm my faith in you.''

''But how will we ever resolve—'' She gulped when his tender nibbles paused at a spot on her neck beneath her ear, causing her knees to go weak.

"Trust me," he said again, his breath hot on her night-cooled flesh.

Trust him? Could she trust any man? "I shall...try," she sighed, attempting to remember why she was upset with him.

Pulling her shabby brown bonnet closer around her face, Annica smoothed the drape of her worn dress. She was indistinguishable from the dozens of shopgirls and fishwives who filled the streets. Hodgeson followed her down a side street and into an open square. The crush of the Saturday crowd closed around them, assuring their anonymity.

Annica took a few coins from her small reticule. "Purchase scones and cider, Hodgeson. We shall have to eat on the move."

He balked, then gave her a curt nod, took the coins and hurried off, his limp more pronounced from their exercise.

She turned her back to the open square and focused on the surface of a shop window to see what was happening behind her in the reflection. Roger Wilkes had led them a pretty chase throughout the afternoon. And now they had followed him to this busy square, where he looked around and sat on a narrow bench. He consulted his pocket watch. Looking bored, he flicked an imaginary speck of dust from his coat sleeve and glanced around. Annica watched his studied nonchalance in the window's reflection and knew with certainty that he was waiting for someone.

Hodgeson rejoined her and offered her a warm scone. "Are we finished yet, milady?"

"Not yet. If you are tired, you may go home. I shall be done very soon."

"I could be of more help if I knew what we were doing."

"I cannot tell you." Annica broke her scone in half and nibbled delicately.

"Does your uncle know—"

"No, and neither does Lord Auberville. This is none of their concern. I would never question your loyalty, Hodgeson, especially after all we have been through together, but do not think of going to them. All you could possibly accomplish would be to upset everyone."

"My concern is for your safety, milady. Surely you do not suppose Lord Auberville will countenance your odd behaviors. He is not the sort who turns a blind eye to impropriety."

"Then he has courted the wrong woman," she muttered under her breath. She turned to face Hodgeson directly. "What have I done that is improper or illegal—today?"

Red-faced, Hodgeson sputtered. "I did not mean...I only meant that, once you are Lady Auberville, your husband might not permit some of your more unusual activities."

"He said he will not interfere. I have his word upon it."

"I would not put Lord Auberville to the test."

"Who will tell him? If he does not know, he cannot challenge me." Annica turned her attention back to the reflection in the shop window.

Roger Wilkes had stood and was carrying on a hurried conversation with a rough-looking individual. The man was short, with an odd foreign cast to his features and a long ugly scar along his left cheek. They appeared to be arguing, but then Wilkes passed a piece of paper to the man and hurried away in the direction of the main street.

Annica tossed the remains of her scone to a flock of milling pigeons and prepared to hurry after him. But just then Scar-face scurried into the doorway of a nearby building. She paused when she saw him hand over the piece of paper to a man whose upper body was obscured in the shadows. Was he playing a double game? Or was he merely a messenger?

"Hodgeson," she whispered, "see which way Mr.

Wilkes goes and hail a coach. Hurry! I will catch up in a moment!''

''But—''

''Hurry!'' she said again. She did not wait to see if he would follow her instructions, but edged closer to the doorway, where a covert conversation was taking place.

'''E says 'e don't dare come out in public,'' Scar-face was saying.

Annica moved nearer, keeping her face averted by studying the goods in the shop windows.

''I do not doubt,'' a deep voice replied. ''He'd be a fool—''

At that moment Annica was bumped from behind and felt a sharp tug at her wrist. She was being robbed by a cutpurse! Anger and outrage overcame good judgment. She whirled to face the culprit indignantly, holding fast to her little reticule.

''Villain!'' she cursed, engaging in a sudden tug-of-war for the worn purse.

''Blimey! Leggo, ye daft wench!'' the ruffian exclaimed. He delivered a backhanded slap to Annica's cheek, and she staggered backward into empty space.

Landing with a hard thump on the cobblestones, she yelped, ''Stop, thief!''

A long arm came out of nowhere, and her purse was snatched back as a blow sent the culprit staggering in a mad dash toward a narrow alley. Before she could protest, strong hands lifted her and set her on her feet.

''Are you quite all right, Lady Annica?'' a concerned voice inquired.

She spun around to stare in disbelief at her rescuer, glancing toward the empty doorway where, only moments before, two men had been exchanging information. Now, however, only one of them—Geoffrey Morgan!—stood facing her, holding her reticule in one hand and slipping a folded piece of paper into his vest pocket with the other.

"Mr. Morgan," she acknowledged, her mind working frantically to find a logical explanation for her predicament. She scanned the square to see if Hodgeson was nearby.

Morgan handed her the little reticule with a curt bow. His dark, brooding eyes swept her shabby costume, then lingered on her cheek, his handsome features tense with concern. "You appear to be unharmed. When we report this incident to Auberville, however, he will likely want you to be examined by a physician."

"Please, Mr. Morgan, there is no need for Auberville to hear about this. I am fine, and I would not want him to worry."

"As you wish," he said. "Where is the rest of your party?"

"Oh! Um…" Annica swallowed and blinked. Would she be able to get away with this deceit? She took a deep breath. "I have come out to do some shopping. My servant is hailing a coach."

"Shopping?" Mr. Morgan asked. His gaze dropped to her shabby costume again.

She glanced into the shop window and her mind registered the goods inside for the first time. Men's riding gear. "Ah, I was shopping for a gift for my cousin Gilbert. I usually dress down when I come here. To discourage thieves, you see."

"That explains it, then." Mr. Morgan smiled, an ingenuous expression that could have won over a lesser woman than she. "You can imagine how surprised I was when I recognized you, Lady Annica, alone and in peril."

"I am neither alone nor in peril, Mr. Morgan."

"As to that, Lady Annica, there is room for disagreement. You will need more than a shabby dress to discourage thieves. I'm bound to say, however, that I admire your courage. Most women would have given up their purse without a struggle.''

"That is not my nature, sir,'' Annica said.

"I can see that.'' He nodded. "You must allow me to escort you back to your party. We cannot risk a repeat of that incident.''

"Thank you, Mr. Morgan.'' Affecting an air of blitheful innocence, she accepted Morgan's offered arm.

"I have received your aunt's invitation to her masquerade ball and have sent my acceptance, of course. You must save a dance for me, Lady Annica.''

"'Tis the least I can do in view of your assistance.''

"Auberville is not the sort of man who would take offense at his intended dancing with another man, is he?''

"Would that prevent you from asking?''

He laughed again, patting her hand where it rested on his arm. "Would it prevent you from accepting, Lady Annica?''

"I suppose we have that in common,'' she murmured.

"I expect you have heard how your negotiations with Auberville have set the 'polite world' in a twitter. There are those who swear you'll never consent, and others who thought Auberville's choice would be more...um, conventional.''

"Conventional? Is that a chivalrous way of saying *respectable?*''

Mr. Morgan looked down at her for a long moment and then gave her a rueful smile. "It is not your way to let an innocent comment pass, is it? Do you challenge everything, Lady Annica?''

"Nearly everything.''

"That must be very uncomfortable for Auberville.''

"He bears up.''

"It is becoming increasingly clear to me just how ideal the Auberville-Sayles match is. I doubt Tristan will ever be complacent again.''

"I was unaware that you are so well acquainted with him, sir." She raised her eyebrows in an expression of interest.

"We have mutual friends," he told her. "He and I served the crown together in the Mediterranean."

Annica's interest was piqued. "Indeed? In the Royal Navy or the Diplomatic Corps?"

"It was quite some time ago, and we were on the same assignment. Our paths crossed briefly."

She was mulling over the fact that he had not answered her question when he leaned closer and whispered, "I would not quiz him on the matter if I were you."

"Milady! Over here!" Hodgeson called as they approached the curb. He had one hand on the open door of a coach and the other was pointing in a westerly direction. "He went that way, milady!"

"M-my cousin Gilbert," she improvised with a surge of anxiety. "'Twould never do to have him suspect what I am giving him for his birthday."

"Never," Morgan agreed.

She looked up at him and felt a twinge of unease. There was more to Mr. Morgan than met the eye.

Try as she might, Annica could not put Wilkes's accusation of Auberville's plot against her out of her mind. Had Auberville, indeed, set out to snare her? Had she been as unwary as the victims the Wednesday League avenged? Oh, he would have to pay for such a treachery!

Grace admitted she had heard a rumor that Wilkes's charge was true, and that Tristan believed Annica's most desirable quality was that she was "capable." She added that she had been told Tristan's treatise on wildflowers was a ruse to become acquainted with Annica and to quell any suspicions she might have of being courted. If those rumors were true, Tristan deserved a dose of his own medicine.

At tea that afternoon in her aunt's private parlor, Annica

smiled, put her teacup down and folded her hands in her lap. "Aunt Lucy, since I am considering marriage, I thought I should consult you regarding proper behavior for a wife."

"Oh! I am so pleased you have asked, my dear," Aunt Lucy twittered. "What, exactly, would you like to learn?"

She did her best to look genuinely interested. "I need advice on personal matters."

"Oh, well, my dear, as to that, there is not much to tell. 'Tis a wife's duty and she must submit. Your husband will know what to do, and will do all the…um, work. I have found that it helps considerably if you have a good-size glass of brandy beforehand and try to think of something else during."

Annica could feel a blush steal up her cheeks. Tristan's kiss had intoxicated her far more than the strongest brandy could ever have done. The sudden memory of his whispered words, *Now you are mine,* caused her heart to lurch, and the clear recollection of the ecstasy he had introduced her to made her hands tremble in her lap. She clasped them more tightly together.

Aunt Lucy's plump hand reached out to pat hers. "Now, now, dear. 'Tis not as bad as all that. Indeed, after a few years you will learn to, well, not mind so much, and once you have produced a few children, Auberville may not trouble you about it at all. Some men are quite considerate that way."

"Gads," she murmured in an undertone, praying fervently that Tristan would never *stop* troubling her about it. That is, if they could reach an agreement on their future.

"Anything else, dear?"

She cleared her head of the unwanted memories and nodded, returning to her original purpose. "What I really want to know, Aunt Lucy, is how to manage a husband."

Aunt Lucy laughed. "We'd all like to know that, my dear. Still, we have our little ways."

"Those *little ways,* Auntie—they are what I want to know about. I never had much time or patience for such things, since I never intended to marry, and I fear I wasn't paying attention when it was discussed. Could you give me a few hints?"

"Certainly. First off, my dear, you must give him credit for everything, whether he deserves it or not."

"But—"

"Then tell him how intelligent he is. How wise. In all things you must defer to him. Ask his advice on even the smallest matters, then tell him how clever he is."

"Will he believe I am so simple-minded that I cannot—"

Aunt Lucy interrupted with a stern shake of her head. "Do not allow yourself to think that way! If you would have him be considerate of your delicate sensibilities, you must not allow him to know how capable you are. He will never put a worm on your hook if he sees you gutting the fish, Annica."

"Why, Aunt Lucy! How very logical of you. I never suspected that you might be so..." She let her voice trail off.

"Practical? Intelligent?" The older woman sat back in her chair and smiled. "Men find that so unattractive, dear. 'Tis much better to let them think they are in charge. *That* is one of our 'little ways.'"

"But why would I want to deceive him about that?"

"Do you want my advice or not?" Lucy sniffed.

Chastised, Annica bit her lower lip. She knew this was her best way of testing Tristan. If he wanted a capable, intelligent wife, what would he do when he thought his carefully laid trap had snared a far different quarry? Would he lose his temper at last? Strike her? Retract his offer? She nodded for her aunt to continue, intending to put Aunt Lucy's advice into practice this very evening.

"Well," Aunt Lucy began, warming to her subject. "Husbands are especially susceptible to fawning and flattery. They adore to be your hero and champion, and you must be quite awed by their strength. They're endlessly amused—in a superior way—over your little trials. Thus, I'd recommend…''

Tristan swept Annica into a waltz and gave her a puzzled frown. "You amaze me, Annica. I had no idea you cared in the least what my favorite color might be.''

She smiled sweetly, making him even more suspicious. "Certainly I care, m'lord. Why, I shall have all my new gowns made in varying shades.''

"Of red? That ought to raise a few eyebrows.''

"Red? Your favorite color is red?''

In truth, he was partial to evergreen—the same shade as her eyes—but he was annoyed that she would employ such a silly affectation, and he did not intend to cooperate.

She frowned and narrowed those wide orbs at him. "What is your *next* favorite color, m'lord?''

Which colors flattered Annica most? Vivid tones set her beauty off like a precious jewel. Softly muted ones gave her the look of an angel. But she wanted to dress in varying shades of a single color. "Blue,'' he said, thinking there was less potential for disaster there—at least until he could discover what her game was.

She nodded and gave him a flirtatious smile. "I do so want to please you, m'lord.''

Now he *knew* she was up to something. He let his gaze sweep the alluring curves of her figure and took note of the temptingly low cut of her coral-pink gown. As always, she was stunning. Perhaps he should have said pink was his favorite color.

He leaned close to her ear as he led her into an unexpected turn. "I like you best in nothing at all, sprite.''

Faltering at his little gibe, she stepped on his shoe. "I cannot go out like that, m'lord.''

"Tristan," he corrected.

"I cannot go out like that, Tristan."

"Then do not go out. Should you accept my proposal, I intend to keep you very close to our bed for quite some time."

Annica's cheeks stained a becoming color that matched her gown to perfection. "I know my duty, Tristan, and I shall do it. You needn't worry over that."

"I was not worried in the least," he replied, amused by her interpretation of their lovemaking. In that aspect, at least, he was confident that Annica was his eager student. "And I am pleased you do not intend to shirk your 'duty.' We shall have to see what we can do about making it more pleasant for you. I'd far rather you look forward to it than regard it as a duty."

"Aunt Lucy said only women of loose morals and mistresses actually enjoy such things."

He smiled and lowered his lips to her ear again. "Do you believe her, Annica?"

She stumbled once more. "I must believe her. How else would I know such things?"

"By using yourself as a yardstick. Did you enjoy what we did? Would you have preferred to feel nothing? Are *you* a woman of loose morals, Annica?"

"Perhaps."

"No, sprite. You have a passionate nature, but you have not abused it. 'Tis one of the reasons I think we are so well suited."

"You have not abused a passionate nature, m'lord? How remarkable. I thought all men were so disposed."

"'Tis true that I wanted to ravish *you* from the moment I first saw you."

Annica's eyes widened. "I cannot imagine why, m'lord. I am really quite ordinary. I am aware that I've been somewhat unconventional, so should I accept your kind offer of marriage, I would want to be a proper wife. One who would not give you cause for embarrassment or regret.''

He watched her face uneasily. There was something wrong here. *His* Annica would never surrender so completely—nor would he want her to. ''Hmm,'' he mused, deciding to test her. ''Since you are in such an accommodating mood, my dear, perhaps I could persuade you to give up your political marches and take up needlepoint instead.''

''Certainly, m'lord.''

Tristan felt the hair on the back of his neck prickle. What little rebellion was she fomenting? Needlepoint, indeed! Not on a cold day in hell.

''And whilst we are on the subject of suitable activities, m'lord, I am wondering when we might be visiting the next specimen.''

''Specimen?''

''For your treatise. Why, now that I am to be more in your company, we should have no trouble at all meeting your publisher's deadline.''

A twinge of conscience pricked at him. ''No trouble at all.''

''Excellent,'' Annica bubbled. ''Oh, we shall have an enviable partnership, Auberville. I intend to do as much credit to your name as you deserve.''

Again he murmured a vague reply, noting the double edge to her words.

''And you waltz so divinely, Tristan,'' she exclaimed, rambling on. ''Are you meeting us at the Lundys' rout later? I am simply dying to introduce you to the rest of my friends. I shall be the envy of every woman in London.''

Tristan clenched his teeth so hard that a muscle jumped along his jaw. ''Will you?''

''Why, yes! Your position, your title, your wealth all combine to make you the catch of the season. Together, we shall have great consequence in society.''

"I was unaware that you cared about such things, Annica."

"Of course I do, silly. I would hazard that you do not know me nearly as well as you thought. All women care about their position in society. Very much the same as men care about their wife's suitability and settlements. You know the polite world will be talking. After all, we have both been the subject of wagers on the betting books. Why, just the other day, Mr. Morgan was saying how everyone expected your choice would be more, um, *conventional,* I believe the word was."

"Morgan? Where did you see him?" Annica was being uncharacteristically annoying this evening, but this little tidbit was interesting.

"I ran into him while I was shopping for a gift for Gilbert. Is something amiss, m'lord?"

"No, not necessarily. Though, as a rule, I wish you'd be more careful in your associations."

"Certainly. You must make me a list. I simply cannot trust my own judgment. Aunt Lucy has said how fortunate I am to have got such an excellent advisor as you."

Tristan looked down into the flawless face. *Who is this woman?* She had Annica's features, Annica's coloring, Annica's luxuriant dark hair, but he could swear she was a stranger. She glanced up, and for a moment he thought he saw a flash of something defiant in the masked eyes.

Chapter Eleven

Glancing over her shoulder to be certain no one had seen her, Annica slipped through the terrace doors into the shadowy garden. Her heart beat a wild rhythm when she thought of the chance she was taking—following Wilkes into the gardens alone—but she had not been able to resist when she saw him steal covertly out the doors by himself.

She heard to her left the sound of footsteps crunching on pebbles, and hurried down the path in that direction, keeping close to the concealing hedge that lined the walk. Even while she prayed she would not be caught, she began fabricating excuses for being in the garden alone.

The rise and fall of lowered voices warned her to caution. She made her way forward with all the stealth she could manage.

"...at Watier's just before closing, eh?" Roger Wilkes was saying.

"I'll meet you outside," a lowered, vaguely familiar voice answered. "Who is the game tonight?"

"Lady Jane Perrin. When we danced, she said she was going on to several routs. We shall intercept her at the Sheffields'. She has a convenient habit of wandering into gardens alone. I shall be waiting and throw a sack over her head, just as I did to Sarah Hunter at Vauxhall.''

Annica covered her mouth to stifle her gasp. It was true! Wilkes *was* the villain they had been seeking! And worse, he was planning to repeat the crime this very night—with more friends of a like mind! Wondering if she dared risk a peek to identify the naggingly familiar voice of his companion, she inched forward.

''I thought you singled out Lady Annica Sayles as the next to amuse our little group,'' the second voice said. ''I was looking forward to that.''

''Damned if she didn't get herself tied up with Auberville. He may be the one man in London we dare not cross.''

''Auberville? Yes, I see your point.''

''He still has all his old connections. He could destroy us utterly inside a week, and he's ruthless enough to do it.''

''That very fact would make Lady Annica a sweeter challenge, Wilkes.''

A low chortle met these words, and Annica retreated again, hugging herself against a sudden chill of fear.

''Oh, I have not given up entirely, you may count on that,'' Wilkes replied. ''Lady Annica's haughtiness is going to cost her dearly, but the victory will be sweeter *after* she is Lady Auberville. His lordship will not be able to denounce her, and will be stuck with a wife who has been used by a good many of his peers. If we catch her soon enough, perhaps she will present him with a son whose parentage presents a question in his mind. That would amuse me for years to come. But we'll have to be careful to cover our tracks—unlike the others.''

Annica shivered as an icy finger traveled up her spine. Just knowing she had been singled out for violation gave rise to near panic. She clenched her jaw tighter.

''We know who is behind their ruin now, Wilkes, and we shall have the edge this time,'' the familiar voice said.

"Nevertheless, I took care that Lady Sarah never see my face, so I have nothing to fear," Wilkes chortled with confidence. "They may suspect, but they will never know for certain. Whoever is investigating for them is damned clever. Could be a rival group. We shall have to make certain they pay for their treachery."

Annica bit her lower lip so hard it nearly bled. She'd heard tell of the secret clubs formed by bored young blades of the ton who roamed London streets in search of danger and mischief—clubs that brought excitement to their jaded lives. No deed was too outrageous, too decadent, too evil. Yes, she had heard rumors of the notorious Hellfire Clubs— "Mohocks" and "Bold Bucks"—but she had never wanted to believe they were true.

The voices grew louder, coming in her direction.

"Tonight, then. Half past twelve. We shall take Lady Jane to the house off Russell Street. Meantime, consider this, Wilkes—if she does not return, she will never tell the tale."

Murder! Dear Lord! They were considering murder now! Annica whirled and fled down the path toward the house. She did not spare a glance over her shoulder until she was safely inside and across the room. Appropriating an abandoned cup of punch from a nearby console, she assumed an apathetic air as she studied a mediocre portrait of their hostess.

As she waited, she struggled to put a face with the voice talking to Wilkes in the garden. Geoffrey Morgan? No. He had been dancing with Constance when Annica slipped away. Nor was it Tristan, Julius, Uncle Thomas or Gilbert— the only male voices she was familiar enough with to be certain.

When Roger Wilkes reentered the ballroom alone and disappeared in the direction of the game room, she put the punch cup back on the console and set off to find Lady Jane

Perrin, praying she had not indulged in her "convenient habit" of wandering into the garden alone.

Smiling over Geoffrey Morgan's shoulder as he swept her into a sedate waltz, Annica watched Lady Jane don her frilled spencer and take her brother's arm as they went toward the foyer. Lady Jane turned, met Annica's gaze and gave a tiny nod, coupled with a grateful smile, before she disappeared outside.

As a further sign that things were going in her favor at last, Tristan glanced her way, then headed in the direction of the game room. She could not help but smile to herself. With Aunt Lucy's advice, she had managed to put the arrogant lord to the test. Rather than stalking her now, he was doing his best to avoid her.

Relieved, she turned her attention back to her partner's conversation. "Excuse me, Mr. Morgan, I did not catch that."

"I was saying, Lady Annica, that I've enjoyed making the acquaintance of a number of your friends. Miss Wardlow and Miss Bennington are especially delightful."

Annica's heart gave a quick skip. Was he telling her that he knew he was being followed? she wondered. She forced an innocent smile. "They are very nice, are they not? Miss Wardlow is so intelligent and loyal to her friends. I believe you have known Miss Bennington for quite some time."

"Not long, Lady Annica. Our families were acquainted. She is a remarkable woman."

"All my friends are remarkable, Mr. Morgan."

"I am inclined to agree, though I cannot think of a uniting thread between you. You are all so very different from one another."

"Our common thread, Mr. Morgan, is our great love of…literature. We are members of the same literary society."

"Now that you mention it, I believe I've heard that you are a bluestocking. That is quite admirable, Lady Annica."

She tilted her head back to look into Geoffrey Morgan's deep hazel eyes and gave him a slow smile, beginning to suspect his game. "You are 'managing' me, are you not, Mr. Morgan?"

He threw his head back and laughed heartily. "I should have known better than to attempt such an obvious ploy."

"Which one of my friends are you after, sir?"

"You do not know?"

"I only know that you have a sudden interest in my circle."

"And I was thinking that your circle had developed a sudden interest in *me*."

Annica kept her bland smile in place. Geoffrey Morgan could not possibly have come closer to the truth. "One of life's odd little coincidences, no doubt."

"Precisely." He favored her with an amused grin. "'Twould be quite egotistical of me to think all your friends might have designs on me, would it not?"

"Quite," she agreed. "Not that you are not eminently suitable, Mr. Morgan. In point of fact, I can find nothing against you."

"Shall I assume you have tried, Lady Annica?"

She winced. Mr. Morgan was a worthy opponent. Precisely who was the hunter and who was the prey here? "Were you following me Saturday when we ran into one another?"

"I wondered the same thing, Lady Annica."

"Why would I follow you, Mr. Morgan?"

"Why would I follow *you*, Lady Annica?"

Stalemate. "I have no idea, sir. I simply thought there were rather too many coincidences to be mere…coincidence. Do you have a theory as to why I would follow you?"

"Like you, Lady Annica, I have no idea. I do not flatter myself that you are interested in me, thus I am left to conclude that you have another motive. I am a very simple fellow. If there is something you wish to know, you need only ask."

Very simple fellow? A bald-faced lie! "Which of my friends *are* you interested in, Mr. Morgan?"

"Perhaps I am interested in all of you," he said.

She looked again into deep hazel eyes that gave nothing away. He could have meant anything by his innocent comment.

The music ended. He led her back to her friends and bowed low, a cynical smile hovering at the corners of his mouth. They were not done playing cat and mouse, she suspected.

"I wish we could emasculate him," Annica sighed after informing Charity of Roger Wilkes's admission in the garden the night before. She stood on a stool at Madame Marie's, inching her way through a slow turn as the modiste pinned her hem.

"That would be a fitting punishment, considering the crime," Charity said. "But I thought we agreed—"

"If ever a situation warranted an exception, this is it. Still, I cannot see you and Sarah holding Mr. Wilkes down whilst Connie and Grace remove his... Well, as appealing as the thought may be, I believe we lack the necessary savagery."

"Not I," Charity denied. "I would cut the man in a trice. Men like Wilkes must be stopped."

Madame Marie spat a mouthful of straight pins into a little dish, shaking her head in disagreement. "Eef you please, *chéries,* I must disagree from you, eh? The man 'oo rapes women ees not a sexual man, no? 'E ees a cruel, violent man. 'E will continue to be cruel and violent, even weethout 'ees testicles, no? So, emasculate 'eem eef that will pay 'eem back, but not to stop 'ees cruelty. For that, there ees only one cure."

Annica gulped. *Only one cure.* "And what would that cure be, madame?"

"You know as well as I, Lady Annica. We shall not speak eet aloud, eh?" But madame drew her finger across her throat in a classic gesture that could not be misunderstood.

"Thank you, Marie. As always, you have hit the nail upon the head. I very much fear we are in too deep here. I am not certain any of us have the stomach for it."

Madame Marie shook her head. "You must not stop, or *le bâtard* weel not 'ave to answer for 'ees offense."

"I assure you, Marie, we have gone too far to quit."

"Bien."

"May we continue to use your shop as a meeting place? Will you receive and pass along information to our runner, Mr. Renquist? You see, Hodgeson's concern for my safety has made him unreliable. I fear he is on the brink of speaking with Auberville or my uncle."

"Mais oui, chérie! Most happily." She sat back on her heels and smiled. "Turn to zee mirror, milady, and see what we 'ave done. *Voilà!* A bridal dress!"

Annica turned to face the large cheval mirror in one corner. The ivory silk dress shot with gold threads she had commissioned before Auberville's proposal had been transformed into a gown suitable for a wedding. Madame Marie had added an edging of exquisite ivory lace and a matching lace chemisette to adapt the evening gown for a morning wedding. Now she placed a lace-trimmed bonnet adorned with tiny gold beads on Annica's head and stood back with all the pride of a sculptor finishing a marble statue.

"Ah," she sighed, "perfection, *n'est-ce pas?* You, *chérie,* are zee most beautiful bride I ever see. Your 'usband weel not be able to take 'ees eyes off you."

Annica stood very still, looking at her reflection. It could not be *her* in a wedding gown! The woman in the mirror was ethereally beautiful. Her skin glowed, her slender figure curved and swelled in all the right places and her eyes were enormous with wonder. The gown shimmered just enough to give the impression of angelic origin. Marie *had* wrought a miracle! Annica looked like an angel, and she knew nothing could be further from the truth.

"Très bien," madame pronounced. "Next I bring your masquerade costume, eh? I go 'urry the silly girls 'oo sew eet."

Alone in the little dressing room with Charity, Annica was nearly overcome with panic. "Oh, Charity! It has just suddenly come to me! The marriage could actually take place. By making his proposal public, Tristan has made refusal more difficult. I could refuse him now, but not without making us both look ridiculous. I really could become Annica Sinclair, Lady Auberville." Tears filled her eyes and threatened to run over.

"There, there, 'Nica." Charity gave her a hug. "'Twill come aright. Lord Tristan is a good man. Julius has said so."

"But do you not see? Once the words are spoken, nothing will ever be the same. I will be bound for a lifetime to a man I barely know. What if…what if he decides he does not like me? What if I cannot be what he needs? He will be angry. He will…strike me."

"Balderdash!" Charity exclaimed. "Why, you are perfectly wonderful, and Auberville is not the sort of man given to abuse. I can vouch that you are the best friend anyone could ever have. I have seen you meet every challenge ever put before you. I'd wager you will exceed even Auberville's highest expectations. You are simply overwrought. Between Mr. Bouldin and Roger Wilkes, you have had quite enough to sort through. Add to that Geoffrey Morgan's teasing,

Constance being peeved and Auberville's proposal—well, no wonder you're falling apart.''

"Yes." Annica nodded, grasping at this rational explanation for her irrational emotions. She wiped at her tears with the back of her hands. "Yes, that must be it. I am unstrung and fatigued by everything that has happened this past week.''

"Once you are settled in with Auberville, 'twill all seem quite ordinary. You shall see.''

"*If* I settle in with Auberville.'' Annica sighed, taking a tenuous grip on her emotions, dreading the evening ahead.

The scar beneath the patch over his left eye looked somehow fitting for a pirate, Annica decided. His full white shirt was edged with a narrow band of lace and tucked into snug leather breeches. Tall buccaneer boots gave him a rakish look and added to his reckless swagger. Yes, Tristan's costume was utterly appropriate. A thick shock of burnished golden hair fell over his forehead as he bowed over her offered hand.

"I see you have caught your true spirit, Auberville,'' she teased.

His voice was a low caress. "And this is how I always envision you, sprite. Fresh, original, elusive, breathtaking.''

Diaphanous layers of flesh-pink chiffon alternately clung to her limbs and floated freely around her, lending her the illusion of near nudity. Freshly cut ivy spiraled around her body from her low bodice to the floor. An ivy crown was perched atop her head, and her dark hair was loosely braided in back to fall to her waist. Little crystal droplets fastened to the garlands sparkled like dew, completing the illusion of enchantment. She had dressed as Tristan's woodland sprite for Aunt Lucy's masquerade.

His warm lips lingered longer than proper on the back of her hand. Her heart leaped into her throat when he suddenly turned her hand over and kissed the palm, trailing his lips upward to the inside of her wrist, tickling it with his tongue. "Auberville!" she gasped. A queer tingling began somewhere in her lower abdomen and her knees went weak.

"How long do you think I will wait to claim what I have already tasted, my dear? I am a man, not a stone. I pray you will give me an answer soon."

It had not escaped her that Tristan had not taken advantage of their new relationship. She had hoped—no! She could not think of that. Every time her mind wandered in that direction, she lost sight of her original objective—to remain unwed.

Music swirled around them as dancers chose their partners for the opening march. Tristan led her onto the ballroom floor with a proud step. She could feel the heat rise in her cheeks. He was remembering. She could see it in his gaze as his unpatched eye swept her appreciatively.

"Once we are married, Annica, you will not be able to leave the house dressed as you are."

She bristled at the proprietary threat. "Why?"

"Because the moment I see you, I will escort you back to our chamber and we shall find our entertainment there."

"Oh." She was momentarily nonplussed, then she remembered her own plans to teach the arrogant lord a lesson. "I was not certain you would like my costume, Auberville. After all, 'tis neither red nor blue."

"Why should that matter?"

"Those are your favorite colors, my lord. Indeed, I've gone to my modiste and ordered dozens of gowns in blue. I shall be having fittings for months to come."

"Ah, yes." Tristan's smile stayed in place, but it had grown stiff and formal. "My housekeeper, Mrs. Eberhart, is quite anxious for your answer. She says she would like a woman to 'do for.' Are you certain you need more time, Annica?"

"Another week or two, I should think."

"You are waiting to see if our…interlude has produced fruit, eh? Will your answer be negative if there are no consequences?"

She glanced up at him again, startled by the hard edge to his voice. She had wounded his pride, and that had not been her intention. "That has nothing to do with my delay. It is just that there is so much to consider. For instance, my position as Lady Auberville."

"Ah. Your position." Tristan nodded.

Her husband-to-be had the look of a much-beleaguered man. *Too bad. He's in for a long siege.* She vowed not to relent until he showed signs of regretting his trickery. Thus, the game was in his hands.

"Aunt Lucy has been giving me such excellent advice on being a proper wife. I am ashamed that I scoffed at her for so long."

"I'd prefer you to ignore her, Annica. I courted *you,* not your aunt Lucy."

"Courted? Did we court? I do not recall that. I was under the impression that we had a business arrangement that had turned into a friendship when you interfered in my affairs and we got ourselves into a pickle in Whitefriars."

"That is a gross oversimplification."

"Is it? Would you care to explain where I have erred?"

"Trust me—there's more to our relationship than that."

"What?"

"This is not the time or place to discuss this, Annica."

He was closer to looking angry than she had seen him since that night in Whitefriars when she had refused to tell him what she was up to. Unflinching, she turned her face up to his. "When shall we discuss it? After a wedding? When it is too late to take back ill-advised vows?"

Tristan's grin was not in the least apologetic. "It is already too late for that, Lady Annica. The die is cast, the walls are breached.''

Her heart skipped a beat at the veiled reminder. ''If you wish to cry off, I will not stop you. I cannot imagine anything worse than a reluctant husband.''

Tristan threw his head back and laughed heartily. ''Not even a reluctant wife—which is what I appear to have? I begin to see what you are doing here. You are afraid. This may be your last chance to break free and remain a spinster the rest of your life. 'Tis no use. Give it up.''

He was doing it again, Annica thought—reading her mind, seeing inside her. Damn the man! She shrugged to indicate her indifference to his advice, and moved on to the next topic she had prepared in order to confound him.

''I went to the printer this morning to order new calling cards, Auberville, but I simply could not decide upon a design. I have brought some samples home for you to see. I thought I should select a design that would be compatible with yours, should we actually marry. Could *you* decide, Auberville? 'Tis confusing when there are so many choices.''

''You cannot make a decision regarding calling cards?'' he asked, a note of disbelief in his voice.

''No. You see, there was a lovely design with a gold fleur-de-lis, and one with a simple gold border. But I got confused when I saw a very pretty flower design. Then, when I tried to remember the emblems on the Auberville coat of arms, well, that's when I became muddled. I was terribly pleased to have you to fall back upon. You are going to be such a boon to me.''

He appeared to be waging a silent war with himself. When he spoke, his voice was tightly controlled. ''Order the gold-bordered cards. And in the future, Annica, whenever you are in doubt, always choose the simplest course.''

''Ah, the simplest course.'' Annica smiled. ''Like the

truth? Or going straight ahead instead of zigzagging? What excellent advice. I wonder why did I not think of that.'' She was pleased to note Tristan's look of consternation.

The processional music ended and the ball was now officially underway. Tristan bowed to her and made an excuse about having to discuss a matter of some importance with Julius Lingate, but she knew he was making an escape before he lost his temper. She could not help but admire his control, and wondered how much longer he would be able to maintain it.

With Tristan safely dispatched to wherever it was that men went to escape their women, she hurried from the ballroom and down the corridor to the conservatory.

Pale moonlight filtered through the glass walls and ceiling transoms. The sound of faint voices muffled by the splash of the fountain drew her toward the far end of the room.

An outraged squeak warned her that all was not as it should be. Annica lifted her pale pink skirts and hurried toward the sound. As she came into the small clearing around the fountain, she was alarmed to see a shepherdess trying to fend off an insistent highwayman.

"Please!" the woman cried, pummeling ineffectively at the highwayman's chest. "Leave me be!"

"You asked for it," a hoarse voice returned. "I've been watchin' you all evening. You want it."

"No! I swear it! I came here to—"

"For me. You knew I'd follow. Well, I did, and now you're going to get what every slut craves."

"No!" Sarah protested.

Annica felt sick to her stomach. The drunken, slurred voice of Sarah's assailant was an echo of her father's voice. She rushed forward and grabbed the man by his arm, tugging him away from her friend. "Stop it! Stop at once!" she cried.

"You!" the highwayman sneered.

Annica was not surprised when she recognized Roger Wilkes behind the mask. She smelled whiskey on his breath, and he made no attempt to hide his malevolence. "Take hold of yourself, Mr. Wilkes. You cannot accost Lady Sarah again."

"I c'n do whatever I please! I know about you an' your friends, an' I know what you did to the others. How long did you think you'd get away with it, Lady Annica?"

She moved between Sarah and Wilkes. "I have no idea what you're talking about, Mr. Wilkes. I only know that Sarah's fear speaks for itself."

Her protective gesture did not escape the drunken man. "Think anything you c'n do will make a difference now, Lady Superior? Think you c'n save her from what she is—a slut who's been used by me an' m' friends?"

"Raped, you mean," Annica corrected. "You and your friends *raped* Lady Sarah."

"Who's gonna stop us?" Wilkes snickered.

"You are unconscionable, Mr. Wilkes. Lady Sarah was innocent as a babe. As a result of the harm you and your friends did her, she has been afraid to come out in public, let alone entertain the notion of marriage. Leave at once!"

"She lied. She wanted it."

"No, Mr. Wilkes, she did not. I found her when you and your friends discarded her. You committed a malicious rape, and you stopped just short of murder."

"Then why have you not told someone?"

"You know the answer to that, Mr. Wilkes."

He gave an evil grin, certain he was safe from prosecution. "Afraid for her reputation, eh? Well, no matter. She'll never be able to marry. Should count 'erself lucky that I still would have anything to do with her."

Sarah began to whimper, and Annica was anxious to dispose of Wilkes as quickly as possible. "Leave before I—"

"You? What c'n you do, you arrogant little harridan?"

He laughed again, at her outrage and anger. ''Y' can't do a damned thing to me without ruining Lady Sarah, too.''

Tristan stepped out of the shadows with Geoffrey on his heels. Annica had not heard them approach over her argument with Wilkes. He shot her a reassuring glance before he turned his attention to Wilkes, and she felt relief wash over her.

''What is going on here?'' he asked.

''Your piece o' fluff misunderstood my attentions to Lady Sarah. Isn' that right, milady?''

Sarah clung to Annica's arm, her eyes wide with fright and humiliation. '''Nica.'' She buried her face against Annica's shoulder and began to cry softly.

Tristan closed the distance between himself and Wilkes with two long strides. He reached for Wilkes's throat and squeezed until the man's eyes bulged and he made choking sounds.

Geoffrey came forward and placed a hand on Tristan's shoulder. ''Easy, Auberville. We cannot afford the luxury.''

Tristan stepped away, controlled fury in his voice. ''See him to the door. Be certain he does not lose his way.''

''Delighted,'' the centurion-garbed man said. He took Wilkes by the arm, a grim smile curving his lips. ''Come along, Wilkes.''

''You won' get away with this,'' Wilkes warned over his shoulder as Morgan led him away, half dragging, half pushing him. ''I've got friends, too. You're not as clever as y' think y'are.''

Tristan came to Annica, his eyes dark with concern. ''Did Wilkes do either of you any harm?''

''How much did you hear?'' she asked.

''Nothing that will ever be repeated, Annica. You and Sarah may count on that.''

''You will not do anything foolish, like calling him out?''

''Are you asking me to let this pass?''

"Precisely," she said. "Calling him out would cause talk, and that is what we must avoid." She lifted her chin and held his gaze, not caring, for the moment, if he saw through her "helpless" charade. "Sarah and I shall find some effective way of dealing with Mr. Wilkes."

"You will bloody well stay away from him, Annica! In view of what he did, how can you even—"

The sound of feminine voices interrupted Tristan's ultimatum. He cursed under his breath and turned to face the women coming his way.

"'Nica! We just saw Mr. Morgan escorting Roger Wilkes toward the front door. Was he here? What did he—oh! Good evening, Auberville," Charity said. Constance and Grace stood behind her.

Sarah still wept against Annica's shoulder, and Annica comforted her as best she could.

"Tristan, could we forget the past few minutes?" Annica asked. "I'm certain the ladies will help me with Sarah. Thank you for your assistance."

Tristan's narrowed eyes told her that their discussion was far from over. "Tomorrow, Annica. Ladies..." He bowed.

Annica waited until she heard the conservatory door close before she told the ladies what had transpired. She paced around the fountain, far too agitated to be still. "Damnation!" she concluded. "Wilkes cannot wait any longer. We shall have to do whatever we can to ruin him. Mr. Renquist is attempting to find his weaknesses and secrets. That would not be a problem if time were on our side, but now that he knows that *we* know he raped Sarah, we cannot wait. Though it goes against our own rules, ladies, I suggest we put our scruples aside. I suggest we do whatever is required to bring Mr. Wilkes down."

"What do you mean, 'Nica?" Grace asked.

"That we contrive an appropriate punishment, whether it has a basis in truth or not."

A Wild Justice

"But if we ruin someone with a lie, that would make us like them," Constance argued.

"On occasion, the ends must justify the means," Grace said. "When circumstances warrant, we may need to do things that go against our principles. What other choice do we have?"

"If Wilkes has grown bold enough to attack Sarah tonight, he could be capable of almost anything. None of us are safe now that he knows of our involvement," Charity said.

"Sarah?" Annica asked. "What is your opinion?"

"Now. We must do it now. I cannot bear the thought that he could be lying in wait whenever I go out."

"I am unsure how to proceed," Annica said. "But there must be a way for us to maintain our integrity, yet dispose of Roger Wilkes as a threat."

She bit her lower lip, remembering Wilkes passing a note to Morgan. Time, she supposed, would be the true judge. Meantime, there was still one source she had not employed, and she would do so immediately.

Chapter Twelve

Grateful for the brown leper's robe that some drunken masquerader had left behind, Annica stepped down from the hired coach in front of the bawdy house and paid the coachman. "I will pay you extra if you will wait a quarter of an hour," she told the man.

"An' what if ye don't come back? Time is money, miss. I'll come back if I ain't got a fare." The driver slackened the reins and snapped his small whip in the air.

Pulling the deep hood farther over her face, and fighting her rising trepidation, she took her bearings as the coach pulled away from the curb. If the lights in the windows and the squeals and laughter coming from within were any indication, the night had just begun in this part of town.

The sounds of jingling harness and rapidly approaching hooves forced her to a decision. She slipped around the side of the building and into the shadows. Pressing herself against the brick wall, she edged toward the back, heading for the kitchen door she had used once before. She heard a coach draw up in front, stop briefly and then continue along the cobbled street.

A boot scraped on the stone casement at the front door, and a firm knock commanded entrance. Annica knew she needed to summon her own courage and go in. Nothing would be accomplished by skulking against a wall except, perhaps, being accosted by some unsavory creature. The way this night was going, that was entirely possible.

A subtle scratching sound carried from the shadows. A cold chill made her shiver as she remembered the threat of the bloodstained note and Wilkes's words to the unknown man in the garden. Propelled by her own fears, she flew around the corner to rap on the kitchen door. When it opened a mere crack, she pushed it wide enough to slip through, grateful to find light and warmth within.

A startled woman with a painted face and stringy brown hair stepped back in alarm. "'Ere now, what's this?"

"I am sorry if I frightened you, madam," Annica whispered, "but I must speak with Naughty Alice at once. Could you fetch her for me, please?"

"An' 'oo shall I say is callin'?" the bawd mimicked.

"She will not know me. Tell her 'tis a friend of Harry Bouldin's."

"Terrible tragedy, that."

"Yes, awful. But could you bring Alice to me? I am in a great hurry. I will pay her for her time."

Heavy footsteps and a series of thumps and shouted curses overhead indicated that someone was throwing doors open and closed in an upstairs corridor. Acutely aware of the business being conducted in this place, Annica retreated to the shadows of a corner by the fireplace, keeping the leper's robes drawn close around her. "Hurry, please," she urged.

"'Nother rowdy one, I s'pose," the woman sniffed. "I'll go tell Alice that Bouldin's friend is waitin' to talk to 'er, but I ain't makin' no promises."

Annica stood very still, her back to a far corner, waiting and praying Alice would be "free." She did not want to stay in this place a moment longer than necessary. And as long as she was praying, she added the fervent plea that Alice would know something useful about Roger Wilkes.

Shrill female voices raised in indignation grew louder as they approached the kitchen. Annica strained to make out some of the words. "We 'aven't seen no one like that, sir! I swear."

"I know she's here, damn it! I followed her!"

Oh, dear Lord! Annica recognized that voice. Tristan had followed her? But that was impossible! She would swear she hadn't been followed. She had slipped away too many times to have made such a careless mistake. And he, above all people, must not find her here! She spun toward the back door and had advanced a single step when the kitchen door flew open with a thunderous bang. A huge, menacing figure ducked under the lintel and stepped through, three scantily garbed women following close on his heels.

Auberville paused, glanced around the room and fastened his gaze on her still form. She knew the shadows of her overhanging hood obscured her face, and hoped that would be enough to deter him. Her knees went weak at the furious expression on his face.

"Well, well," he said in a deceptively soft voice. "Is this the place for a woman of your ilk, Lady Reckless?"

"I…"

"Should you not be in one of the upstairs rooms living life on the edge of disaster, as is your wont?" he asked.

Her only chance at escape lay in deception. "Sir, I do not take your meaning," she whispered.

A low, dangerous chortle was his only reply. He advanced on her slowly, as if savoring his moment of triumph. "It will be my pleasure to explain my meaning in great detail. And then you, milady, will explain your presence here to-night."

"I believe you have mistaken me for someone else." She

took another step backward, her heart pounding wildly, but found herself blocked in the corner.

He reached out and threw her hood back, revealing her ivy-crowned head and sending a sprinkling of crystal drops bouncing across the stone floor. A quick pull of the strings at her throat loosened the leper's robe. She made a futile grab at it as it slid to a puddle at her feet.

"Your costume is appropriate in this setting. All that remains is for us to find an empty room upstairs."

Annica was disconcerted by the looks of horror on the faces of the women who had followed him into the kitchen. They were too terrified to intercede on her behalf, and she did not blame them. She was terrified, as well—this time she had pushed Auberville too far. She cleared her throat and remained calm.

"I'd prefer to go home. If you would be so kind as to summon me a coach?"

"I have no intention of allowing you out of my sight, Milady Reckless. I'm done giving you credit for common sense. You are out of hand, and 'tis time someone brought you under control."

Her heart leaped into her throat. All she could think of was her father, and his abuse of her mother. Annica summoned every ounce of courage and stood her ground. "Do not play the fool, sir. You will never get away with this. Now stand out of my way."

"Excellent strategy! Seize the offensive. What a pity your talents are wasted on someone with my experience. But in answer to your question, no—I most certainly will not stand out of your way. You are at my mercy, and now you will learn what that means. We are going upstairs, little wanton, not home."

She placed her hands on her hips and narrowed her eyes in her most intimidating manner. "You will not risk a scene. I doubt your reputation could survive such a scandal."

"*My* reputation? *Bloody goddamned hell!*" he thundered. He withdrew a gold sovereign from his vest pocket and tossed it on the table. "A room, if you please," he snarled to the old woman, his eyes never leaving Annica.

"Oh, sir—" the woman began.

"A room!"

"Seven. Room seven," she squeaked.

He leaned down, scooped up the leper's robe and threw Annica over his shoulder before whirling toward the hallway.

She squealed in protest and pounded his back with her fists as he carried her up the narrow stairs and past a row of closed doors. His shoulder pressed into her stomach, and his arm trapped her legs and prevented her from kicking. "You are mad! Put me down!" she demanded.

At the end of the corridor, he kicked a door open and stepped through. A moment later, he leaned forward to deposit her on an indecently large, intriguingly soft, bed.

She pushed herself into a sitting position as he dropped his greatcoat on a chair and turned to shut the door. One corner of her soul filled with dread, remembering the ugly, hurtful scenes between her mother and her father. But another, more visceral part of her could not believe that this man would ever really hurt her, and she took courage from that.

The room, dimly lit by a banked fire in the fireplace, was swathed in varying shades of pink, from blush to deep rose. A single window was hung with a heavy rose-pink brocade. Even the walls had been covered in a garish fuchsia peau de soie. There were a series of lewd pictures hanging along the walls, depicting a naked couple engaged in various sex acts. The silk coverlet on the bed was slippery and cool to the touch. Aside from a quick glance when she and Charity had tracked Farmingdale here, Annica had never seen the inside of a bawdy house, and she was fascinated.

Tristan locked the door and wedged the back of a chair beneath the knob for good measure before he turned to face her, a cold anger gleaming in the clear hunter's eyes. Dear Lord, but he was handsome when he looked so fierce!

"What were you thinking!" he roared.

What, indeed? "That is my affair—"

"You are wrong there, madam. Your affairs are mine now."

"This is precisely why I shall never marry," she snapped. "I will not countenance anyone calling me to account for my actions and dictating what I may do. 'Tis *my* business, sir, and no one else's!"

He leaned over her and narrowed his eyes, his voice a soft rumble. "It is not a ring that makes you my business, milady. 'Tis honor. You gave yourself to me—willingly— ten days ago, and I took you. *That,* if nothing else, makes you my business."

"How like a man to—"

"Therefore not only are you my business, Annica Sayles, you are my lover. Evidently I must remind you of that. This is what comes of giving you time to come to terms with your future. I should have followed my impulses to ravish you at every turn. Well, it is not too late. I shall not lose *this* opportunity."

"You would not dare!" She stole a quick glance at the door, wondering if she could dart past him and make an escape. If he touched her, if he made love to her, she was lost. The mere memory of the first time made jelly of her middle.

"Dare?" He laughed. "I would without thinking twice, madam. And if you think for a moment to discourage me with outrageous pranks, you are wrong there, too. If I ever find you engaging in such folly again, I shall send you to Scotland to rusticate in my hunting lodge! There's not a single valid reason for you to be here. Have you any inkling what could happen to you? My God, Annica! There are dark things unfolding in this part of town. A woman is not safe alone. That fact cannot have escaped you. Why did you come here?" He threw her leper's robe atop his own coat and began pacing at the foot of the bed.

"I must say I have never seen you in a temper before, Auberville, and I do not think I like it."

"As for seeing me in a temper, madam, you have not seen *that* yet. I suspected you were plotting something, went home and got rid of my costume, returned and waited outside your home in time to see you step into a coach and ride away. I followed you, madam, not daring to believe you could be so heedless as to sneak off in the night, knowing full well what became of you last time. But a bordello, Annica? I am speechless!" He shrugged out of his jacket and added it to the growing pile of garments.

"I wish you truly were." She spared a quick, nervous glance at the discards.

"Do not even try to divert me. It is useless." He drew her slippers off and threw them on the heap. "How often have you come here? What is your purpose?"

How could she lie to him? But how could she tell him he was trying to obtain information she could use to bring Wilkes to heel? Would he settle for half-truths? "I came to inquire if Roger Wilkes frequented this place, and if so, if he had any peculiar habits."

"Peculiar habits?" Tristan stopped dead in his tracks and fastened her with a look of utter disbelief. "You cannot be serious!"

"I thought knowledge of that sort could work as a caution or restraint on Mr. Wilkes. If necessary, of course."

"Blackmail?" His eyebrows went up nearly two inches. "You were going to *blackmail* Wilkes to stay away from Sarah?"

"Do you have a better idea, Tristan?"

He took a deep, controlling breath. After one long, unpleasant moment he spoke. "I wish I had killed the son of a bitch! But where is the woman who asked my help in choosing calling cards? How is it that poor little inept thing has taken on the task of avenging a friend?"

Annica looked into his eyes and winced. She had just given her game away. Tristan was so deucedly focused that she was never able to deceive him for long.

He resumed his pacing as he loosened his cravat and tossed it aside. "Here's an idea. Did it occur to you for a single moment to ask my help? Before you risked your pretty neck by coming to a brothel, did you consider that I might be of some assistance to you? Will you ever trust me?"

"I am not accustomed to answering to anyone else, nor am I accustomed to asking others to handle unpleasant tasks for me. And trust—"

"Try it, Annica. 'Tis not as difficult as you may think.'

Trust? Could it really be that simple?

"Tell me what drives you to such absurd lengths." He leaned over her and tilted her chin up to him, denying her the comfort of looking away.

The faint smell of brandy on his breath startled her, and for one awful moment, she saw her father looming over her instead of Tristan. Quick tears filled her eyes and rising panic clogged her throat. Would he hurt her? Would he actually hurt her?

"Trust me," he said again in a soft, compelling voice. "I will not disappoint you."

Tristan was not her father. He was a man of conscience and honor. She took a deep, steadying breath and focused on her clenched hands, too ashamed to meet his eyes. "My…my father was a vile man who abused and demeaned my mother in every possible way, and…and punished me too. I cannot recall him ever being kind or helpful to either of us. He only used kindness when he wanted something, or when he was trying to trick us. It was easier…it did not hurt as much…if we simply did not allow ourselves to trust him, or to believe that he might be genuine.''

Tristan's hands clenched and unclenched. ''I am sorry for your pain, Annica, but I am not your father. I will never let you down.''

She took another deep breath and rushed on, anxious to have it over with before she weakened. ''There's more, Tristan. You asked why I cannot simply leave Mr. Wilkes alone. You see, the day my mother was killed, we were coming back from paying a call on the vicar and his wife. Father had been at the local public house. He caught up to us, took Hodgeson's place on the box, and seized the reins from our driver. He was blind drunk and behaving like a madman. I think he meant to kill us all. Within half a mile, we knew he was hell-bound. Hodgeson threw me from the coach, but he could not reach my mother in time. She died in my arms, Tristan, and I could not help her.'' She held fresh tears back with grim determination. Tristan reached out to her and she waved him away, knowing his sympathy would be her undoing.

''I learned then that no woman should be at the mercy of a man, and I vowed that there would be justice for such heinous acts. I could not save my mother, but I can stop injustice when I see it. There is nothing more important to me than that. So, you see, I cannot just ignore Wilkes. It is a point of honor. He must pay for what he did to Sarah. He *must.*''

Tristan came back to the bedside and gazed down at her. ''Annica, I understand your need for justice, but you must leave it to the courts.''

''Can you not understand? There *is* no justice for a woman in an English court. So stay out of my way, Tristan.''

She swung her legs over the side of the bed, knowing her chances of escape were growing dimmer. It was now or never.

He placed one hand on her shoulder and pushed her back onto the pillows. "Oh, no, Annica. You are not going anywhere. You haven't told me how you knew where to come for your information or how often you've been here." He lifted one diaphanous layer of sheer, flesh-pink silk and tugged. The delicate threads popped and crystal drops scattered across the pale coverlet.

She kept her expression neutral, refusing to give him the satisfaction of a reaction.

There was a bare twitch of a muscle in his scarred cheek as he flicked a finger and another seam gave way. This time the crystals rolled to the floor. The air was cool on the newly exposed flesh of her shoulder and arm. She cursed herself for a fool. How could she feel so elated at the sensations sweeping over her and yet so afraid of a will stronger than her own? With great difficulty, she grasped the essence of his question and launched another counterattack.

"I...I merely began here, Auberville. I was prepared to visit every brothel in London if necessary."

"Are you playing me for a fool, Annica?" He popped the studs at his cuffs and collar, then ran his long fingers through his hair. "That would be a serious mistake."

She swallowed hard in an attempt to still her jangling nerves. Had he been serious? Did he mean to...to *take* her? "I've never thought you a fool," she said, dismayed by the wild tattoo her heart began and the hunger building in her blood.

"What is your game, then?"

He was not going to give up. "'Tis not a game, Tristan...." She wavered as he turned his attention back to her costume. "I am deadly serious. Though you might not believe me, I cannot help what I am. Nothing is more important to me than justice.''

''Nothing, Annica? Me? Us?''

She gulped. ''I...I collect this is what is meant by 'acting in haste and repenting at leisure.' You involved yourself with me before you learned my true nature. I release you from your offer. Society will believe me flighty enough to botch the negotiations, thus you will come off without damage to your reputation.''

Her shoulder seam split under his skillful dissection. '''Flighty?' Sweet Jesus! Are you mad?'' A slow smile curved the sensuous lips and he leaned over her with fatal emphasis. ''Do not toy with me, Annica, or I am apt to lose what little control I have gained over my temper.''

Her mind reeled at the mere thought of Tristan out of control. In a very squeaky voice, she managed to state, ''It was an honest offer, Auberville.'' She was a little afraid and entirely fascinated. Oh, dear Lord! When had his shirt come open? When had his cold eyes begun to burn with a different light? And what wanton inside her was responding with a primordial instinct?

''I am beginning to think you concocted this whole episode in an effort to be rid of me. I see your game now. The fear in your eyes tells me what you will not. You are afraid of me. Despite that you take risks, you are afraid of the greatest risk, afraid of taking that chance. Whatever else your father did, he instilled an unwillingness to join the game. That's what's behind the absurd risks you take. It has become your substitute for emotion, your excuse to stand outside the passions of life at its wildest and most exciting. Oh, no, Annica. I won't let you wither from dead emotions. Come into the fire.''

''I—you are wrong,'' she choked out. Tears sprang to her eyes and she turned to run, but his grip on her arm was strong and steady. There was no escape, no hiding from the truth.

His mouth claimed hers with a soft, cherishing touch that made sparks fly along her nerve endings. She could not catch her breath unless she drew it from him.

His lips moved against the flesh of her cheek and throat as he whispered, "I have never been more right, Annica. Tell me. Tell me what he did to destroy your innocence and turn you against marriage. What did he kill in you that breathes life only in a challenge or a reckless chance?"

"Nothing," she gasped, feeling cornered and surprised. Was he right? Is that what she had done—deaden herself to emotion? "He…he was just a man—like any other man."

Tristan uttered a muffled curse and shook his head. "Is that what you believe? That every man is like your father?"

"Given the right opportunity, yes."

"Not on my worst day, Annica. Now the rest makes sense—your shunning of callers, surrounding yourself almost exclusively with women, embracing unpopular causes in order to make yourself a social pariah. Oh, you knew just how to frighten men away, did you not? And now that I know your fatal flaw, you are an open book to me. You cannot hide from me again, Annica. Do not even try. Mark my words, we shall marry tomorrow, will you, nil you. Thank God for the special license."

"Tomorrow? But…" She stopped, panicked, and he looked as if he would relent. Almost.

"Tomorrow. Morning," he affirmed, running his hand down her arm.

She shivered with the new sensitivity he was awakening. "I am…likely to…shame you, Auberville. You will want to murder me two…weeks into our marriage," she moaned.

His mouth lowered and he cherished the hollow of her throat. He trailed his tongue downward to the slope of breast above the flesh-colored silk, causing a weakness to invade her limbs. "I want to murder you now."

"Oh." She gulped, trying not to think of how her breasts were tingling and puckering in response to that calculated move.

"'Twill pass. You wanted to take risks, so 'tis time for you to learn what comes of visiting brothels in the middle of the night," he whispered. "But in the morning you will stand before a minister and pledge your troth to me."

But even as she shook her head, her hands cupped his shoulders to draw him closer. "I do not think I can—"

"You have got so completely out of hand that I dare not leave you on your own another day. We shall marry in the morning. Are we understood?"

Never. But there it was again—that fluttering, weightless feeling somewhere deep inside. "I...I really think that would be...ill-advised."

Tristan broke the stitches on her other shoulder and peeled away the silken layer. His lips brushed the exposed skin. "Marry me, Annica," he said again. "Come into the fire."

Annica bit her lower lip to hold back her consent, and the gesture was so revealing that he nearly claimed victory. He read indecision in her eyes, uncertainty in her actions and utter fascination in her quickened breathing. She was a woman of her word and, once given, she would honor it. It was time to press his advantage—not to take pity on the little bluestocking.

"Say yes, Annica."

"Tristan...oh, Tristan," she moaned, when he bent to taste her lips again.

He was instantly tumescent at that soft litany, half prayer, half plea. Dear Lord, how he wanted his little bluestocking as he had wanted no other. A lifetime of self-discipline and caution came to naught when Annica sighed. When Annica smiled. When Annica laughed. "Marry me." The words came from his deepest soul, not from his carefully laid plan, and he was surprised by his own fierceness. *"Marry me."*

"No...never," she murmured against his lips. Her arms clung to him as if he were her life. She turned her face to the side, giving him access to the soft, tender dip directly below her ear where her neck met her shoulder.

He ran his tongue over the spot and she shivered, her whole body rising with goose bumps. "Marry me."

"N-never..." she gasped. He kissed the spot again and she began trembling. "Tristan, please..."

"Marry me," he insisted. He slipped a finger beneath the fragile fabric of her décolletage and silently thanked her dressmaker for the delicate stitches and fine fabric that split open with the barest insistence. One rosebud-crested breast lay exposed to his gaze. "Marry me, Annica."

"I...never. No, never." But she arched to his hand.

He covered the heaving peak with his mouth and nipped gently. She whimpered and tangled her fingers through his hair to draw him closer.

He was growing impatient with this game. His own need was threatening to take over. Firmly controlled and in charge of all other facets of his life, he was barely above savage when it came to making love. He'd managed to hold himself in check last time, when he knew it was Annica's first, but the burning in his belly was raging out of control now, fueled by abstinence and need. "Say it, Annica. Say you'll marry me."

"If ever...I married...'twould be to you." She writhed when he skimmed his hand down her belly, pushing the torn fabric aside. "Make love to me, Tristan."

"That is what I want, sprite. To make love to you. Every morning, every night, all day. Always. All ways. Marry me."

"'Tis not…a ring that binds…." she whimpered.

"'Tis a vow," he finished. "Marry me." His mouth went dry when his gaze swept the form he had just bared. More than life, he wanted to drink his fill of the wonder of her perfect body—the tender pink of her virginal breasts and the dark triangle of hair against the soft fairness of her skin. By all that lived and breathed, he needed her—now. This instant. "Marry me," he groaned.

Trembling fingers slipped inside his shirt to push the fabric over his shoulders and down his arms. She blushed and gave a shaky sigh when, at last, he was naked and her gaze dropped to his erection. "Please," she whispered in a faint, tremulous voice, never betraying what it was that she asked.

He wanted to oblige her, to drive into her with all the abandon of an unschooled youth, but he could not treat Annica like a bawd. Clenching handfuls of her glorious chestnut hair in his fists, he paused to worship at one heaving breast on his way downward, repeating over and over in his mind, *Slowly…do not frighten her…patience….*

Her small hands pressed him closer when he reached that sweet destination, and she arched her head back on the pillow. With a sudden change of mind, she slipped her fingers through his hair, tugging him upward, away from her mons veneris. "Please! Oh, please!"

"Do you like that, sprite?" She was an amazing creature, both courageous and cowardly, prim and sensual. Her unexpected contradictions fascinated him, and he could not live without her.

"Yes!" she gasped. "It…it is beyond anything!"

He parted the fleshy petals with one finger and stroked the little nub. Annica uttered an incoherent cry. "And that? Do you like that?"

"Yes! Yes…"

He slipped his finger down and inward, entering the hot, wet center of her. "And that?"

"Yes!" She was crying now, with a need so intense that he knew she was on the brink.

Again he slipped his finger inside her, deeper this time. "And this?"

"Yes..."

He could feel her tremors begin, and pulled back, denying his touch. A soft scream ripped from her throat as she surged upward, trying to find him again.

"Marry me, Annica," he moaned, and before he could prevent them, the words he had never said before were out. "I love you."

"Yes! Now, Tristan...*now!*"

"Marry me, Annica," he asked again, just to be sure.

"Yes! I said yes! Tristan—*please...*" She gave an inexperienced thrust upward with her hips in a blind search for the pressure that would give her release.

Tristan felt his tenuous control slip inexorably away as he moved up the length of her to fit his body to hers. "Christ," he murmured when he sank into her, burying himself deeply within the snug warmth of her body. He moaned and jerked with the pure ecstasy of the joining.

Annica went very still for one endless moment and, jaw clenched, shaking with the effort, he prepared to withdraw. Her fingers bit into his buttocks, holding him to her, and her legs entwined with his, denying him exit. Her muscles convulsed around him. "Sprite?"

"Yes, Tristan," she wept. "Yes, yes!"

He knew her affirmation had little to do with his proposal, but he reveled in it anyway, only a little ashamed that he had used her passion to gain his ends. He gritted his teeth and waited for her spasms to ebb. When her chest was no longer heaving, he withdrew slowly to the tip of his shaft and slid downward again, feeling goose bumps rise on his arms from the sheer deliciousness of the sensation. She was so tight, so hot and wet, that he feared he would lose control before he could bring her to that primal destination again.

"Oh!" she gasped. "There cannot…be more?"

"Do you want to find out, Annica?"

"Yes. Dear Lord, yes!"

All discipline, all restraint, vanished. Annica felt it, too, he saw—this wild quest for completion. He'd never known a woman who could match his passions as quickly and instinctively, never known anything remotely like the perfect joining of flesh and spirit he felt with Annica. He surged into her again, obeying her throaty pleas. "Marry me," he moaned.

"Yes," she cried in an unrestrained release as new, deeper, more intense, tremors wracked her body.

In a blinding, scalding rush, he spent himself within her. "My sprite," he answered, his voice a hoarse cry of triumph.

Annica's breathing slowed and evened to a sated level, and her erratically beating heart steadied in measure against his chest. He buried his face in the fragrant tangles of her hair and in every line of her body felt her surrender. Dear God! He had always meant to have her, but how had he come to love her?

Near dawn, Tristan's coach drew up in front of the Sayles home and he lifted a drowsy Annica, wrapped in her heavy leper's robe, down to the pavement. When she started around the house to the trellis, he took her arm and led her up the front steps.

"Tristan! They will know—" she protested.

He smiled at her, proud of the soft afterglow of lovemaking in her sleepy eyes. "'Twill make no difference at all, Annica. This time the error will be corrected before anyone knows it was committed."

He knocked sharply several times before Hodgeson answered in his nightshirt and robe, a nightcap askew on his graying head.

"Hodgeson, I will be coming for Lady Annica quite early. We shall be married without delay. See that her bags are packed for the journey to Clarendon Place, and arrange for the moving of her personal items. You and her abigail will be coming, too. For the moment, see her to her room, please, and keep an eye on her."

Hodgeson gave his mistress a wary look before he nodded. "I shall do my utmost, Lord Auberville, but that has not always been an easy task."

"So I gather, Hodgeson. Together, you and I may yet make something of her." He smoothed her hair back from her cheeks and gave her a teasing smile when she sniffed and looked away.

"Yes, milord. One can always hope," the beleaguered servant sighed.

Chapter Thirteen

Lady Auberville? Soft candlelight played across Annica's features when she faced her mirror. Could it really be true?

Mary brushed the elaborate curls from her hair, her expression dreamy. Annica's glance kept wandering to the large bed with deep green hangings and the door to the adjoining chamber. How in God's name had "No, never" become "Yes, oh yes"? Had it been his single, barely audible "I love you" that finally pushed her over the brink? And, oh, she loved him, too! Surely he knew that. He knew everything else about her. But now she was stuck with the results of her own recklessness. She certainly had not weighed *these* risks!

She was grateful, at least, for the fact that Tristan was not the sort to gloat or wield control just for the sake of it. He had not denied her a single reasonable request when he came for her that morning. In fact, he had granted everything—except to recant her agreement.

He had collected her like a neatly wrapped parcel, taken her, along with the special license to marry without banns or delay, to his minister, married her without ado and deposited her on his doorstep. And he accomplished all this while Aunt Lucy and Uncle Thomas still slept. By the time they rose at noon, it was a fait accompli. With every appearance of deep regret, he said he had other business. Urgent business that he had neglected far too long.

She was left to conclude that he would not be an overattentive husband, and she couldn't decide if that fact relieved her or annoyed her. Roger Wilkes's warning now gave her greater pause for thought.

Her breasts began to tingle with the memory of the previous night. She cringed at the knowledge of how Tristan could reduce her to a limp rag with a kiss and turn her into a demanding wanton with little more than that. She could not bear that he could have such power over her. Nor could she help it.

Her glance wandered to the bed again. The canopy was hung in heavy fabric that, when drawn, would hold back the daylight, and the surface of the bed looked exceedingly soft and inviting. Her whole room, in fact, was inviting. It had been decorated in evergreen and splashes of soft pink and white roses. A lovely vase of pink rosebuds and lily of the valley stood on the small table by her bed as a welcome from Tristan's servants. Every detail was enchanting. Arranged by Tristan? Or his housekeeper, the quiet, motherly Mrs. Eberhart?

Annica fidgeted, far too distracted to sit still for long. "Are your new quarters comfortable, Mary?" she asked her maid.

"Oh, yes, milady. Mr. Hodgeson's room is nearly plush. He and Mr. Chauncy, Lord Auberville's valet, are getting on like great chums. Mr. Hodgeson says the man is an old freebooter. What's that, milady?"

"A freebooter is a…well, a pirate. But I am certain Auberville would not employ a man of questionable reputation."

"Aye, milady. And Mrs. Eberhart is a dear woman, for all that she had her beginnings in a tavern."

"Mrs. Eberhart? Are you certain?"

"Aye, mum. Seems as if all of his lordship's servants have a 'past,' if you take my meaning."

Annica smiled faintly, approving of Tristan's willingness to give people a second chance. "Who oversaw my move to Clarendon Place?" she asked.

"Me an' Hodgeson, an' Mrs. Eberhart. Your writing table and books are in his lordship's library. Your paints and canvases are in the nursery. Mr. Chauncy said the light is very good there in the morning. Shall I lay out for the morning?"

Morning! Annica could not even think past this moment, this night. "No, thank you." She glanced again toward the adjoining door, feeling anxious and apprehensive at the same time. A thin shaft of light appeared and her heart took a leap. Having no idea what Tristan had been thinking all day, she could not even guess at his state of mind by now. "That will be all for tonight, Mary."

Alone, she went to her window and pulled back the heavy draperies. No escape here, and no soft landing in the cobblestone courtyard below. She dropped the draperies and turned back to her room.

Her thin nightdress was sufficient for the summer night, but she pulled a velvet robe close about her for protection of another kind. She took a deep breath and knocked softly on Tristan's door.

Chauncy appeared on the other side and bowed to her. "Yes, Lady Auberville?"

She felt the heat rise in her cheeks. "His lordship?"

"I regret, milady, that he has not yet returned."

She glanced over the valet's shoulder to see that he had been turning down the bedding on a huge four-poster bed and banking a fire in the fireplace. "Oh. I...I was just going to, ah, say good-night."

"You are retiring, milady?"

She frowned and rubbed one temple. Was she supposed

to wait up? Oh, she should have paid more attention to Aunt Lucy's endless advice!

"Ah! A headache, milady? I shall have Mrs. Eberhart bring you some headache powder."

"Thank you, Chauncy." Perhaps Tristan would come to her. Did he even care, now that he had got her neatly trapped? She turned the thick gold posy ring on her finger. Studded in emeralds, the inside bore the motto Only You, but she suspected the sentiment was the jeweler's, not Tristan's.

"Will that be all, milady?" Chauncy asked, furrowing his brow in concern.

"Yes, Chauncy. I just...thank you."

The door closed again, and Annica went to her bedside and turned down the wick on the oil lantern.

Deeply fatigued, she lay back against her pillows and closed her eyes to contain her tears.

The message from Madame Marie on Monday morning caught Annica by surprise. Mr. Renquist had arranged his affairs to meet with her during her appointment with the modiste. She refolded the note and put it aside with a nonchalant shrug of her shoulders, then glanced at her aunt Lucy and Ellen over her teacup. They had come to call upon her and assure themselves that she was none the worse for wear as Lady Auberville.

"From Madame Marie," she said, explaining the interruption. "My new blue gown is ready for a fitting."

"Ellen and I shall come with you," Aunt Lucy bubbled. "Ellen will be needing some new lingerie for her trousseau."

Annica cast a glance at her delicate cousin. The girl was stirring her tea rather more vigorously than necessary to dissolve the sugar.

"Thank you, Aunt Lucy, but I must meet Charity. She is

helping with the design, and we set this appointment last week. Perhaps I could arrange a fitting for Ellen on Thursday. Would that suit you, Ellen?''

Her cousin kept her gaze lowered, and Annica suspected she was hiding some strong emotion. "Thank you, 'Nica. Thursday would work well for me.''

"Capital!'' Aunt Lucy proclaimed, standing and dusting the cake crumbs from her lap. "Annica dear, I am delighted to find you so well. It appears that marriage agrees with you. I am sorry to have missed Auberville, though. I thought he would bring you back after your wedding to have a celebratory cup, but I suppose he was anxious to, ah…'' her aunt managed a very convincing blush ''…be private with you. Will we see him tonight at the Lawsons' fete?''

"I cannot say, Auntie. I am certain he will try to put in an appearance, as it will be our first social engagement as a married couple. He has some sort of meeting earlier. Constance is accompanying me.'' She stood to walk her guests to the door. "Would you care to join us, Ellen? Gilbert, too, if he'd like.''

"Y-yes. That would be very amusing.''

"How jolly,'' Aunt Lucy said, taking her gloves and reticule from a servant in the foyer. "Thank you for arranging an appointment for Ellen with Madame Marie. She is by far the most popular modiste in London these days. And thank you for including Ellen in your plans tonight, 'Nica.''

In truth, Annica wanted a private talk with her cousin. Ellen's peculiar behavior indicated that something was bothering her. "We shall call for you at nine o'clock, Ellen. Will Lord Dennison be at the Lawsons', too?''

"I believe he intends to stop by on his way to his club.''

"I shall be sure to look for him.'' Annica gave her a benign smile over the top of Lucy's head.

Twenty minutes later, Hodgeson declared he would wait on the street outside Madame Marie's. "I am confident no harm can come to you in a dressmaker's shop, milady. There is little mischief for even you to find in such a place.''

Annica gave him a fond pat on the arm and smiled. "Thank you, Hodgeson. I am impressed with your diligence."

A shop bell above the door rang to announce her presence. She took a moment to glance at herself in a cheval mirror placed in an alcove and turned from side to side. Was she different today? No, she looked the same.

Then why hadn't Auberville come to her since their marriage? From adolescence onward, she had heard tales of wedding nights fraught with bliss and some with disaster. Never indifference. Had she imagined his tentative admission of love?

Or had her behavior the night before their marriage so shocked and dismayed him that he no longer found her desirable? Had the revelation of her past disgusted him, and had her commitment to justice unsettled him? Well, two could play at that game!

"Such a dark look!" Charity exclaimed as she entered the shop and gave Annica a quick hug. "Who has crossed you, 'Nica?"

"Auberville, I suspect."

"Speaking of Auberville, you will never believe the absurd rumors going about!" Charity laughed. She removed her gloves and waved them as if to dismiss the notion. "The ton has it that you and Auberville were wed Saturday!"

"We were, Charity."

Charity's eyes grew round in amazement. "Good heavens! But you said you'd never—that is, you swore that—"

"We were engaged in negotiations. The marriage should not have come as such a complete surprise."

"That is how Auberville crossed you, is it not? Did he coerce your consent? Did he trick you?"

Marie's arrival saved Annica the necessity of a reply. The modiste led them to the dressing room nearest the back entrance and opened the door for them. "I like your man, Renquist, *mes chéries*. 'E ees very 'andsome, *n'est-ce pas?*"

"*Oui.*" Annica smiled. The Frenchwoman was irresistible to men, and Renquist would fall victim to Marie's charms in short order, Annica knew. Within a month, she and Charity would be treated to all the details of Renquist's techniques beneath the sheets. While discreet to a fault regarding her clients, Madame Marie had no such scruples where her own life was concerned.

The door closed behind them and Francis Renquist came out from behind a tall dressing screen. "Ladies," he said.

Charity got right to the point. "Hello, Mr. Renquist. According to Madame—"

"She's a corker, that one," Renquist interrupted, beaming.

Annica grinned. "Yes, she is quite amusing, Mr. Renquist, but hold fast to your heart. She is not the marrying kind. Now, what have you found for us?"

"As requested, milady, I put several men on Morgan, and also on Wilkes."

Annica frowned. "The villain is Wilkes. The whole affair is out in the open, and it is no longer necessary to keep up a pretense of friendship. We need to know how to destroy him as quickly as possible. 'Tis a whole new game, Mr. Renquist. No longer 'who,' but 'how.'"

"I can see that, milady. But, to the point, I sent for you because I have a bit of information that might be right up your alley regarding the missing women—"

"Frederika Ballard? Or missing women in general?" The fine hairs on the back of her neck stood on end.

Renquist shook his head. "One of my men, in the process of investigating Wilkes and Morgan, came across an odd set of coincidences. Twenty-eight women have gone missing in the past two months. That this fact came to light while investigating your suspects suggests a connection, milady.''

Annica's heartbeat accelerated. "Go on, Mr. Renquist."

Renquist's face revealed an internal struggle, further evidenced by his hesitation and eventual sigh. "There *is* more, Lady Auberville, but I would prefer not to say what it is at this point. It could be dangerous."

"Please, Mr. Renquist," she asked, "keep us informed of any developments. If there is treachery afoot, we had best know it. But remember, Wilkes is our primary objective at the moment."

Renquist gave her a curt nod. "I will be in touch, milady," he said on his way to the door. "Very soon."

"How queer," Charity said when the door closed behind him. "What are you thinking, 'Nica?"

"That this may have something to do with Frederika, and Madame Marie's seamstress. And that, if Geoffrey Morgan had reason to call upon Constance, he could have met Frederika."

"Met her and wooed her?" Charity tapped her cheek with an index finger. "You may have something there, 'Nica. You've always said there is more to him than meets the eye."

Amused by her instant acceptability, Annica received well over ten invitations—including a voucher to Almack's—within an hour of her arrival at the Lawsons' grand ball. Society, it seemed, had decided to forgive all her political and social indiscretions and give her a second chance in view of her marriage to the eminently respectable Lord Auberville.

"The invitation to Almack's has already met the dustbin, but I shall be able to take advantage of one or two invitations before I fall from grace again," she told Ellen with an ingenuous smile as she smoothed the drape of her elegantly cut, midnight-blue gown. Matching velvet roses nestled in her dark curls, and she had chosen a sapphire-and-pearl necklace to complete her costume. Tristan had sent word that he would meet her here later, and she wanted to do him credit despite the fact that she had planned a little revenge for his absence the night before.

"Fall from grace? 'Nica, are you planning something outrageous?" Ellen asked.

"Nothing out of the ordinary…for me," she said. "It is the tax march. I have not yet told Auberville."

Ellen's eyes widened. "Good heavens! He will be very angry," she warned.

Annica shrugged, wanting to reassure her cousin without actually lying. "Ellen, you need not worry about me."

"I am glad, 'Nica. I worried when Papa told me you and Auberville were wed. All your talk of marrying for affection and such, and then to accept a proposal—well, I vow I thought there was more behind the whole thing than I was told. Indeed, I feared that Auberville had compromised you in some way. I have heard whispers that he is a very deliberate and relentless man, and that he always achieves his goals."

"Yes, he does have that reputation, Annica," Constance agreed. "I have seen strong men, confident men, stand down from an issue when your husband takes the opposite side."

Annica shrugged. "Do not trouble yourself over it. I have no problem standing up to him. And now the deed is done, I am more comfortable with the concept."

"You *are* fond of Auberville, are you not?" Ellen persisted.

"Quite over the top. He is really rather amazing. He is very accomplished, and has talents I could not possibly have guessed." Annica smiled, thinking of their night at Naughty Alice's brothel.

Constance rolled her eyes and laughed. "On those words,

Lady Auberville, I think I shall go find Charity and Grace. I am anxious to hear who has come tonight, and who has not.''

Annica knew Constance was referring to Roger Wilkes. ''I shall join you in a few moments, Constance.''

Ellen was still focused on her questions regarding Annica's marriage. ''Was your match the *coup de foudre* you spoke of? The thunderbolt of love?''

''Yes, indeed,'' she admitted with a sigh, ''though I did not immediately recognize it as such.''

''Then I envy you, 'Nica.''

''Pardon me?''

''Well, to have found such an illusive thing as love...while I have come to believe that such vaunted emotions do not exist, or that I am simply incapable of them—''

''Oh, Ellen! I was afraid of that. You must not wed Dennison. You are young yet. There may be more for you.''

''Annica—'' Ellen began.

''Gads! It must run in the family!'' Annica exclaimed.

''What runs in the family, Lady Annica?'' a masculine voice asked.

Completely disconcerted, she turned to find Geoffrey Morgan standing at her shoulder. ''Um, our looks, Mr. Morgan.''

He laughed. ''Ah yes, I can see it. If not for the difference in hair color, eye color, height and weight, you could be twins.''

Ellen smiled and excused herself, saying she had promised this dance to her fiancé.

Morgan bowed to Annica. ''Since I find you alone, Lady Auberville, may I prevail upon you for a dance?''

''Actually, Mr. Morgan, I was hoping I would see you tonight and that we might have a few words together.''

''This sounds serious. Would you prefer to converse on

the dance floor, or should we find a quiet spot where we can speak uninterrupted?''

''In the interest of discretion, perhaps we could take a cup of punch to a quiet place?'' she suggested.

''My pleasure.'' He offered his arm and led her to the punch bowl near the terrace doors.

When he had filled two cups, they went out into the balmy night and sat on a stone bench, near enough the doors to be within the bounds of propriety. This was something Annica had never worried about before, but she suspected the possibility of causing embarrassment to Tristan would keep her from doing a great many things she used to do.

Geoffrey Morgan took a sip of punch and regarded her with a thoughtful smile. ''I must say I am intrigued, Lady Annica. What could you have to say to me that requires privacy?''

''''Tis about Sarah.''

''Ahh.'' He nodded, a strange light in his deep hazel eyes. ''What about Lady Sarah?''

''At the masquerade, when you and Auberville came across us in the conservatory, how much did you hear?''

''Enough to answer a few questions.''

''What questions?''

''Why Lady Sarah cannot tease and flirt as other women her age. Why there is always a member of your bluestocking society lurking somewhere about her.''

''Lurking?'' she huffed.

''Your instinct to protect her is quite admirable, but have a care not to smother her. Too much protection could keep her from regaining her self-confidence.''

''And not enough protection could cause her to be a recluse, afraid to venture out at all. Believe me, Mr. Morgan, we are doing all we can to help Sarah regain her pride and self-confidence. I am surprised that you, who barely know her, presume to know what is best for her.''

"I meant no insult, and I am sorry if you took it as such. In truth, I presumed such a thing owing to my affection for the lady," he said in a conciliatory tone.

"Affection!" she scoffed. "What underhanded deeds have been done in *that* name, I wonder? Just answer my question, please."

He glanced around and lowered his voice discreetly. "I heard what was done to her, and that there were others in addition to Wilkes. I deduced that her friends have kept it secret to protect her good name and position."

"What will *you* do with that information, Mr. Morgan?"

"What did you expect, Lady Annica? That I would take an ad in the *Times* to expose her? Or did you think I'd whisper it abroad? Perhaps you feared that I'd use the information to force her to unpalatable deeds, as Wilkes attempted to do?"

Annica could feel heat creeping up her cheeks. Lord! What *had* she thought? "Please, Mr. Morgan. I barely know you, certainly not well enough to make any assumptions about what you might or might not do. My purpose in speaking with you was to ask if you will keep her secret."

"What will you offer to buy my silence? Hush money? Your favors, perhaps? Now there's an interesting idea."

"I was relying upon your honor as a gentleman."

"What did you think I would do?" he repeated.

Warranted or not, Mr. Morgan's anger was a little frightening. And she had questions of her own, though she dare not ask them. *Where were you when Mr. Bouldin was killed, Mr. Morgan? What do you know about missing women?*

But she had to respond to his question. "I feared you might repeat what you witnessed in casual conversation."

"Did I not tell you that I have a fondness for Lady Sarah?"

"Yes, but that could mean almost anything. Especially now that you know what has happened to her."

"Good God! You think me that malicious?"

"Not malicious, Mr. Morgan, just thoughtless. Men are rarely careful of a woman's name, future and well-being, especially when they believe her worth to be diminished."

"I pity you, Lady Annica, if this is any indication of your experience with men. What high, thick walls Auberville must have had to breach to find that withered suspicious heart of yours."

She could not apologize for her instinct to protect her friend, but she winced at those well-deserved words. "Sarah has friends who are prepared to deal with any wrong done her."

"I am one of those friends." The handsome man gave her a cold smile. "You had better accustom yourself to me, Lady Annica, because I do not intend to abandon Constance Bennington or Sarah Hunter."

"I shall count upon that."

The recipient of occasional snubs from pious society matrons, Annica was not used to dealing them out. She'd never given anyone the cut direct in her life. But when the audacious Roger Wilkes stood in her path on her way to the ladies' retiring room, it did not seem enough. She opted for the cut sublime.

"I must talk to you, Lady Annica," he said.

Though aware of him, Annica kept her eyes directly ahead, as if looking through him. Her face remained impassive and she did not falter so much as a fraction of a second.

"You cannot—" Wilkes's voice broke as he began to understand what she was about to do.

She slapped her open fan across her left palm, closing it in a bored gesture of disdain. The toe of her slipper nearly touched Wilkes's shoe as he moved to block her way. Her back was stiff and straight and her chin lifted imperceptibly, but she did not break her stride. Her gaze met that of Lady

Winters, who was coming down the corridor from the retiring room.

"You will be sorry if you do not listen," Wilkes hissed. "There is more to this than you know. I—"

With a little twitch of her shoulder, Annica cleared the human obstacle without ever acknowledging him. Her actions said that, as far as Lady Auberville was concerned, Roger Wilkes did not exist. She noted the desperation in his stance, and she knew how society would judge this tableau.

The hiss of whispers behind her indicated that the gossip had already begun. The cut sublime was sufficiently rare and severe as to be remarked upon.

She inclined her head to Lady Winters in passing and said clearly, "Brace yourself, Eloise. There is an unaccountable stench ahead."

More than one gasp met this denouncement. Lady Winters blinked and looked away from Wilkes. "Thank you for the warning, my dear."

"I will remember this," Wilkes snarled in a low undertone.

Annica shivered at this threat as she closed the retiring room door behind her. The cut sublime was little enough punishment for the cad, but it was a beginning.

Grace was sitting before a mirror tucking stray wisps of chestnut hair back into her artfully arranged coiffure, while Charity and Constance watched. They looked up when she entered.

"Here you are!" Charity smiled. "Connie was just telling us how very entertaining you are finding Lord Tristan."

Annica laughed. "Entertaining. Now there's an interesting description if ever I heard one."

"Where have you been, 'Nica?" Grace asked, finishing the final repairs on her hairdo.

"Giving Roger Wilkes the cut sublime. And before that, speaking with Geoffrey Morgan."

"The cut sublime? Heavens! How did he react?" Constance's eyes widened with surprise.

"He was furious, but as we were public, he could do nothing. We cannot destroy him yet, but we can make it uncomfortable for him to mingle in society."

Grace nodded somberly. "That is a good idea, 'Nica."

"What did Geoff have to say?" Constance asked, changing the subject. She stood and shook the folds of her emerald evening dress into a graceful drape.

Annica glanced around the room. "Where is Sarah?"

"She went to Oxford for her grandmother's birthday. She should be back tomorrow in time for our meeting," Charity told her. "Is something amiss?"

"I wanted to be certain she would not overhear us."

"Well?" Constance prodded. "What about Geoffrey?"

"I meant to ask him if he would keep Sarah's secret, but somehow the conversation got out of hand. We ended with an argument, and he threatened to remain in Sarah's life."

"I would not call that a threat, Annica," Constance snapped.

"As hard as I try, I cannot rid myself of the suspicion that he is engaged in some secret purpose."

"You did not always have such a bad opinion of him," Charity reminded her.

"I did not always feel as if he were up to something."

"Oh, for pity sake! Let it alone, can you not?" Constance gave Annica an exasperated look and raised her eyes heavenward, as if looking for help from that direction. "I find Auberville as suspicious as you find Geoffrey. He was in town when Sarah was attacked, and left soon after. And he returned about the same time as Geoff. Furthermore, you and Sarah witnessed at the masquerade that he is capable of violence. According to your criteria, that is more than enough to cast suspicion."

"'Nica has her reasons," Charity stated, jumping to her defense.

"I shall explain tomorrow," Annica promised. "There are a good many things we must sort through, and some decisions we must make."

Annica's first inkling that Tristan had arrived was the hush that fell over the ballroom. She turned to see him scan the crowd in search of...her? Society was ready to judge their match based on what they witnessed tonight. For the first time in her life, she cared very much what society might think.

He caught sight of her and cut through the crowd, heading straight in her direction. Her heart pounded madly. She had no idea what to expect, considering that he hadn't come to her last night—or their wedding night.

"My dear." He gave her that lazy, crooked grin, took her hand and lifted it to his lips. This time he lingered over the kiss to a scandalous degree, and heat swept over her. "I am pleased to find you so well. Chauncy informed me of your devastating headache again last night. I trust you are fully recovered?"

Hope washed over her. Perhaps he had not snubbed her, after all. Perhaps he had been considerate. She had to clear her throat before she could speak. "Lord Auberville. How...how pleasant that you could join us."

"I would not have missed it, Lady Auberville. I certainly did not want to wait until...later."

Annica knew beyond doubt that she was blushing. The heat was unbearable. She snapped her fan open and waved it rapidly. She did not realize how revealing their little exchange had been until the ladies began giggling behind their hands. Everyone would now assume that their wedding night had been a monumental success. Annica wanted to both slap him for embarrassing her and thank him for saving her pride. Society would now conclude that theirs was a love match.

He swept her into a graceful waltz that made matrons sigh with envy. "You must forgive me, my dear. I came home as soon as I could break away from my appointments tonight, only to find that you had given up waiting and gone on without me. I hope you will not think that I will be a neglectful husband."

"N-no," she said. In truth, she was so new to the concept of marriage that it hadn't even occurred to her that Tristan might *want* to escort her to the nightly festivities of the social season. Most husbands did not escort their wives. "You were gone when I woke this morning, and I thought you would not...that is to say, that you did not care if..." She gave up. "I do not know what you expect of me, Tristan. I thought I was to go on with my life as usual, except that—"

"That you now sleep at Clarendon Place?" He grinned, and his hand tightened around her waist. "Well, that is a start, Annica. But perhaps you would consider going home with me?"

His roguish grin made her blush and his teasing references to going home made her tremble with anticipation—facts, she noted, that were not lost on observers. But his invitation reminded her that she had waited for him on their wedding night, and he had not come. What—or *who*—had been more important than her? And he still had not confessed his trap.

"I cannot, my lord. I have promised my friends that I will accompany them to the Morton crush." A flicker of hurt passed through the compelling blue eyes and she could not bear that she had caused it. "I shall cancel and they will go on without me."

"No."

"They will understand, Auberville."

"I will not have you break your word on my account. And there are promises I should be keeping, as well," he said.

She wondered if he was simply being gracious. "Are you certain?"

"As certain as I am of anything, my dear."

The dance ended and he escorted her back to the sidelines. Again he bent over her hand. "I shall count the minutes," he said in a voice loud enough to be heard by those nearby.

She adored him for that gesture. To be so openly attentive to one's wife was a sure sign of defeat for a man, and victory for a woman. Tristan had made her look victorious. How could he have known how much that would salve her pride?

Grace was waiting with her wrap, and Annica smiled at her husband over her shoulder as her friend led her to the door. She wanted to make some gesture that would restore Tristan's esteem in the eyes of his peers, but she couldn't think how. She would have to ask Aunt Lucy.

The balance of their group had shifted, with Ellen continuing on to another party with a group of her friends and Gilbert departing for a gaming hell. Constance and Charity were waiting at the curb as they summoned Grace's coach.

"I cannot wait to see if the news of your cut to Wilkes has been told as far as the Mortons' crush, 'Nica," Charity whispered, a satisfied smile on her lips.

Before Annica could reply, a raised voice near the street corner drew their attention. Roger Wilkes was deep in conversation with the foreign-looking man with the scar. She stepped closer to her group and inclined her head in Wilkes's direction.

Constance gasped, gripped Annica's arm and said in a low voice, "That odd little man has shown up several times since I have been investigating Frederika's disappearance. I have been referring to him as 'Mr. X.' If he has a connection to Frederika *and* Wilkes…''

''Wilkes might be involved with Frederika's disappearance.'' Annica finished the half-formed thought for her friend. *Wilkes? Or Morgan?* Cold dread filled her. What was afoot?

''But Wilkes is such a swine!'' Charity said. ''How could he ever persuade a woman to run off with him?''

''He may have help. When he attacked Sarah, he had three other companions, and there was another man in the garden with Wilkes the night I heard him confess to raping Sarah. And I've seen Mr. X act as a liaison between Wilkes and someone else.'' Annica stopped. She did not have the heart to battle Constance again. Tomorrow would be soon enough.

Constance took a deep breath and let it out slowly. ''I will inquire of one of my sources. If there is a connection, we shall know it by tomorrow.''

''Who is your source? Who have you been using, Constance?''

She merely pressed her lips together and shook her head.

Chapter Fourteen

Jane Austen's *Mansfield Park* lay on a corner of Tristan's desk, the bloodied note left pinned to Mr. Bouldin's chest safely tucked inside. Annica had a new scheme and she wanted to present it to the Wednesday League at their usual Wednesday meeting this afternoon.

She pushed Tristan's chair back and tried to open the middle drawer in search of a pen. Locked. How odd, for a man who trusted his servants implicitly. Did he have something to hide? Was it she that he didn't trust? Was something of great importance hidden in the drawer? Or in the library?

She gazed around. Unlike most dark and somber libraries, this one was awash with light and color. No dark paneling and stingy oil lamps here, but tall, wide windows separating the bookshelves, letting bright natural light stream in. Tristan's massive desk was placed in one corner near the fireplace so he could enjoy both light and warmth. Deep Oriental carpets warmed the polished wood floors, and vases of multihued flowers provided bright splashes of color. Chairs and a sofa were grouped near the fireplace, inviting lazy afternoons and cozy evenings.

She could discern no hidden panels, no false walls, nothing sinister or that signaled a hiding place. She tugged at the drawer again, thinking she might not have been forceful enough.

Feminine laughter echoed in the foyer, announcing the arrival of Charity and Sarah. Annica gave a guilty start. She stood and hurried to gaze innocently at a row of books on one shelf, then felt foolish for the deception. This was her home now. She had a perfect right to look for a pen. What had got into her? The locked drawer?

When Chauncy opened the door for Charity and Sarah, his scarred face was relaxed in a pleasant smile. "If you do not mind my saying so, Lady Auberville, 'tis nice to have females about the place. Mrs. Eberhart is seeing to your tea and pastries, though Hodgeson is set upon bringing them to you. Shall I say you are ready?"

"Thank you, Chauncy." Annica smiled. "But Miss Bennington and Mrs. Forbush will be arriving soon. We shall wait for them."

Charity and Sarah arranged themselves on the sofa while Annica took one of the chairs facing them.

"That sky-blue frock is quite lovely on you, 'Nica," Sarah exclaimed.

Annica groaned and adjusted the ribbon beneath her breasts. "I am growing so weary of blues—from robin's egg to midnight—that I could scream, but Tristan simply will not confess. He is either more stubborn or more tolerant than I suspected."

"How are you liking married life, 'Nica?" Sarah sighed dreamily.

"Once Auberville and I have settled accounts and adjusted to considering another person, instead of just our own plans, I believe we will be compatible."

"Of course you will." Charity leaned forward and patted her hand. "Why, it is not as if you and he are still in nappies."

The door swung open and Grace strode in, Constance in her wake. "Nappies?" she asked, lifting her eyebrows nearly to her hairline. "That was quick work, even for you, 'Nica. Are you carrying the Auberville heir?"

Hodgeson, following Constance with the tea service, faltered for a moment, but managed to keep the teapot and cream upright. Annica realized that he had been harboring that particular fear. Torn between chagrin and annoyance, she shook her head. "You need not gift me with rattles and blankets just yet. Thank you, Hodgeson. Put the tray on the table, please. Shut the door on your way out and, if you will, see that we are not disturbed."

"Yes, milady," Hodgeson said, bowing and closing the double doors behind him, a look of utter relief on his wrinkled face.

Annica poured the tea and passed the cups. "We have much ground to cover today," she sighed. "We had best begin, but I hardly know where. Wilkes? Morgan? Mr. X? Frederika?" She sat back and sipped her tea. "Madame Marie's seamstress?"

"Constance, what was the result of your errand last night?" Grace asked.

"My source has met with an accident. A coach ran him over three days ago. I cannot help but wonder if his accident is connected to the questions he was asking."

"What does all this mean?" Grace asked, rubbing one temple.

"It means," Charity said, "that yet another man has died, and the information to destroy Wilkes is just beyond our grasp."

Annica's heart twisted. Her inability to help Sarah made her feel as impotent as she had as a child, unable to help her mother. Sarah had a fine spirit and a brave heart, and she deserved better than what the Fates had given her.

"I believe Mr. Morgan was next on our agenda," Sarah prompted.

Annica chose her words with care, painfully aware that Sarah, as well as Constance, would take exception to what she would say next. "The foreign man with the scar that Constance refers to as 'Mr. X' is not unknown to me. In the course of following Mr. Wilkes, I witnessed a meeting between the two. When Wilkes departed, Mr. X relayed a message of some sort to a man waiting in the doorway of a small shop. That man was Geoffrey Morgan."

She paused for a deep breath and forged ahead. "I am sorry, Constance, but I believe Mr. Morgan may have a connection to this whole affair. Mr. Renquist also believes there may be some connection—if not with a Hellfire Club, then with twenty-eight missing women. Most certainly with Wilkes."

"Twenty-eight missing women? But what implicates Mr. Morgan?"

"He told me once that he served in the Royal Navy with Farmingdale and Wilkes, to be specific."

"For heaven's sake, 'Nica, would it not stand to reason that an entire regiment served with Wilkes and Farmingdale? I'd venture to say there are several more of the ton who served with them. We were at war with France, if you recall," Constance said. "Why, your very own husband was in the Royal Navy. I cannot believe that Geoff would—"

"Constance has a blind spot where Geoffrey Morgan is concerned," Charity snapped.

"Do you think that I would jeopardize women for the sake of a personal prejudice?" Constance huffed. "And what evidence could you possibly have against Geoffrey?" she asked, an angry glint in her eyes.

Annica sidestepped the question in favor of presenting her plan. "There is a way to eliminate him as Mr. Bouldin's murderer." She retrieved *Mansfield Park* from Tristan's desk, removed the bloodied note and held it up for all to see. "I propose we acquire a sample of each man's handwriting and compare it to this note."

"An excellent idea!" Grace exclaimed.

The library doors swung open and Tristan strode in. He flashed his crooked grin and bowed to the group at large. "Ladies. Please excuse my intrusion. I was not aware that we had company. I have need of some papers in my desk. I will only be a moment."

Annica folded the note with an air of calm unconcern and slipped it back between the pages of her book. She smiled sweetly and nodded. "Of course, Auberville. 'Tis your home, after all."

"And yours, madam," he acknowledged absently. He sat at his desk, withdrew a small key from his waistcoat pocket and unlocked the middle drawer. After rummaging for a moment, he folded a sheet of paper, slipped it into the inside pocket of his jacket, relocked the drawer and returned the key to his pocket.

"Sorry for the interruption," he said. Halfway to the door, he turned back and smiled again. "Ah! The Wednesday League, is it not?"

"Yes. 'Tis Wednesday," Annica said.

"Would you care to join us? We're just beginning our discussion," Charity offered with an innocent smile.

"I have an appointment or I should be delighted."

"What a pity," she giggled. "We so seldom have the benefit of a male viewpoint."

"Perhaps I could spare a moment," Tristan allowed. He went back to the carafe on his desk and poured half a glass of claret.

Annica shot Charity an exasperated look before pasting a bland smile on her face.

He took the vacant chair beside her. "Pray, continue."

"Thank you, Auberville. We were just discussing the Marquise de Sade's *Misfortunes of Virtue,* also known as *Justine,*" she improvised. "What is *your* opinion of the work?"

The quirk at the corner of Tristan's mouth and the barest hint of a blink were the only signs that she had surprised him. "Did you know that work is considered pornographic and was banned last year?" he asked evenly. "But what is your opinion, Annica?"

"It is an interesting premise, Auberville, that virtue must be its own reward, since there are no *other* rewards for it."

"Do you believe that?"

"We have noted how goodness and right do not always triumph, and how wickedness appears to thrive," she said evasively.

"Did you find Justine virtuous? I thought her foolish. Trusting where she had no basis for trust and thus participating in her own betrayal. Altogether an incapable woman."

"Incapable?" The ultimate indictment! "That is an interesting opinion, Auberville. Then you did not find the work particularly enlightening?"

Tristan laughed as he stood. "I shall tell you exactly what I thought tonight, madam. We can discuss it at length, if you wish. But I do not have the time at the moment. I really must go. Ladies." He bowed to the group again.

As one, they gave him polite smiles and nods. Silence prevailed until the door closed behind him. Then the room exploded.

"'Nica! What were you thinking?"

"*Justine?* Good heavens!"

"He will forbid you to associate with us," Charity gasped.

"You asked him to stay, Charity, not I, and I do not think

he would dictate my friends.'' Indeed, if she read the signs correctly, he actually seemed to be amused. But if he thought she would succumb to his charms tonight, he was mistaken. No. Not until he admitted that he had trapped her.

''Perhaps he is not as stodgy as I thought him,'' Charity allowed.

Constance picked up the conversation where they had left off. ''I will write a note to Geoffrey requesting a meeting to discuss a matter of importance. I shall ask that he respond by return post, naming a place and a time. Will his return letter give you what you need, Annica?''

''Yes, thank you.''

''While we wait for the results, I think I shall begin inquiries into the connection of our suspects with the Royal Navy. I am certain there must be a clue there, somewhere.''

Annica nodded. Constance would be well served to have a task that would keep her busy until Mr. Morgan could be cleared of suspicion. ''Who will tackle Wilkes? I could write a note saying that I want our hostilities to end as long as he keeps his silence regarding his use of Sarah.''

''After your cut, that would be foolhardy, and he would recognize it as some sort of trick,'' Grace said. ''*I* shall take Wilkes in hand. I will write him telling him I think the cut sublime was cruel and unnecessary.''

''That is a good ploy, Grace. He will be desperate for a kind word from anyone.'' Annica took another deep breath. ''As for the missing twenty-eight women, there is not much to tell. Mr. Renquist discovered the coincidence while investigating Frederika's disappearance. We cannot be certain yet if there is a connection, but we suspect there is.''

''We are forgetting something else,'' Sarah said.

''Wilkes's Hellfire Club.'' Annica nodded, seeing the fear in Sarah's soft eyes. Her heart went out to her friend. ''Oh, if I could only place the voice I heard! We *must* find out who was out there.''

My dear Constance,
I will be happy to meet you at any time and place you
desire. Our friendship means a great deal to me and, if
there is any matter with which I might be able to help,
I would be pleased to do so.

I urge you to use care in selecting a meeting place,
as I would be grievously unhappy should your reputation suffer harm on my account. If you have no better
solution, may I suggest Hyde Park tomorrow afternoon? I will be waiting on the bench nearest the south
entrance at four o'clock.

Yrs., G.M.

Annica sighed and folded the letter. The handwriting did
not match the threatening note pinned to Mr. Bouldin. She
dropped Morgan's letter in the orange flames of her fireplace
and pulled her wrapper a bit closer before reclining on the
rose chintz chaise.

She was both relieved and disappointed that Morgan had
not written that threat. Relieved because, although she was
certain he was up to something, she did not think it was
murder. And disappointed because they were no closer to
identifying Bouldin's murderer than they had been weeks
ago. Try as she might, she could not shake the certainty that
disaster loomed ahead if a solution was not quickly found.

She closed her eyes and pressed her fingertips to her temples, her head throbbing in an unrelenting rhythm. Tomorrow Grace would likely have a reply to her note, and that
would mean an end to their newest scheme—for better or
worse. If that note did not match the note she'd received,
she would have to conclude that there was an unknown person involved. Most likely the unknown voice in the garden.

A soft draft signaled the opening of Tristan's adjoining
door. He had returned from whatever late errand had taken
him out. She opened her eyes and turned her head, certain

she'd see him standing in his doorway, but he was suddenly next to her, as silent as always.

"I'm a fortunate man to have a wife who waits up for my return. Your presence gives me a reason to come home, Annica." He sat on the edge of the chaise and dropped a soft kiss on her lips. Cool fingers brushed her forehead. "Not feeling well?"

"Headache," she answered.

"Again? In another woman I might think that was an excuse," he said, "but not you, my dear. You would tell me if you simply did not want to accommodate me, would you not?"

"I shall always be as honest with you as you are with me, Tristan. You deserve that much."

His lips quirked in a sardonic smile. "Thank you, madam. There will be other opportunities. Very soon. In the meanwhile, I have brought some reading material I thought you might find entertaining."

"Oh?" She sat up and watched him disappear into his own room and then return, carrying several tomes. The amused smile should have warned her.

"I was surprised by your taste in reading material this afternoon, Annica. I had not suspected your interests would be quite so...exotic. If pornography is to your taste, I know several men who have extensive libraries in that genre, and who would be willing to open them to you. If you appreciate gentler, more erotic material, I can make other recommendations. Sappho's poetry, for instance, or Ovid's *Ars Amatoria.* Shakespeare's *Venus and Adonis,* or Marlowe's *Hero and Leander.*"

Annica swallowed her embarrassment and assumed an air of sophisticated interest. It would never do to have him find out that she had deliberately misdirected him.

He placed the stack of books by her chaise and sat on the edge to take her hand. "I have bought you copies of those

I recommend, but, just for the sake of discussion, may I recommend the *Kama Sutra* by Vatsyayana? I would enjoy exploring that particular work with you privately, and in detail.''

"The *Kama Sutra?*" she repeated with a frown. "I do not believe I have heard of that.''

"I would be surprised if you had.'' He chuckled and an endearing dimple appeared in one cheek. "But I feel certain you will find it fascinating. 'Tis told mostly in pictures.''

Her curiosity got the better of her again. "But prithee, Auberville, you have not answered my question regarding *Justine*. You said you would give me your opinion tonight.''

"I was barely twenty when I read it. I did not care for any character in the story. Justine, of course, was the most sympathetic, but I even lost patience with her as she made one foolish mistake after another, apparently unable to learn from her experiences,'' Tristan said, watching for Annica's reaction. He ran his hand down her bare arm, leaving goose bumps in its wake.

"Did you not think her mistakes were born of her natural innocence, and that her very virtue kept her naively trusting?'' she asked, baiting her trap.

"God forbid any woman should be so 'virtuous' that she make Justine's mistakes.'' He stood and went to the fireplace, leaning one arm on the mantel and fondling the glass of cognac he'd brought with him. "In my opinion, Justine was a simpleminded woman, lacking the capacity to learn from her errors or make intelligent decisions, and trusting to a fault with no reason. Virtue should not be confused with stupidity. Justine was an incapable woman.''

Annica shivered at his denouncement. There it was again. An incapable woman! The sort that drew his disgust. "Thus deserving of her trials?''

"I did not say that, Annica. No man or woman has the right to victimize or defile another.'' He abandoned his glass of cognac and sat beside her again, leaning forward with his forearms resting upon his knees. "I believe *The Misfortunes of Virtue* was written solely for the purpose of stimulating man's baser nature, to awaken hidden and forbidden desires and give birth to the commission of criminal acts. In short, I am of the opinion that de Sade's work is simple pornography, devoid of literary value. And you, madam? What do you believe?"

"The author's opinion and use of women is offensive. Though I do not hold with censorship, there are certain works that never should have seen print. *The Misfortunes of Virtue* is one."

"I am relieved you think so," he laughed. "In future, you need not use that particular ploy when you wish to be rid of me. I will be happy to leave without shocking your friends."

Annica bit her lip. "Was I so obvious?"

"To me," he said, brushing her hair back from her forehead. "There are still many things I do not know about you, things I may never learn, but you are not crude or vulgar. Nor are you helpless or silly, however much you pretend to be."

She held her breath, wondering what to say. He was inviting an explanation. "I do not know what you mean," she uttered, sounding even more stupid than she intended.

"Do you not?"

"How can you know what is feigned and what is real, Auberville? Has it occurred to you that your judgment may not always be correct, or that you might have made a bad decision?"

"Many times, my lady, but not about you. Never about you. When you are ready to tell me what is behind your little game, I am ready to listen."

She gave him a feeble smile. "Perhaps I just want to please you, Tristan."

"Wear green on occasion, Annica. That would please me." He kissed her again and went to his door. "Good night, my dear, and sweet dreams."

Punishing Tristan by withholding her favors was a two-edged sword. Frustration rose in her every time she saw him. It was beginning to appear as if she wanted him more than he wanted her. Or was he spending sleepless nights as well?

She heard a sudden crash from the adjoining room, as if a glass had shattered against a fireplace.

Annica permitted herself a small smile before she sat up and slipped the top book off the stack he had left by her chaise. "Hmm." She read the title. *"The Kama Sutra...."*

Chapter Fifteen

The following afternoon Annica watched as Ellen stepped onto the low stool in front of the mirror at Madame Marie's shop. Ellen blushed and dropped her gaze to the floor, turning on the little stool so the seamstress could mark the hem. She was everything a bride should be—sweet, naive, modest, demure, biddable. *Poor Ellen.*

"Ah! Perfection, *n'est-ce pas?*" Madame Marie clasped her hands to her bosom and sighed. "Dennison ees a lucky man, eh?"

"Have you and Dennison set the date, Ellen?" Charity asked.

"August 11," she told them in a voice so soft she could barely be heard.

"That is time enough, then." Annica nodded.

"Time enough for what?" Ellen's blue eyes widened in surprise that she might have forgotten something.

"To change your mind," Charity teased.

Annica's laughter died when Ellen burst into tears, her narrow shoulders shaking. Annica swept her cousin up in a comforting hug when she teetered off the stool.

"Ellen," she crooned. "Hush, dearling, hush. 'Twill come a' right."

"Oh, 'Nica! I cannot cry off! Papa would never speak to me again, and Mama would fall into a decline. They are counting upon this marriage. The scandal would kill them," Ellen wept against Annica's shoulder.

"No, sweet cousin," she contradicted. "They may be disappointed and angry at first, but they will forgive you. They do not want you to be miserable. After all, 'tis your life. You must not live it in a manner repugnant to you. Stand up to them, Ellen."

"But they will shout at me and—"

"Refuse to be bullied! Aunt Lucy will sulk and Uncle Thomas will growl, and two months hence they will have forgotten all about it. I doubt Gilbert will even notice, he is so consumed by his own life. Anyway, in the end, you know they will all blame me."

Ellen gave her a tentative smile. "Yes, but do you not mind that Mama and Papa will blame you?"

"I have always worn blame like a badge of honor."

Charity laughed and patted Ellen's shoulder. "You know it is true, Ellen. She takes great pride in it. And, now she is wed to Lord Auberville, your parents cannot even punish her."

"I ask one favor, Ellen. If you refuse Dennison, warn me ahead so that I may prepare for the inevitable denouncements."

"'Nica, how could I ever live this down?"

"Easily, so long as you do not make Dennison look a fool. He does not deserve that for simply finding you wonderful enough to wed. You must put as good a face on it as possible, and not make an enemy of him. After all, I credit my great social success to the fact that I always put a good face on matters, and I never make enemies."

Ellen and Charity both laughed at Annica's outrageous explanation. The lighthearted jest was just the right tone to allow Ellen to pull herself together.

"I do not understand," Madame Marie said. "Weel zere be zee wedding?"

"Perhaps." Annica helped Ellen back onto the stool. "But it will not be to Dennison. Take your time, Marie. In fact, make a very special tea gown for my cousin first, and bill Auberville."

Ellen giggled. "Will he not be angry?"

Annica shuddered, remembering the demon-possessed man who had thrown her over his shoulder and carried her up the stairs of the brothel. "I have seen him angry only once, Ellen, and that took considerably more than a gown. I guarantee, I would not provoke him like that again. Nevertheless, I shall speak to him at once to apprise him of your situation and discuss possible solutions. I will not have him called to account for my actions without his prior knowledge."

"Shoo! Off weeth you." Madame Marie made a sweeping movement with her arms. "You and Mees Wardlow wait outside, eh? I strip Lady Ellen down for zee measures, and I call you when we are done. Go now! Give us privacy. Shoo!"

Annica and Charity exited with a promise to wait in the adjoining fitting room. A clock chimed three times when they closed the door behind them and entered the room nearest the back door. As arranged, Mr. Renquist was waiting for them.

"Afternoon, ladies." He bowed. "I'm afraid I have nothing new to report. Wilkes is either damned clever or he has friends."

Charity emitted an unladylike snort. "He is horrid."

"He is lucky." Annica dropped her reticule on a chair and shrugged out of her light spencer. "God knows we have not left him with a single friend."

Mr. Renquist shook his head in dejection. "Be that as it

may, ladies, we are in the same situation—what to do next?
Do we continue, or move on?''

''We change strategy,'' Annica said. ''Mr. Renquist, find
out what you can about the people around Wilkes. Who are
his closest friends? What clubs, organizations and social
groups is he associated with? How has he spent the last
twenty years? Does he receive letters? From whom? Does
he post letters? To whom? Where is his family and what do
they think of him? Somewhere, Mr. Renquist, there is a
connection to a Hellfire Club. And amongst those people
will be the source of the familiar voice in the garden and
the man with the scar.''

''There comes a time when one must cut one's losses and
move on,'' Renquist said. ''One must use sound judgment
to determine when one is in over one's head, if you take
my meaning.''

''Thank you for the caution, Mr. Renquist. I will consider
it very carefully. Is there anything else?''

''Regarding your friend's abigail and the other missing
women, have you heard of white slavery, Lady Annica?''

''White slavery?'' Charity repeated. ''What do you mean?''

''The kidnapping of English women to be sold into the
harems and brothels of rich Arabs and North Africans,''
Renquist sighed. ''Longshoremen whisper of women crying
and calling at night from ships along the docks. Ships bound
for the Mediterranean. I am inclined to believe them. White
slavery is profitable.''

Annica leaned forward with earnestness. ''Can you bring
me names? And the names of the ships?''

''That's the pity of it, Lady Annica. I could post a man
at every dock and wharf, but looking for a particular ship
is like searching for a particular grain of sand on a beach.''

She opened her reticule and withdrew all the cash she had
brought with her. It amounted to nearly twenty-five pounds,
and she handed it over to the Bow Street Runner without

blinking. "Keep on, Mr. Renquist. Hire more men if you must. Send them to work at the Surrey docks and tell them to keep their eyes and ears open. Whatever it takes, Mr. Renquist, *do it.*"

"Aye. I will, milady. The situation is out of hand. Did you hear that a woman disappeared Friday night and another on Saturday night?"

"No, Mr. Renquist, I had not. I am afraid I've been somewhat distracted. Who were they?"

"Working class, Lady Annica. A governess and an upstairs maid from the Kensington area. Just the sort that make good victims."

She stiffened her spine and lifted her chin. "If you do not send for me before then, we shall meet here again on Thursday at two o'clock."

"Very well, Lady Annica," Renquist said. "One more thing."

"Yes?" Annica turned back.

"That tavern where my man met the dock worker? There was another man there, too."

"Who?"

"Geoffrey Morgan."

Her mind reeled. Everything just kept becoming more and more complicated. "Please determine if there is a connection between Mr. Wilkes and Mr. Morgan, and the missing women."

Renquist narrowed his eyes. "What do you suspect, Lady Annica?"

"I am of a divided mind. A part of me cannot credit Geoffrey Morgan with rape and murder, but another part believes he could be dangerous and that he is engaged in something nefarious."

That evening, at the Lundy soiree, Annica watched the elegant widow dodge the approach of Roger Wilkes. Grace was in a very uncomfortable position, having pretended sympathy to obtain a sample of his handwriting. Now she faced the unpleasant consequence—Wilkes's annoying gratitude.

Taking pity on her friend, and knowing Wilkes would not dare subject himself to another cut, Annica waved and called, "Over here, Grace! Heavens! Where have you been?"

The look of utter relief on Grace's face was comical. She headed straight for Annica, glancing neither right nor left. "Annica, my dear! I feared you'd forgotten me in the crush."

She slipped her arm through Annica's and led her toward the game room, chatting pleasantly about the excellent weather and how the almanac had predicted rain.

Once they were safely out of sight, Annica unfolded the note and scanned the scribbled lines. Blotched, heavy strokes together with a cramped style told Annica everything she needed to know. The words were unimportant. "*Curses!* I was so certain!" She crumpled the paper in her fist.

"Not the same at all, is it?" Grace agreed. "But if the murderer is not Wilkes and not Morgan, who could it be?"

"I cannot even imagine. There is no shortage of villains in the world, but finding one particular villain in the crowd is becoming a great problem."

Grace nodded enthusiastically. "And now we have another investigation looming ahead. Find the *fifth* man—the one who wrote that warning."

"At least we are free to finish with Wilkes."

Grace's Cupid's bow lips curved in a satisfied smile. "Shall we go tell Sarah and the others?"

"The sooner the better. I am anxious to have it done."

"What if he slanders Sarah?"

"I would like to cut his tongue out! I have the heart for it, Grace, but not the stomach. That is why, should it become public, I shall swear Sarah was with me the night she was assaulted. I do not like to lie, but I shall do it with a straight face and my hand upon a Bible, if I must."

"Nick!" a voice called as they passed the game room on their way back to the ballroom. "I say, old boy, come join us in a hand, eh?"

Annica spun around to see Julius Lingate, Geoffrey Morgan, Horace Lundy and Alfred Neeley sitting at a green, baize-covered card table. A nearly empty bottle of port stood at Julius's elbow and he wore a silly grin. She wondered if he was in his cups. With a promise to rejoin her shortly, she let Grace go on without her and went into the game room.

"'Pears to me as if your table is full, Jules," she observed, mimicking a male voice.

Horace Lundy got to his feet and held his chair for her. "You may have my place, Lady Auberville. Morgan has already relieved me of the last of my ready, and Clara will be looking for me to play host. Besides, I have no idea how to play the games that ladies play."

Annica sat and watched Mr. Lundy hurry from the room. When she turned back to the table, she was amused to find Geoffrey Morgan and Mr. Neeley looking at her with disbelief. Julius, however, watched her with approval. He, at least, was learning.

"Well, gentlemen? Were we playing ladies' games?" she asked.

"No," Neeley told her. "We were playing—"

"Vingt et un," Morgan interrupted.

"Lingate was just giving Lundy a graceful exit. He lost more than he should," Neeley explained. "Geoff is unbeatable tonight."

Annica turned to Morgan. "So you are having a run of good luck, eh, Mr. Morgan?"

His eyes, a bit golden tonight, met hers. "Until now, Lady Annica. Have you come to change my luck?"

She raised her eyebrows at the veiled challenge. "Why would I want to do that, Mr. Morgan?"

"Because you like to win?" He gathered the cards from the table and began to shuffle.

"Not enough to—"

"Cheat?" he finished.

Annica did not flinch. She regretted her harshness with him at their last meeting. Now, in the face of his apparent innocence, his anger seemed justified. She could not atone for her suspicions, but she could try to restore a measure of civility between them. For Constance's sake.

"I was not going to say that, Mr. Morgan. I was going to say that I like to win, but not enough to *gamble*."

"You do not like risk, Lady Annica?" Morgan persisted.

"One is never more alive than when there is something at risk. But a card game hardly qualifies, sir. And the things I cherish cannot be gambled."

"I beg to differ, Lady Annica."

"How?"

"You made a great show of cherishing your freedom over the past several years, yet you gambled all that Auberville would not exercise his right to remove it when you said your vows." He slid the deck of shuffled cards toward her.

Accepting the challenge, she cut the deck and slid it back across the green cloth to him. "You have me there. It would appear I *do* gamble."

Alfred Neeley pushed his chair away from the table and stood. "Sounds too serious for me."

Julius sat back and crossed his arms over his chest. "I fear the stakes have just got too high for me. I am out."

"Vingt et un?" Morgan asked.

She nodded. "As you know, I learned it a few weeks ago. The wager?"

"Shall we wager something you truly cherish, Lady Annica?"

The first uneasy stirrings of fear raised the fine hairs on the back of her neck. "What did you have in mind, Mr Morgan?"

He dealt one card facedown for each of them, then placed the deck on the table between them. "Your judgment."

Confused, she tapped one cheek with a finger and pursed her lips in a thoughtful pose.

There was a trap here—she was certain of it—but it eluded her. How could she lose her judgment? "Deal," she said.

He took one card, a seven, off the deck and placed it faceup on top of her other card. The next card, his, was a nine. Annica lifted a corner of her first card and peeked. A five.

Geoffrey Morgan watched her, cool and confident, not bothering to look at his own bottom card.

Annica calculated the risks quickly. Sixteen of fifty-two cards could put her over. Therefore, thirty-eight were safe. Three of those could be accounted for, leaving thirty-five. Fairly good odds. Better than two-to-one.

"Lady Annica?"

"Again," she said.

His graceful fingers flipped the top card off the deck to land atop her other two. A jack. Twenty-two. The odds had failed her. She kept her face impassive as she waited to see what her opponent would do.

Very slowly, very deliberately, he turned his bottom card up. It was a queen. Nineteen points.

Annica took comfort from the fact that she would have been defeated whether she had drawn from the deck or not. Ah, but she had to give Mr. Morgan credit for nerves of steel. She hadn't turned her card up, so he couldn't know she was over.

A niggling of doubt began to tease at the back of her mind. She had heard of marked decks, where only the marker knew how to read the secret clues on the backs, hidden in the patterns. She narrowed her eyes as she studied the red-patterned deck for any irregularity.

In one fluid movement, Morgan spread the entire rest of the deck across the table, to facilitate her suspicious study. Julius laughed, a wink telling her that he knew, too, what she had been thinking.

"Best two of three, Lady Annica?" Morgan offered, the hint of a smile playing at the corners of his mouth.

"No, thank you, Mr. Morgan. You won—fairly, I suppose. Now you must tell me what is it that you've won."

"The benefit of the doubt." He gathered the cards again and began shuffling. "You see, Lady Annica, the next time you are faced with such a choice, you will remember this conversation, and that you owe me a debt of honor. You cannot help but consider a better motive for my actions than you are accustomed to ascribing to me. An element of doubt may cloud your usual certainty. I may benefit from it, or I may not. But..." he grinned at her with all the charm he possessed "...you will have considered it. And that is what I have won."

She smiled. Mr. Morgan was more clever than she'd thought. And more dangerous. And now she owed him a debt of honor!

Chapter Sixteen

The midafternoon sunlight did not penetrate the dim alley where Annica's coach waited. There was little risk of her being seen by anyone she knew in this part of town. After matching wits with Mr. Morgan the previous evening, Annica decided to take action. If she could clear him of suspicion, then her debt to him would be paid.

Naughty Alice arrived, climbed up into the coach, pulled the door closed and left the stuttering, white-faced Hodgeson standing on the cobblestones.

"Drive, Hodgeson, and do not stop until I tell you," Annica instructed.

She fished through her reticule, brought forth a sovereign, then turned to the blowzy blonde and pressed the coin into her palm. "Here. I know your time is valuable, and I would not want you to suffer for helping me."

"So it's you, eh? I had a note from Nick," the woman said.

"I am Nick," she admitted, somewhat ashamed of her ploy. "I thought you'd be more likely to meet me if you thought I was male." She glanced out the coach window to find Hodgeson still standing at the curb. She took note of the lengthening shadows on the brick wall in the alleyway.

She would have to be home for supper soon. Mrs. Eberhart was preparing her special mutton stew, and Tristan had left a note this morning promising to tell her stories of his youth. "Hodgeson, are you just going to stand there?"

"He thinks I ain't no sort for the likes of you to be seen with," the woman guessed. "Are you the one that come looking for me a while back? The one what got carried upstairs?"

"Yes, Alice. That would have been me."

"Edwina said you was real brave. The man who took you was ever so fierce."

Annica shivered at the memory and wondered briefly what Tristan would do if he knew about *this* meeting. Still, she had honored his wishes by not going to the bawd's place of business. She had brought the bawd to her. "Alice, you helped us with Mr. Farmingdale, and I hope you will be able to help us with one or two of his friends."

"An' who might they be, yer ladyship?"

"One is Roger Wilkes. Another is Geoffrey Morgan. And, of course, anyone else who kept company with them."

Alice's lips compressed into a thin line. "I did not know Mr. Morgan went about with the others. As for the rest—that's a bad lot, yer ladyship. Mr. Morgan, too, but not in the same way."

The coach rocked as Hodgeson climbed into the driver's seat. Annica waited, but there was no further movement. Hodgeson was going nowhere. He really was becoming quite unmanageable. The staff at Clarendon Place were proving to be an inspiration to him. They appeared to walk a fine line between friendly compliance and cordial disobedience. Hodgeson had hinted that they'd been hired for their discretion rather than their subservience. He was learning their techniques.

She returned to the matter at hand. "Bad lot? How many

are in that lot, Alice? Farmingdale, Wilkes and...who else?''

"I ain't sure," she said evasively. "Most of 'em don't use their true names. Men of that sort do not tell the truth to women of my sort. But women of my sort have our ways of finding out things."

The pragmatic statement made Annica smile.

"Farmingdale's a wicked one. I wouldn't put nothin' past 'im. Like as not, all those that run with 'im are as bad," Alice continued. "Wilkes is, for certain. So was Taylor. There was some others that used to come with 'em, but I never knew all they was up to. Wish I could be more help, Lady Annica."

"You've been of immense help," Annica told her. "Truly, we could not have ruined Farmingdale without you."

"I ain't so sure I did you a service there, milady."

"Lord only knows how long he might have continued his perfidy."

"He's still alive, milady."

"I know." Annica tensed as a burning began in her belly. Farmingdale might not be a threat to Englishwomen, but it would never do to start thinking of unlucky Jamaican women just now.

"As for the rest," Alice was saying, "Wilkes comes, once in a while, and the girls draw lots to see who'll take him."

"Can you find out who else was associated with Roger Wilkes?''

"I could, but I ain't sure I should."

"Alice, we are desperate. Frightful threats have been made against my group. Murder has been done. Women have gone missing. I am very afraid all those events may be linked and have something to do with Wilkes or someone he knows."

Alice pondered this while she patted her brassy curls into place. "I'll think on it, milady. 'Tisn't that I'm loath to help, but our customers are our livin', if you catch me. If word got out that we repeated names—well, you can imagine what that would do to business."

"I can assure you, Alice, that my source would never be revealed."

"An' yer servant?" Alice gestured toward the driver's box, where Hodgeson sat unseen.

"Hodgeson is the very soul of discretion. He would never betray me. Never."

"I'll think 'pon it. How can I reach you, milady?"

"Leave a message with Madame Marie LeBeau at her shop off Piccadilly. Or send a message to 'Nick Sayles' at the Auberville residence, Clarendon Place. Be certain to seal it."

"Auberville?" Alice's face drained of color. "You're related to Lord Auberville?"

"He is my husband," she admitted.

"Harry Bouldin never told me that," Alice gasped. "He said you was gentry, and a spinster."

"My marriage to Auberville is a recent development, Alice. It came about after Mr. Bouldin's untimely demise."

Alice composed herself with aplomb and accorded Annica new respect. "I believe I'll send to Madame Marie, if it's all the same to you, milady."

"Do you know my husband, Alice?" Annica asked uneasily.

"By reputation, milady. Blimey! I never would have guessed he'd countenance his wife in such an undertaking! But there's no figurin' the Quality, eh? Him, doing what he does—and you, doing what you do. It's a peculiar world."

"What do you mean, Alice? What does Auberville do?"

Alice sobered. "I only hears rumors, milady."

"He has taken his seat in the House of Lords, if that is

what you mean. In truth, my activities could cause him embarrassment if they were known.''

Alice gave her an odd look, as if there had been some sort of misunderstanding. ''As you say.''

Reassuring the woman was foremost on Annica's mind. ''He has no idea about my secret activities, Alice, nor must he *ever*. Do you understand? He would take exception—''

The expression on Alice's face turned to one of horror. ''Lord! 'Twere Auberville who carried you up the stairs that night! Edwina and Fanny said it was a demon, but I thought they fancied it. They was closer to the truth than they knew!''

''Alice! Collect yourself! Auberville is a perfectly ordinary—well, not *ordinary,* perhaps—but harmless—oh, well, not precisely harmless, I suppose—but reasonable… Oh, never mind. Shall we just say that he is ignorant of my pursuits and must remain so?''

''The last thing I want is trouble with Lord Auberville,'' Alice vowed. ''But he ain't a good one to try to keep a secret from. He just seems to *know* things, if ye catch my meaning.''

Annica picked up a bottle and dabbed rose water behind her ears. Her dark hair was arranged in a fall of little ringlets down her back and lay in stark relief against her French-blue gown. Lord, but she was sick of blue!

She needn't have hurried home from her meeting with Alice. Tristan had sent his apologies that he would not be able to join her for dinner. Business. Again. Who was punishing whom? She went to her dressing room, determined to find something red, orange or chartreuse—anything loud and tasteless!—to wear down to dinner. Tristan never need know.

Mary found her there, rummaging through wardrobes and bureaus. ''Milady! Your aunt is below demanding that you receive her at once. She's in the front parlor, and Master Gilbert is with her.''

Annica had a sinking sensation. She abandoned her plan to change her gown. Something was afoot, and she suspected what it was.

She hurried down the stairs and into the front parlor to find Lucy pacing and wringing her hands, while Gilbert slumped in a chair with a scowl on his young face. "Hello, Auntie. Gil. Is something wrong?''

Lucy turned to her and threw her hands up. "This is *your* fault! I know it is!''

Annica stopped in her tracks, her premonition fulfilled. Ellen had made her decision. Gathering her wits, Annica assumed an innocent air as she sat on the velvet settee and folded her hands in her lap. "What have I done, Aunt Lucy?''

"'Tis Ellen! She is locked in her room and will not be allowed to leave until she comes to her senses. Thomas is beside himself.''

"How am I responsible for that?'' Annica asked.

"Ellen would never think of this on her own.''

"Think of what?''

"She announced this morning over breakfast that she had decided not to marry Dennison after all—hoped it would not be too inconvenient making the announcement and nullifying the contracts. What *can* she be thinking?''

"That she does not love Dennison?'' Annica ventured.

"Does not *love* him!'' Lucy exclaimed. "Yes, that is just what she said!''

Gilbert nodded. "And that's how we know *you* are involved.''

Annica squared her shoulders and lifted her chin. "Then I am proud to have been of service.''

Gilbert catapulted out of his chair. "You see? I knew she would not help,'' he told his mother.

"Help? Did you come here to ask me to speak with Ellen? Change her mind? Persuade her to go through with a loveless marriage? *Me?*" Annica did her best to hold back a laugh.

"My dear, you have made a brilliant marriage. Ellen is not so fortunate. She does not have your vibrancy, your wit, your humor, your—"

"Unfortunate manners? Eccentricities? Reputation as a bluestocking?" she finished for her aunt. "Think, Aunt Lucy. Ellen, with her sterling reputation and flawless beauty will have whoever she chooses. Whoever *she* chooses," she repeated for emphasis. "And she does not choose Dennison."

"Who is behind this, Annica?" her aunt asked, intent on fixing the blame.

She shrugged and suppressed her guilt—not on account of supporting Ellen, but guilt at defying her aunt and uncle. "I suppose 'twas me. How many times have I said I would never marry without affection? If she has adopted my opinion—"

"She has no right to make decisions," Gilbert huffed. "Girls do as they're told. They are not equipped to—"

"Oh, Gil! Do not prove your ignorance with a parroted speech from Mr. Wilberforce." She looked at her cousin and sighed. Would a man ever understand all that a woman gave up when she said her vows? Perhaps she could help them look at the problem in a different way. "If Ellen has come to the conclusion that she simply cannot spend the rest of her life lying beneath Dennison and submitting to his will and intimacies, I cannot wish it of her. And I am amazed that anyone who claims affection for her *would* wish it."

Lucy collapsed on the settee beside Annica, utterly defeated. "Dear child! How can you see malice in her parents wanting what is best for her?"

"If she does not love him, Dennison is not the best."

"He will be furious!"

"Then we should set our minds to finding just the sort of woman who could love him—one whom he can love in return."

Lucy wrung her hankie. "But Ellen—"

"Ellen will prevail, Aunt Lucy. How could she not? She has the benefit of your excellent training and guidance. By the time she is done, Dennison will be thanking her. Meantime, Auberville and I will set out to find just the right woman for him. I promise, Aunt Lucy, he will be married before Ellen, and pleased with his good fortune."

"How?"

"'Tis just a matter of matching interests and goals. We shall find a woman who adores horses and cannot wait to have children. One who favors slightly stuffy, humorless men with very old titles. We shall make him a brilliant match. Now, please go home and tell Uncle Thomas to unlock Ellen's door. She will not disgrace the family. I promise, Aunt Lucy. That is not her style. 'Tis mine."

Tristan's right arm slipped around the stranger's throat and tightened. Only discipline kept him from snapping the neck. The old anger, the darkness, was very near to taking control again, and he had to remind himself that he was in Whitefriars, not Algiers. He lowered the unconscious man to the ground, easing him onto his back.

"Sweet Jesu! I've never seen him before," The Sheikh said when he finally got a good look at the man's face.

Tristan searched the unconscious man's jacket pockets, looking for a clue. A wad of banknotes, a few coins, a watch, a match safe—nothing to give the man's identity away. "A professional, I'd guess. He knows the tricks."

"Who would follow Wilkes?" The Sheikh asked.

"An unlucky woman's husband? An angry father?" Tristan pushed the items back into the man's pocket. "Where is Lord Ian Hunter these days?"

"Lady Sarah's father? Thought of that, Auberville. He and his sons are in Scotland at their hunting lodge. No, this is not the work of Sarah's family. As I understand it, they know nothing of what was done to her."

"If Wilkes knew we were following him, and hired this man to find out who we are..." Tristan speculated.

"If he was following *us,* how could we have taken him by surprise? He was as dumbfounded as we were."

Tristan felt for the man's pulse. "How the hell will we explain this to Kilgrew?"

They dragged the stranger into the shelter of a dark alley. They couldn't leave him alone in this part of town until he began to regain consciousness, so they prepared to wait.

"We may as well pack it in," the man continued. "Go home to your wife, Auberville. She must mark your absence. I am amazed she has not asked about your odd hours."

An unaccustomed tweak of conscience troubled Tristan. He regretted begging off on their rare dinner at home that evening. "She assumes I spend time at my club and Parliament. Chauncy covers for me. Still, I think I will not be able to deceive her once she is accustomed to marriage and my habits. She has a way of sensing trouble." It helped that she was still miffed at him for the way he had coerced her into marriage. Withholding her favors was working to his advantage, if not suiting his disposition.

The unconscious man moaned and moved his head from side to side. Tristan looked down at him. "He'll be coming around soon. Time for us to disappear."

"Tomorrow night?"

"I'll meet you at the King's Head Tavern," Tristan said, pulling the collar of his coat up and scanning the eastern horizon, where a violet-pink dawn was breaking.

"We are coming very close," his companion informed him.

Tristan smiled grimly. "We know everything but the name of the mastermind of this little scheme."

Annica's heart thumped painfully. Her throat constricted and she glanced furtively toward the front of the book store to be certain they could not be overheard before she whispered, "Was it…could it have been Mr. Bouldin's murderer? Dear Lord, is he onto *you* now?"

Renquist rubbed the bump on the back of his head. "Doubtful, milady. Whoever hit me over the head last night had the opportunity to kill me, and did not."

"You must quit, Mr. Renquist!" Annica argued. "For your own safety. Leave town. I could not bear it if I were the cause—"

"Stop right there, Lady Annica. Bouldin was my friend. Hired or not, I will find the filthy swine who—"

"Enough, Mr. Renquist." Anxiety churned in her stomach. How could the Wednesday League risk another life? Yet he swore to continue, whether working with her or not. "Very well, sir. But promise you will be careful. You…that is, when one shares certain perils and secrets, one grows attached, and—"

"Say no more, Lady Annica. I have regard for you, too."

She hoped his sentiment would not cost him his life. Trying to cover her embarrassment at the awkward admission, she straightened her spine and assumed a brusque manner. "Did you have any news, Mr. Renquist?"

"Quite a lot. Better sit down."

She perched herself on a sturdy box containing books and waited expectantly.

"I asked a man I hire once in a while, a member of the gentry who has occasional need of extra, er, income, to make some inquires. He looked into Hellfire Clubs, milady.

Young bloods who belong to such things are secretive about it. Still, we managed.'' He paused dramatically before continuing, holding her in breathless anticipation.

''No Wilkes,'' he said at length. ''No Taylor, Harris or Farmingdale. There may be more clubs than we found, but not likely. My man was intrigued by the problem, and was very thorough. He did uncover another possibility.''

''What?'' she asked, drawn into Renquist's drama.

''A regimental club. Wilkes, Farmingdale, Taylor and Harris all served in the same battalion years ago. They were all officers, all served in the same area, and all were discharged within months of each other.''

Annica knew there was more by the way Renquist held his breath. She sat forward, anxious to hear it all. ''Come, Mr. Renquist. All of it!''

''They served in the Royal Navy. In the Mediterranean.''

''That's it!'' Annica murmured. ''*That's* the connection.'' And another connection Auberville shared with the villains.

Chapter Seventeen

Standing before his cheval looking glass, Tristan arranged the folds of his cravat. Chauncy stood by, holding his waistcoat.

"She asked when I would be home?" he questioned his valet. "That is very wifelike of Annica. Did she say why?"

"No, my lord. I gather she wished to speak with you."

Tristan glanced at the closed door that adjoined his room to Annica's. "Hmm. I fear our schedules have been in conflict the past several days. Make no appointments for me on Saturday, Chauncy. I want to spend the day with my wife. Odd to say, but I miss her company."

Tristan smiled, glad that he had had Chauncy to rely upon. The man had been his aide in the Royal Navy and had served him ever since—as valet, confidant and messenger when required. "I require your assistance now, Chauncy. Lady Annica has made an enemy of Roger Wilkes. Should he call here, he is not to be admitted. Keep alert to any unusual activity or events. Should my wife so much as stub her toe, report it to me at once."

"Would this be related to your earlier warnings regarding trellises and vines, my lord?"

"No, Chauncy, although do not relax your vigilance on

that score. At this point in time, I more fear the danger from outside than Annica's occasional recklessness.''

"As you say, milord.''

Chauncy's face did not betray his emotions, but the twinkle in his eyes did. Tristan knew the man must be thinking that his employer had got what he deserved. After years of yearning for peace and quiet, he had deliberately courted Annica Sayles. After seeking a woman who would bear his children, stay out of his way and amuse herself, he had found Annica. And, after guarding himself against betrayal and desertion, he'd opened his heart and invited Annica in. Annica, with her record of renunciation, doubt, willfulness and distrust...

He was insane!

"Ask Mrs. Eberhart to keep her eye on my lady, too. I've already had a word with Hodgeson. We cannot be too careful.''

"Of course, my lord.'' Chauncy held Tristan's waistcoat as he shrugged into it.

A soft knock on the door from Annica's room drew both men's attention. "Yes?'' Tristan called.

His wife peeked around the panel. Her night-dark hair fell in loose waves around her shoulders and over the thin lawn of her nightdress. Her eyes were heavy-lidded and shadowed with sleep.

Chauncy, always sensitive to the moment, whisked a nonexistent piece of lint from Tristan's jacket and excused himself with a perfunctory bow.

"Come in, Annica.'' Tristan straightened his cravat.

She came to him on bare feet, standing close enough for him to smell the warmth of her skin mingled with rose water. He was seized with the desire to gather her into his arms and make love to her all day long. God knew how much he had longed for that. But he was nearly desperate to conclude his business for Kilgrew so he could give his full attention to his bride.

"Tristan..." she sighed sleepily.

He scooped her off her feet and carried her to his still-rumpled bed. He pulled the covers over her and kissed her cheek. "And good morning to you, sprite."

She smiled—a heart-squeezingly vulnerable smile. "Tristan, stay. I've been trying to catch you for days. There are things we must discuss. You must know what is afoot with—"

"Christ," he groaned, and stepped back before his resolve vanished. He'd never seen her in his bed before—only in hers—and the sight sent his blood pumping. There wasn't a single part of him that didn't ache to do as she bade. But duty called. "I have urgent business, Annica. I shall be tied up for another day or two."

"These are important matters, Tristan. They cannot wait."

"I shall look for an opportunity sooner than that, milady. Not tonight—I have a previous commitment. Tomorrow night? Will you be at Beatrice Caldwell's dinner party? We could steal away for a few minutes for a private word."

Annica blinked and pushed herself up against his pillows. "Steal away? But—"

"Whatever it is, you can handle it, Annica," he said, taking another step backward.

"But—"

"I should have been in chambers an hour ago."

"You have no idea what is happening in your own home!" There was a sharp edge to her voice.

"Annica, I received a bill for a dress for Ellen. If your aunt and uncle are in dun territory, ask what they need. Of course we will help them through this rough patch."

"It is not a 'rough patch.' It is Ellen! She—"

Tristan cursed under his breath. Annica, her color heightened in anger, her delicate hands tightened into little fists, was the most beguiling sight he had seen since last week, when she had—no! He could not think about that now. As it was, he was finding it difficult to stand straight. He gave himself a mental shake. His courtship of Annica had required more attention away from his investigation than he'd bargained for, and now he had to make up for lost time. The lives of innocent women were hanging in the balance.

"Ellen? Ah, yes. The dress. If your uncle cannot afford a gown—"

"He can afford a gown, Tristan."

"Then why did your dressmaker bill me?"

"I told her to."

Tristan took his pocket watch out and glanced at the time. Nearly ten o'clock. He was half an hour late. "I know you must have had a reason."

"Yes, I did. And that is what we must discuss before there is a disaster. You see, Ellen has—"

Disaster? In a dress? Only a woman would see such consequences. "Not now, Annica."

"Now!" she demanded. "You have asked me to keep you informed. I am trying to do so."

He spoke over his shoulder on his way to the door. "I do not have time for your 'helpless' game just now. Whatever it is, handle it. I shall try to be home by midnight or shortly after, and will be at your disposal then, Annica."

Her toneless voice brought him back around. "Perhaps *I* will not be here, Tristan. Perhaps *I* will not have time for *you.*"

His blood thinned to ice water, and cold anger flashed along his nerves. It had taken her long enough, but she had finally found his weak spot, his greatest vulnerability. "What are you saying, Lady Auberville? Do you think you can leave me?"

"Do you think you could stop me?"

Tristan was halfway down the stairs before the echo of his slamming door died into an awful stillness.

The dark gray burnoose billowed behind Tristan as he urged his horse to greater speed, The Sheikh riding closely on his stallion's heels. Their sense of urgency grew in the moonless night. The warning they had received from one of their informants mere minutes ago may have come too late.

A woman—a "Nosy Parker" who had been meddling in the disappearance of other women—had been marked for removal, their source had said. She was to be lured to a private place, and then eliminated.

Tristan had not been surprised to learn that a woman might have become involved in this case. He had long expected a mother, an aunt, a sister, a friend, to raise an alarm. But according to their informant, this woman had come close enough to the truth to be a real danger. Something about this made Tristan uneasy, as if there was something he should remember, something just out of his grasp.

They dropped their surveillance of Wilkes at a seedy tavern and galloped across London Bridge to the Southwark side. Following their informant's directions, they came to a deserted street two lanes off the Thames. The area was quiet, the closest tavern being three streets away, and only a bawdy house or two nearby. Most buildings were warehouses and shipping offices.

Tristan dismounted and waited for his companion to join him. Was this a trap laid for them? His jaw clenched at the soft scrape of metal when the blade of his midshipman's dirk slipped from the scabbard. He could hear the lapping of the river, the faint music from the tavern, and a soft shuffle of movement somewhere behind him.

"Well?" The Sheikh asked him in a whisper.

"I'll take the left. You go right." Tristan gestured to the narrow lanes that opened off the street.

A Wild Justice

The absolute darkness of a moonless night made the going slow. Every sense Tristan had was alert. Every instinct warned of disaster. Danger was thick in the air. It jangled his nerve endings and quickened his heartbeat.

Tristan detected the soft gurgle of expelled breath, a grotesque and all too familiar sound. A slight movement drew his attention to the darkest corner, behind a row of stacked wooden crates. A scurrying rat? His instincts said not. He went forward.

A pile of rags was heaped in a far corner, and Tristan could well imagine what an excellent breeding ground that would make for vermin. A darker patch atop the pile glistened wet, and Tristan knew with dark certainty what it was.

"Over here!" he called in a hoarse whisper.

"What is it?" The Sheikh asked.

Tristan pointed to the tangle of rags. He dropped his stallion's reins and started forward. "Cover me," he said.

The click of the hammer being drawn back on The Sheikh's pistol was only mildly comforting.

Tristan poked at the pile with the toe of his boot and got no response. The density and weight of the rags drew his memory back several years. To Tunis. To the Algerian affair. Swallowing the bile that rose to his throat, Tristan knelt on one knee beside the heap.

No pulse, and the body was still warm. His fingertips came away sticky and dark. He turned the man's head to see his face. The man's face—eyes still opened in surprise, mouth agape in a silent scream—was familiar, but he couldn't place it. He passed his hand over the man's face, closing the eyes.

"Too late," he said. The Sheikh's footsteps came up behind him. "Look at the knife work. Remind you of anything?"

Easing the hammer back into place, The Sheikh knelt

beside Tristan. "Tunis. The Turk." He turned the dead man's face toward him. "Kauffman?"

Kauffman? Where had he heard that name before? Eyes fully adjusted to the dark corner, Tristan made out a second shape in the pile of rags. Leaving his comrade, he inched forward, to find another, smaller form.

The Sheikh's attention was riveted on the dead man. "Good God! It *is* Kauffman! He's Constance Bennington's footman. What can he have to do with this?"

Tristan lifted the second body out of the formless heap. Building fury took control of him. A primal growl rose in his chest. "Christ…!"

Dark red hair tumbled over his arm. A light violet gown was blotched with blood, and he gathered the slight form against his chest, his howl echoing off the buildings around them.

The Sheikh came to his feet, pain and incomprehension registering on his face. "No. No, Tristan."

Tristan groaned, "I cannot credit this. It makes no sense." *Annica!* he thought, fighting a sudden panic. *Dear Lord, is she safe? Is she in danger, too?*

"Constance…" The Sheikh's voice held an audible ache as he took the limp body from Tristan's arms and held it in his own. He dropped to his knees, laid his cheek to hers and closed his eyes, rocking the woman's body back and forth. He turned his face upward and shouted for the heavens to hear. "Damn you to hell, Turk! Damn your mother and damn your father!"

"I'll summon the night watch." Tristan reached for the reins of his horse.

"Go home, Auberville. Look to your lady. I will handle this," the man said, his voice now cold and calm. "The night watch will be on the way after the noise we made."

"The questions—"

"I will handle it. I want to stay with her, Auberville."

* * *

The wild gallop home in the darkest part of night seemed endless. Tristan's imagination played havoc with his emotions. After what he'd just seen he could not help but wonder what he would do if Annica had been harmed. How could he live with that?

He thought of her as she'd been that morning—soft, warm and sweet-scented, lying against his pillows, dwarfed by the massive four-poster bed, her delicate beauty luring him from duty with nothing but a soft plea. *Tristan, stay.* God, how he wished he had! Now her veiled threat took on monstrous proportions: *Perhaps I will not be here, Tristan.*

Was Annica somehow tangled in this morass of violence and intrigue? Was she in danger? Was this what she had wanted to discuss this morning? If she came to harm because of his inattention or negligence, he would never forgive himself.

He dismounted in the courtyard and threw his reins to a sleepy groom who'd waited up for his return. Chauncy, fully clothed and upright, sat dozing in a chair by the back stairs.

"Go to bed, Chauncy," Tristan growled on his way by, not wanting a witness to his humiliation. Because if Annica were gone...

He took the stairs two at a time, anxiety rising with every step. Letting himself into his room, he went directly to Annica's door. Dim light from her fireplace shone along the bottom edge.

Her bed looked empty. Cold settled in his stomach, an emptiness more devastating than any he had ever experienced. It gave rise immediately to a barbaric anger. The betrayal, so basic to every hurt he had ever endured, was doubly cutting from Annica.

His steps took him to her bedside. There, nearly indistinguishable beneath a feather comforter, lay Annica. He felt the tension and anxiety drain from his strained muscles.

Her tangled hair curled around her oval face, and her long lashes curved in a delicate sweep against the flawless cream of her cheeks. Slightly parted lips looked deliciously soft and inviting. One hand lay on the pillow beside her face, the fingers curled toward her palm. The other arm was flung across the empty space beside her, as if searching in her sleep for the reassurance of an absent mate. As if searching for him…

He experienced a fierce swelling in his heart, a primal passion for which there were no words. As he stood studying her, his hunger grew, even while his fear sharpened his need to affirm life, to celebrate the senses, to honor love.

He gripped the canopy post and tightened his hold. The bed moved as his muscles tensed, and the wood groaned in protest. A smoldering log dropped in the fireplace, sending up a small spray of ash and glowing cinders. Annica turned at the sound, her lashes fluttering as she came awake.

An apparition dressed in a dull, formless garment with a pointed hood hovered in the darkness beside her bed. A long dagger in a sheath hung from his waist. Dark smears soiled the front of the robe, and Annica smelled blood. She shivered. The apparition stood absolutely still, as if carved from gray marble, one hand gripping the post at the foot of her bed.

The other hand came up to brush the hood back. Her husband's face emerged, looking like an avenging angel fresh from a fight, and intent on some divine purpose. His hair curled over his forehead and the scar across his cheekbone was a pale gash in the dim light. His features were impassive, unreadable. But his eyes! Dear Lord! They shone with a hunger and need that she could not hope to understand.

This was Tristan, yet somehow *not* Tristan. And he was waiting, every muscle strained and tense, for a sign, an acknowledgment.

Excitement danced along her nerves. Her breasts tingled beneath his bold, possessive study. When she exhaled a shaky sigh from breath held too long, his gaze shifted from her eyes to her mouth.

"Tristan?" she whispered into the stillness.

He fell upon her with a hungry moan. His fingers tangled in her hair and one hand cupped the back of her head while his lips cherished hers, then traveled to her eyes, her ears, her throat.

She melted against him, plucking at the ties of his robe. "Tristan," she whispered again. For all her intentions to punish him, her need was far greater.

The sound of his name cut the invisible threads of restraint still remaining, and Tristan became filled with an exquisite urgency. He yanked the covers away, annoyed by the layers between them. That done, he turned his attention to her nightgown, ripping it down the center to lay her bare to his eyes and touch. He parted from her long enough to remove his own clothes. Then he was beside her again, stroking and kissing her.

He laced his fingers through hers and held her hands against the pillow. He wanted—no, *needed*—to command tonight, surrounding her in a vortex of ecstasy where he teased, tempted and denied her until she cried out from the deepest wellspring of her own need.

"*Now…*"

Consumed as he was with the compulsion to fuse into one flesh, his first thrust—sure and strong—caught her off guard. Even as he reveled in the deliciousness of burying himself deep within her, the sultry eyes fluttered open. He held her gaze, an odd mingling of triumph and reverence filling him when she flushed with pleasure.

Deeply rooted within her, he thought he would explode with the building need. Need that made him relentless as he continued his tender assault, drawing her into his world of danger and desire. She matched him measure for measure, and when the pleasure became too intense for her to keep pace, she wrapped her legs around his hips, refusing him withdrawal. He was glad—nay, *eager*—to bear such a sweet burden.

"Yes, sprite…surrender to it…to me," he moaned.

His passion poured into her at the same instant she cried out and arched, gasping with the power of her own rapture. He could not hear above the thundering of his own beating heart, but her lips moved and he thought he read, *I love you, Tristan.*

He released her hands and rolled aside, dragging her with him. She nestled against him and sighed sleepily, one small hand resting on his chest. His breathing steadied and slowed. He stroked her and buried his face in the fragrance of her hair.

"That was an eloquent apology, m'lord," she sighed. "I accept and tender my own. I am sorry we argued this morning."

His arms tightened about her instinctively. "I thought you might not be here."

She glanced at the mantel clock. "Where else would I be at this time of night, Tristan?"

Where else, indeed? He rested his cheek against the top of her head in the darkness. Where had Constance gone?

Constance. "Hush." He laid one finger over Annica's lips to still her words and then applied his mouth to hers to silence her. He could not talk about her friend now. Could not tell her, after what they had just shared, that Constance had been murdered. Nothing could be accomplished by saying words that would rob Annica of her last few moments of blissful innocence. He would let her have this short respite before the approaching day destroyed her peace.

Chapter Eighteen

Charity dabbed at her eyes with a silk hankie and her shoulders shook as she gave in to another fit of weeping. Grace patted her back in a motherly fashion and poured another cup of tea before bursting into tears herself. Sarah seemed to have melted into one corner of the sofa, staring expressionless and dry-eyed at the unlit fireplace. She had said very little since arriving at Clarendon Place in response to Annica's summons an hour ago.

Annica knew this devastating event could immobilize them with fear and guilt. She straightened her spine and swallowed the lump in her throat. She had to be strong enough to hold them together and to find the villain. She could never give up now! Constance's murderer would pay if it was the last thing the Wednesday League accomplished! If it was that last thing *she* accomplished.

"When did you hear, 'Nica?" Grace asked.

"Mr. Bennington's valet came before we had risen. Constance's mother is not accepting the news. She sent him to inquire if Constance had spent the night here. She is certain there must be some mistake. Mr. Bennington had gone with the authorities to…to identify her. I sent word to all of you immediately."

"We must go to Mrs. Bennington," Grace sighed. She took a fresh handkerchief from her reticule and dabbed at her tears.

Annica closed the draperies, finding the sun too bright for eyes swollen with weeping. She sniffled and shook her head. "Tristan has gone to see what he can find out from the authorities. Perhaps they will know who is behind this. He swore he would be back soon. I cannot credit this," she murmured.

"Murder. I cannot comprehend…" Sarah agreed, her soft voice barely above a whisper.

"She said she would call upon me this morning to begin our inquires into Frederika's disappearance," Grace explained to no one in particular. "What could she have been doing in that part of town in the middle of the night?"

Annica thought of her own forays into predawn London to gather information or meet an informant. Could Constance have had a lead? About what—or whom? Was it mere coincidence that Constance had been murdered scant hours after she had begun an investigation into missing women?

Annica removed her copy of *Mansfield Park* from the bookcase and withdrew the bloodstained note from the leaves. "I cannot help but think Constance was a victim of our investigations."

"Oh!" Sarah wailed. "What have I done? Because of me, Mr. Bouldin and now Constance—"

"Do not say it." Annica held up her right hand, palm outward, tears filling her eyes again. "Do not even *think* it, Sarah. We have all made the choice to take whatever risks are necessary. This may not even pertain to your case."

"How can you be certain?"

"Aside from Wilkes's ruin, we are finished dealing with your misfortune. The problem with which we have begun grappling is the fifth man—the man in the garden—and the abductions."

"Wilkes! It had to be Wilkes," Charity pronounced in a low, angry voice. "He followed her and then attacked her."

"But her footman was with her," Grace said. "Could that little weasel have killed them both?"

"Perhaps he had help," Grace suggested.

"Who would help him? It isn't as if we have left him with a single friend," Charity sneered.

"*There* is a question to ponder," Annica said. She refolded the note and slipped it back into the pages of her book, leaving it on a corner of Tristan's desk. She went to sit in a chair facing Sarah and Grace. "The murderer could have been the fifth man. Wilkes and he may be involved in abducting women, as well as attacking them. And we were not regarded a threat until we uncovered this kidnapping scheme."

"Then why did they not kidnap Constance? Why kill her?" Sarah asked.

"I cannot guess that, Sarah."

Hodgeson knocked softly and opened the doors, admitting Tristan. His expression was grave as he came to kneel by Annica's chair and take her hand. She looked down to where their hands were joined, startled by how much such a small gesture could comfort her. The warmth of his touch reached clear to her heart and brought fresh tears to her eyes.

"What did you discover?" Sarah asked. "Was it Connie?"

Tristan nodded. "The constable will want to question you in a day or two, Annica. They will want to talk to all of you."

"Why?"

"They will ask…" Tristan stopped and shook his head. "I cannot allow them to put you ladies through this. If you can talk to me, I will relay the information to them."

Annica looked at the three other women. Each of them gave her a tiny nod of agreement. "Very well, Tristan. You may ask whatever you wish. We will answer you to the best of our knowledge."

He glanced over his shoulder to the hovering servant. "Hodgeson, brandy for the ladies. Tea will not be fortification enough."

Charity began to cry again.

Hodgeson poured out the requisite number of brandies in small crystal glasses and brought them on a silver tray.

Tristan gave the ladies a moment, then asked, "Shall we begin?"

"Yes," Annica sighed.

"Do you know why anyone would want to hurt Miss Bennington?"

Annica shuddered and a little prickle of fear went up her spine. "Tristan, who would want to strangle Constance?"

"Strangle? Did I say she had been strangled?"

Not strangled? Mr. Renquist had said that all the other missing women who had been found had been strangled. All but... She glanced toward the corner of Tristan's desk, where her copy of *Mansfield Park* lay. She blushed and stammered, unable to meet his gaze. "I cannot remember. That is, you must have... Perhaps I assumed."

"She was not strangled, my dear."

"Then how...?"

"Annica, I do not think—"

"How, Tristan?"

"A knife."

"To her heart?"

"Her throat."

A quick glance at the others told Annica they had caught the importance of the method of Constance's murder: it linked Constance to Mr. Bouldin's murderer. Charity and Grace both looked as if they had been turned to stone. Sarah, though still pale, had an unfamiliar look in her eyes. In another, Annica might have described it as the light of battle.

"I see," she said. She glanced down again, masking another sudden rush of tears. "Well, the answer remains the same. We do not know why anyone would want to kill Constance."

"Chauncy informed me that Miss Bennington was here late yesterday afternoon for your weekly meeting. Did she mention what her plans were for the evening? Or discuss anything unusual?"

Annica bit her lower lip. "We discussed our usual subjects. She mentioned that she had plans for the evening, but she did not tell us what they were." She disengaged her hand, swallowed her brandy, winced as it burned its way down her throat, and handed the empty glass to him.

"'Nica, she seemed a little restless," Sarah interjected. "Perhaps *nervous* would be a better word."

"Did she say why?" Tristan asked.

"No, but I recall thinking that she might be hiding something, or holding back."

"Do you know what?"

"'Twas only a feeling."

Tristan nodded. "Thank you, Sarah."

Annica nodded in agreement with Sarah's statement and waited for the next question.

"The authorities believe this incident may be related to a case currently under investigation. Did Constance ever mention anything like that?"

"Like what?" Annica asked. She held her breath, keeping a tight rein on her fears.

"Did she ever talk about…missing women?"

Dear Lord! The authorities knew. They were aware women were missing, and they had gathered enough details to suspect a connection to Constance. How long before they discovered the rest? Annica's nerves jangled. Tristan had to know before he ran afoul of trouble, too. "Tristan, we have been—"

"Missing women?" Sarah interrupted with a guileless look. "Oh! I believe she did mention that her abigail, Frederika, had disappeared. She had not come back from her day out."

"When was this?"

"Just after 'Nica began keeping company with you, Lord Auberville."

"Had Constance made any new acquaintances?"

Only one name came to mind. Annica hesitated.

"I can see that there is something on your mind, Annica. It would be best if you would just say it."

"Geoffrey Morgan. But she has known him several months, and he did not wish her harm. To the contrary, he was fond of her."

"Geoffrey Morgan! Oh, heavens!" Sarah gasped. "He was sweet on Connie. We cannot allow him to hear this from the gossip mills or to read it in the *Times*."

"Everyone will know by tonight, Sarah. This will feed the gossipmongers for at least a month," Grace said.

"I must go to him at once. He will be devastated."

"I will tell Morgan." Tristan leaned back against his desk and crossed his arms. His thigh pressed against *Mansfield Park*, nearly toppling it from its precarious perch on the corner of his desk. He lifted it and held it carelessly in one hand. "Then you have no idea who might want Miss Bennington dead?"

Annica stared at the little book and held her breath, praying Tristan would not open it. She glanced at her friends. Though it had not been spoken aloud in her presence, she knew that they had not missed that Tristan, too, had served in the Royal Navy, that he had been sent to the Mediterranean.

''What are you thinking, Annica?''

She came back to herself with a start, then shrugged and glanced around at the group again. ''Only one person we know might wish any of us harm. Roger Wilkes. 'Tis common knowledge that I gave him the cut sublime, and most of us have done so since. Mr. Wilkes could easily wish us dead.''

Tristan seemed to think this over. He frowned, then shook his head. One errant blond curl fell over his forehead, and he smoothed it back absently. He was so handsome that Annica could almost feel her heart breaking. How could the Wednesday League ever suspect him?

''It could not have been Wilkes,'' he said.

''Tristan, his is the only name I can think of. If not Wilkes, then who?''

He shook his head, complete bafflement showing on his face.

Grace gave him a skeptical look. ''Perhaps it was a vicious footpad. That makes as much sense as someone wishing her harm.''

He nodded. ''Perhaps you are right, Grace. I shall report your answers to the constabulary. Nevertheless, it would have been nigh on impossible for Wilkes to have committed the crime. You see, I bumped into him last night.''

Annica's heart stopped for one long moment. She noted the guarded looks that Charity, Grace and Sarah exchanged. *Auberville and Wilkes? Together?*

''I'll find Morgan immediately after I've dealt with the authorities. Annica, I'd prefer it if you would not go out today. Humor me, my dear. I should be home by midafternoon. I believe there was something you wished to discuss with me.''

The room remained silent until he had gone, and Hodgeson with him. When the doors closed with a soft click, the ladies expelled their breath with an audible sigh.

Charity gulped her brandy and set her glass down with a bang. "What were you thinking, 'Nica? You nearly gave us away."

"Tristan could help us. If we just tell him—"

Grace cut her off and addressed the others. "She told him nothing he would not turn up with a little investigation. Mr. and Mrs. Bennington will remember about Frederika. All of creation knows we've been cutting Wilkes. Julius would be able to tell them about Constance and Morgan. None of these matters should undo us."

"Undo us? Do you seriously think Auberville is the enemy?" Annica was nonplussed.

"He must suspect we know more than we are saying." Charity ignored her and paused to blow her nose before she continued. "And he'd be correct."

Sunlight streamed through the dormer windows. The nursery had a hollow, empty feeling despite its conversion to an artist's studio. Annica sat with her back to the afternoon light and continued to work as Tristan paced the length of the long room.

"So I gather you suspected Ellen's defection from Dennison?"

She nodded.

"And you did nothing to discourage that notion?"

"No." She mixed yellow and red with a flat-edged palette knife. "I...I encouraged it."

"And this is why you wanted to speak with me yestermorn?"

She added a dab more of red to the mixture and blended again. "I wanted to apprise you of the problem, m'lord, as I suspected the blame would be placed at my door. *Your* door, sir, now that you are held accountable for me."

"Are you are still angry that I did not make time for you?" he asked. "I will not make that mistake again."

Tears filled her eyes, glimmering at the edges but not spilling down her cheeks. Her emotions were so heightened that they were unreliable. One moment she was calm, the next she approached hysteria. She could not answer.

His voice was soft when he spoke again. "I thought, after last night, you had forgiven me."

"I...cannot get the shade right," she whispered. She pushed the jars in her paint box around, looking for another color to add to the mix. "I thought I had umber."

"Annica, talk to me." He took the palette and knife from her hands and set them aside. "Yesterday morning I could not shut you up, and today you will not say what is in your heart."

"Please, Tristan. I must finish this before..."

He looked at the canvas and winced. She had sketched the outline of a woman standing on a windswept bluff overlooking the ocean. A closed book was held to her heart in one hand, and the other lifted an edge of her gown, as if she were walking.

He touched Annica's shoulder. "You are afraid you will forget how Constance looked, are you not?"

She nodded, tears finally spilling down her cheeks.

"Do you want to talk about it?" he asked.

She shook her head and wiped her hands on a paint-smeared rag. The pain was still too raw to voice.

"Annica, you needn't hide your grief from me."

Hide? She and Tristan had both done their share of hiding—emotions, actions, motives—and the knowledge frustrated her. She slammed down the lid on her paint box and dropped a cloth over the unfinished painting.

Tristan stared at her for a long moment, as if he could not decide her mood, and she felt a stab of regret. She tried for a neutral subject. "Are you angry over my support of Ellen?"

"Very well, my dear," he said after a pregnant pause,

"since you are determined to discuss it, I have only one objection."

"And what is that?"

"That you accept the blame." He began pacing again. "Ellen begged off on her own. I will not have you the scapegoat for Ellen's folly. I will put out the story that Dennison had second thoughts. That should salvage the man's pride. Do not contradict me."

"But it will make Ellen appear less desirable."

"I am sorry for Ellen, but she must face the consequences of her own actions, Annica. This is her mess, and I won't have you or Dennison suffering for it."

"If you wish," she replied wearily.

"Most men complain that their wives are matchmakers. I will not have society saying my wife is a match*breaker*."

She lifted her chin and shrugged. "I'd already delayed in order to discuss this with you. Talk had begun. The suspicion regarding my involvement was being whispered abroad, especially after Uncle Thomas locked Ellen in her room."

"I appreciate that, Annica, but you are never to paint yourself in an unfavorable light again."

"I selected that story for the express purpose of sparing the Sayles and Sinclair names. I knew full well that society would not blame you for your ungovernable wife's actions. That, I thought, is a better alternative than to have the ton thinking Ellen fickle. Since you were indifferent to the problem—"

"Bloody hell! I was not indifferent! I had business, Annica. There are other people depending upon me. I have more important things to do than indulge a demanding wife. You must be honest with me."

"You are a fine one to lecture me on honesty!" she cried, her greatest fears surfacing.

"What, prithee, are you suggesting? Speak, Annica. Say it aloud and have done with it."

"Very well, then! How can I be honest with you when our friendship began with a lie?" She turned to the wide school table and placed her hands, palms down, on the folio lying there.

He came to stand across the table from her, his face stony. "What was a lie?"

She opened the folio, seized one botanical canvas and sent it sailing across the room. "This!" she snapped. One by one, she did the same with the other canvases, almost relieved to have the subject in the open at last. "And this, and this, and this!"

"How did you find out?" he asked with a guarded expression.

"You were overheard discussing it and the tale was repeated to me. Aside from that, did you think I was so simpleminded that I would not notice when you ceased to take me to conservatories and gardens?"

"What were you told?" Tristan's voice had gone flat.

Her heart fell with a breathless thud. Then it was true. "That you set out looking for a capable wife. One you would not have to supervise. One who would not make excessive demands. I gather you needed a woman to provide and raise your heirs with little fuss. And certainly my dowry played no small part—"

"It did not factor in at all, milady," Tristan interrupted. "Of all my faults, I am not a fortune hunter. While it is true that I set out to find a capable woman, I fail to see the crime in that."

"You had a right to look for whatever sort of woman you wish," she agreed. "The crime lies in your deliberate hunting of me, and in your deception. I had a right to know your intentions, but you kept me unwary whilst you laid your trap."

"Annica, I did not mean to hurt you. But how else was I to get past your defenses?"

She sank onto her little stool again. *How, indeed?* She had hardened her heart to the point that no man got further than a dance. "I had a right to know," she repeated. "Why do you despise incapable women so?"

"I do not despise them, Annica. I simply do not have time for them."

"Because you think them inferior?"

"Because I think them untrustworthy. If a woman is dependent upon a man, then she will shift her allegiance to whoever offers her the greatest attention and comfort. Incapable women are loyal to none but themselves."

Annica felt her indignation fade as she recalled Tristan's admission that his mother had left him. Somehow he had connected her weakness with dependence and disloyalty. How deeply he must have felt her betrayal.

"Did you think I would leave you, Tristan?"

He ignored her question. "If it is any comfort to you, my lady, before my trap was sprung I had come to the conclusion that you were going to be a great deal of trouble, and that, despite your reputation, you were not especially capable. I decided to go forward based on the fact that, notwithstanding those insufficiencies, you are intelligent and—"

"Manageable?" she guessed.

"You?" he scoffed. "Manageable?"

"You had no trouble at all backing me into a corner. You compromised me at the first opportunity, then demanded I marry you."

Of all her accusations, Tristan called her to account for only one. "Do you mean to say that you'd never have married me had I not 'compromised' you?"

She saw the trap in his question and sidestepped with a

charge of her own. "Had you allowed things to progress in a natural way—"

"Natural?" he mocked. "There is nothing natural in making progress with you, Annica. You were set on spinsterhood. You were not about to let any man close enough to love you."

"You did not require love—only a capable woman who would manage your home and your family, while you are off…doing *what,* my lord?"

Tristan ignored her question. He placed his hands on the school table and leaned toward her. "We have both had our little deceptions, eh? And you, Annica? What is your game?"

"I do not—"

"Hold! Think first, Annica. I may not always know what you are up to, but I always know when you are lying."

She stood and moved away, uncomfortable with his nearness. He had a way of unnerving her that always gave him the advantage.

"What is wrong, Annica?" he asked. A frown knit fine lines in his forehead and puckered the scar beneath his eye in a sinister fashion.

"Do you want it out in the open, milord?" she parried with a reckless toss of her head. "Very well. When I learned that your only requirement was a capable woman, I decided to see what you would do—indeed, if you would get rid of me altogether—if you thought your trap had snared a far different animal. I was as silly and simpering as some society brides I have observed."

"Ah. Dressing in my favorite color, vacillating regarding calling cards and stationery, and asking my advice on trivial matters? I see. Then why have you not taken up needlepoint?"

She shrugged when she recalled her foolish promise. "Some things are simply too absurd to pretend."

"I am relieved to know that you have limits." Tristan straightened and folded his arms across his chest. "How long were you going to continue your little charade?"

"Until you confessed your scheme."

"And if I did not?"

"Then you would be stuck with a simpering, inept wife. I must give you credit for more patience than I anticipated."

"And now that your plan is exposed, what is next?"

"I shall likely not be able to find another way to confound or confuse you."

Tristan smiled. "Do not discount your talents, milady. I have always been quite impressed with your resourcefulness."

"Aside from your trap, what are *you* hiding?" she asked.

A veiled look settled over his features and he moved to distance himself from her. He turned when he was shrouded by the shadows between the dormer windows. The maneuver was almost more instinctive than contrived. She realized that Tristan was a man accustomed to hiding his emotions.

"If you have a question, Annica, you will have to be more specific," he told her in a deep, even voice.

She shrugged. "Tell me what you do all day. And where you spend your evenings of late."

"Different things and different places—as circumstances require."

She tilted her chin, ready to do battle. "What were you doing with Roger Wilkes last night? How can you be so certain that miscreant did not murder Constance?"

"That is no concern of yours, Annica."

"No? Then what, exactly, *is* my concern?"

He came forward, his face a study in regret. "Believe me, if it were possible to set your mind at ease, I would. All I can tell you is that you must not interfere with my business."

Her eyes filled with tears again, but this time they were

not for Constance. "Perhaps I shall take matters into my own hands, Tristan. With the right questions, I could find out nearly anything."

"You will do no such thing, Annica. Questions could be dangerous. Remember Constance."

She stared at him for a long moment, defying his edict wordlessly.

He reached out to her with one hand, looking as if he would touch her cheek or apologize. Long years under her father's tutelage made her shrink away, and Tristan stopped in his tracks, a look of misery on his handsome face. He shook his head and dropped his hand.

"Soon, Annica, we shall settle this," he murmured on his way to the door.

Chapter Nineteen

"Going to see Wilkes alone is not simply half-witted, it is insane," Grace said. "I cannot imagine what has possessed you."

"I am determined, Grace," Annica answered. "Justice is everything. If the murderer thinks he has frightened us off, he is sadly mistaken."

The interior of Grace's coach was dim, and the blinds were pulled, affording her a measure of modesty as she tucked her shirttails into the waistband of her trousers. Grace stuffed her discarded gown and slippers into a small satchel.

Sarah held the vest while Annica slipped her arms through the holes. She nodded her agreement to Grace's statement. "Why do you think he will give you any answers?"

"Money, Sarah. Mr. Wilkes needs traveling money. And he does not know he is meeting me. He thinks he is meeting a man named Nick. This outrage has gone on too long. Women are in grave danger, and no one seems to be able to do anything about it." She buttoned the snug vest over her breasts, smoothing and diminishing their contours, before she donned the coat jacket. "I will be perfectly safe, Sarah. For one thing, I am not without protection." She took

her small pistol from the inside pocket of her jacket. '
doubt I will have to use it. Mr. Renquist arranged for us
meet in a public place, and he will not be far away. Anyway
Wilkes has an alibi for Constance's murder.''

"Yes. Auberville," Grace sighed. "I cannot believe I a
saying this, but—who will vouch for him?''

"I will," Annica said, ending that topic. "Leave m
gown and slippers with Madame Marie. She will packag
them as a new delivery, wrap them in blue and send the
to me by messenger.''

"We shall wait for you," Grace stated.

"No! A private coach waiting outside the Bear and Bu
would draw too much attention.''

"Annica is right," Sarah admitted. Her firm little chi
jutted out with the air of decision. "I shall go to Madam
Marie's tomorrow and have a pair of trousers made for my
self. You should not have to go on these errands alon
Annica. I shall go with you in the future.''

Annica cringed, well-acquainted with Sarah's feeling
After all, risk was what had made her feel alive until Au
berville had taught her a "far more interesting way to fli
with disaster.'' But Sarah had little experience to back u
her new confidence, and there was a murderer and kidnappe
loose. "I pray that tonight will be the last time I resort t
a disguise.''

"What would Auberville do if he caught you?''

"I cannot even imagine.'' She shivered and put th
thought away before her own fears could get the better c
her.

The coach slowed in the heavy traffic and she glance
out the window. She pushed her hair up under her cap an
felt in her jacket pocket for the wad of banknotes. Every
thing was ready. When the coach stopped, Annica pushe
the door open and hopped down. "Tomorrow!" she prom
ised, then merged with the crowd.

Though nearly midnight, revelers and bawds caroused in noisy groups and called to one another across the narrow streets. Annica walked boldly toward the Bear and Bull, her heart beating so hard that she could barely hear the jingle of harness and the clip-clop of hooves as Grace's coach pulled away.

Annica did not hesitate, but entered the tavern with the air of one who had done so many times before.

The tavern's central room was crowded and raucous with laughter and arguments. No one paid attention to the slight 'lad' who made his way through the throngs. Francis Renquist stood with one arm on the wide counter, holding a pint of ale. He nodded, then let his gaze sweep toward the back of the room.

Wilkes is waiting, Annica thought, her heart pounding harder. She went to the small table in the farthest corner and ordered two pints of ale—the arranged signal. Only when she had two tankards in front of her did she squint into the smoke-filled shadows to identify her quarry.

Roger Wilkes stood near the fireplace, his eyes darting right and left with a nervous twitch. The man was a shadow of his former self! He was gaunt and drawn, and obviously hadn't shaved in several days.

Waiting until his eyes darted back in her direction, she nodded to the vacant chair opposite hers. He noted the two tankards on the table, looked right and left again, as if he were afraid someone might be watching, then approached. After taking the offered seat, he leaned forward, squinting through red, hazy eyes to identify the face beneath the brim of her hat.

"You!" he exclaimed. "What the hell—"

"Have a care, Mr. Wilkes," she warned in an undertone. 'I have friends about the room, ready to come to my aid, and I am armed, so do not even contemplate treachery."

"What do you want?" he snarled.

"Answers, and I want them quickly. You will serve m
in this, Mr. Wilkes, and I will reward you with cash—
commodity my agent informs me you are in sore need of.

"Why should I help you with anything?"

Annica shrugged. There was no use in denying it. "W
shall have justice for Sarah. Make no mistake, this is not a
offer of friendship or forgiveness. You have information.
need it, and will pay for it."

Wilkes gave her a grudging look. "How much money?

"Twenty pounds for each answer. Mark me well—I hav
done extensive investigation and I will know if you are ly
ing. Your information need not be new, only accurate."

"Ask, then." He gave her a wary look. "I must leav
town, and the sooner, the better."

"Why now?"

"Things have got out of hand. I didn't count on any c
this happening." The nervous twitch beneath one eye inter
sified.

"Any of *what* happening?"

"You know goddamn well what!"

"Do you mean Sarah? I overheard you conspiring to a
tack another woman not very long ago."

"Ah. That's when you found out? The garden at…"

Annica nodded. "I could not see who you were with, M
Wilkes. Who was it?"

He shook his head and scanned the room again. "If tha
is one of your questions, I will not answer."

"Very well. Then who is behind the kidnappings?"

"Kidnappings? I do not—"

"That's a lie."

"How did you find out? We were careful. If they go
suspicious and tried to escape, he'd kill them. He didn't lik
to do it, since they were as good as money in our pocket
but there could not be anyone left to tell tales, he said."

Dear Lord! Francis Renquist was right. White slaver

Here in London. "The disappearance of Constance's maid and Madame Marie's seamstress put us on the track," she admitted, fighting her revulsion. She could not imagine how Wilkes could be so lacking in conscience. "Tell me about the murders."

"I did not bargain to become involved in anything like that. It was not my idea. I have to leave town...get away." His eyes widened and he licked his lips.

Annica was disgusted by the man's duplicity. "You would not stop at rape or assault, but murder is beyond you?"

"We just wanted to turn a profit on a few skirts nobody would miss. The men who bought them will take good care of them. How bad a life could it be to please a man?"

How bad could it be, indeed! She fought her rising anger. "A little harmless kidnapping and slave trading, eh? When, and how, did it get out of hand?"

Wilkes looked at her, his eyes clearing momentarily, as if he just now remembered to whom he was speaking. "Cannot talk to you about this. You will..."

"What, Mr. Wilkes? What will I do?"

"Christ! If you found out...."

A shiver ran up Annica's spine. "*Who*, Mr. Wilkes?"

"He'd *kill* me, for God's sake!"

"Did he kill Constance? And Mr. Bouldin?"

Wilkes appeared not to hear her question. He shrank lower in his chair, pulled his hat down over his eyes and scanned the room again. "She learned too much. She had to die, he said. We could have got a good price for her, but he said if she was missing they'd keep looking until they found us. They had to find her body so they'd stop looking. Now he's suspicious of me. He's been watching."

Annica wondered if the alleys were crowded with people who were following Roger Wilkes. "Who has been watching you, Mr. Wilkes? Who killed Constance and Harry

Bouldin? Who is behind the kidnapping scheme? Who are
you so afraid of?''

Completely distraught, he toppled his chair backward as
he stood. ''I should tell you. It would serve you right.''

Annica held her breath and waited.

''But I'm a dead man if I tell. I tried to warn you, you
know.'' He was rambling on, almost incoherently. ''The
night you gave me the cut, I was afraid something like what
happened to Miss Bennington would happen to you, and I
tried to tell you, but you wouldn't listen.''

''Shh,'' Annica warned, with a glance around the dining
room. ''Tell me now, Mr. Wilkes. I must have that name.''

Wilkes was fairly foaming at the mouth. ''The money!
All of it for the answer.''

Annica reached into her coat, seizing the banknotes in an
inside pocket. ''The name, Mr. Wilkes.''

He glanced over his shoulder. His whole body stiffened.

Alerted by his reaction, Annica leaned forward and
peered around him to scan the far end of the room near the
entrance. A figure in a black cloak was disappearing out the
door.

She gave Renquist a quick nod in that direction, indicating that he should follow the unknown man, then turned
back to Wilkes, the wad of banknotes in her hand. Wilkes'
eyes were round and he had gone pale.

''I should not have come,'' he muttered. ''I should have
known he would find out. Damn his eyes! He *always*
knows!'' He backed away.

''Wait,'' Annica called after him. She stood and waved
the banknotes, certain that would bring him back to the table. ''The name! Say it! He's already seen you. Tell me,
Mr. Wilkes!''

''He's seen you, too—seen us together. You will find out
soon enough, Lady Auberville. He's always been the dangerous one, the sly one. In the Royal Navy, he...'' Wilkes

hook his head and turned away, merging with the crowd
o quickly that Annica did not have time to protest.

She lunged after him, heedless of the fact that now she
was quite alone.

"Damnation!" Tristan snarled in an undertone. "She's
done it again!" His stomach twisted and a hole burned
through the center. He was nauseous with fear for her—*he,*
who had feared nothing during his years with the Foreign
Office. Good God! Was she insane to wander out alone with
a murderer on the loose? Had Constance's fate not affected
her at all?

"What is it?" The Sheikh whispered.

"My wife! She said she could find out nearly anything
with the right questions. That is Annica following Wilkes."

Tristan's companion followed him around a corner and
down an alley, traveling in a parallel line with the erring
wife. He pulled the brim of his hat down to shroud his face.
"As if we do not have problems enough! Wilkes is supposed to meet The Turk tonight, not your wife. You said
you could manage her, and that she'd not present a problem," he accused in a low, angry tone. "Damn it, Auberville, we cannot compromise this investigation because your
wife is up to some bluestocking prank. We finally have a
chance to unmask The Turk."

"I want that as much as you. More. Do you have a suggestion for saving my wife?"

"A few," the other man gibed, "but none that you'd
take. And we haven't the time to be diverted now."

Having made better progress down the side lane than
those in the crowded street, they turned a corner to intercept
their prey, halted and stepped back into the shadows to wait.

"I'll take Annica from behind. You follow Wilkes. We'll
rally at Whitechapel later," Tristan instructed.

The Sheikh hesitated. "I'll attend to her. I can see murder

in your eyes. This may not be the best time for you to dea with Lady Annica.''

"And have to explain your role in this? No. She's mine— and all the trouble that comes with her," Tristan growled Finding Annica as he'd found Constance would spell h end for certain. He'd go insane. "Leave her to me. She wi present no further interference.''

His companion raised his eyebrows. "I am grateful I an not in your wife's shoes. Have you considered telling he everything and relying upon her good sense to keep out o the way?''

"Annica has more valor than good sense. She believes is her duty to champion injustice. I would never be able t keep her out of this.''

"Champion injustice? Is that why—''

"Shh! Here's Wilkes.''

Wilkes rushed by, unaware of them in the shadows. Th Sheikh was poised to sprint the moment Annica had bee detained.

Tristan tensed at the sound of light footsteps approaching every muscle strained for action. Anticipating her nex move, he suspected she would duck into the alley to catc her breath and escape any glance Wilkes might spare ove his shoulder—a calculated risk, but one necessary to re maining undiscovered. She was good at this. His annoyanc peaked when he wondered how much practice she'd had.

Almost too easy, he thought when his wife passed him i the dark. He lunged out of the alley behind her, slipped on arm around her waist, the other over her mouth, and dragge her back into the shadows. Without missing a beat, Th Sheikh stepped into the street and adjusted his pace to th unwary Wilkes.

Tristan was ready for Annica's pointed little elbow an dodged to the side, so it came backward and struck bric wall instead of his ribs. He smiled at her muffled curse.

Her booted heel came down sharply on his instep. He bent his head to whisper a caution in her ear. "Easy, Annica. 'Tis me. Auberville."

Her struggles ceased for a moment, then strong, even teeth bit the hand across her mouth.

"Ouch!" The palm of his hand stung and he resisted the urge to throttle the little hellion.

She attempted to jerk away, and he tightened the arm around her waist. "Disavow yourself of the notion that you can escape, madam, or that I would not give chase if you did. You will have to face me sooner or later. I recommend sooner."

Slowly, by inches, Annica seemed to relax against him. Her arms went slack and her muscles untensed. She nodded agreement to his offer.

He knew better than to trust her completely. "I am going to uncover your mouth. Cry out for help or do anything to call attention to us and you will regret it. I know where to apply just enough pressure to render you unconscious, and you will find yourself waking up at Clarendon Place. Do you understand?"

She nodded again.

As he loosened his grip, his hand grazed a hard object in Annica's pocket. He reached inside, recognizing the shape and weight. "Good God, madam! A pistol? What were you thinking?"

"That I might need protection," she snapped.

"Your recklessness astounds me. Had this discharged accidentally, you could have been killed."

There was anger in her stance and voice. "I am not a complete novice, sir."

"Damn it, Annica! When I found you at the bawdy house, I told you there would be no more forays into Whitefriars." He slipped the pistol into his own coat pocket.

"I weighed the risks of this particular endeavor and found them acceptable."

He pulled her into the street with one hand around her wrist and hailed a passing coach. "You weighed the risks against what, Annica? What did you hope to gain?"

"I—"

"I saw Wilkes. You met him, did you not? Were you asking him about Constance? What do you think he could possibly know?"

"More than I, Auberville, but that wouldn't take much."

He pushed her into the dark recess of the coach and sat beside her on the worn leather seat. Leaning forward, he knocked on the driver's box and called, "Clarendon Place off Hyde Park. There's money in it if you have me there in a hurry."

"Aye, Guv'nor," came the reply. The coach jolted into motion and reached a steady clip.

His attention free, Tristan turned to regard his wife's impassive face through the gloom of the coach interior. She had removed her hat and allowed her dark hair to fall down her back. Her cheeks burned a warm pink and her dark lashes fluttered nervously as she gazed out the window. He could smell the fresh herbal scent of her soap—juniper, moss and wildflowers—made more intense by the warmth of her skin. He shivered with the sweetness of his response. He wanted her. Every minute of every day, he wanted Annica.

She had invaded every facet of his life, just as her scent and soft sighs did now, leaving him no peace at all. She was in his mind and heart every waking moment. He could not think for the memories of her that crowded his mind. He could not concentrate for worrying about her. And he feared he could not do justice to this case with such a sweet distraction to divert him. He braced himself against the temptation to sweep her into his arms and make slow, deliberate love to her.

The opposition of duty and desire confounded him. Annica—all-woman; soft, fragile and small—dressed in rough clothing designed to make her look like a man. The effect was astonishingly erotic, and he was suddenly angry with her for that, too. He needed her as much as he needed the air he breathed, in spite of the fact that he had promised himself that he would never need a woman again.

"Tristan...oh, Tristan," she sighed, turning from the coach window to gaze into his eyes, with an unaccountable sadness in hers. "Where has it all gone wrong?"

Her lament sobered him. This episode was not some frivolous game for Annica, but a dangerous blunder that could cost her her life. He had to make her understand that she was in over her head.

Composing himself, he demanded, "Why did you meet Wilkes?"

"I had to find out about Constance. I suspected that Wilkes would know something, despite what you said."

"I only said that Wilkes did not do it."

She continued to face him, her gaze never wavering. "The night Constance was killed, you came in late, looking ever so fierce. And bloody. If you were with him, where were you, Tristan? How can you know Mr. Wilkes is innocent? What were you and he doing together?"

Tristan bit back a curse. How much did she know, and how much did she merely suspect? For Annica to have even a little knowledge would be dangerous to her. "You will have to trust me, Annica."

"I have done that." She shook her head and gave a self-deprecating laugh. "But you cannot return the sentiment, can you?"

She had cut to the core of his dilemma. His fear of betrayal. He dared not tell her, yet he could lose her if he did

not. How could he make her understand the seriousness o
her actions and the consequences they carried, without ex
posing government secrets? There were grave matters hang
ing in the balance—treason, kidnapping and murder.

"Your silence is answer enough," she said after a mo
ment.

"If you will recall," he snapped, "you were to keep m
informed of your activities."

"I would have informed you, Auberville, but you wer
not available. And you swore you would not prevent m
from acting in accord with my convictions," she said. "
am doing so."

"What conviction could compel you to meet Roge
Wilkes in a Whitefriars tavern dressed as a man?"

"Justice, Tristan. Plain and simple." She turned away t
look out the window.

Justice. Of course. Annica, sitting on a pink-covered be
with tears in her eyes, saying, "I could not save my mother
but I can fight injustice when I see it. There is nothing mor
important to me than that." With Annica, justice was a poin
of honor. And a point of honor with Annica was sacred
Still, he was better equipped to deal with the man. "Leav
Wilkes to me."

Her shoulders lifted and dropped in a shrug. "I cannot.
thought you understood."

"I understand your need for justice, but I did not think i
had to be got by you. I will deal with him."

"I have the matter in hand."

"What is it you propose to do?"

"I shall expose Roger Wilkes for the cowardly rapist h
is and let society do the rest. Then I will be free to dea
with Constance's murderer."

His heart grew cold with fear. "Stay away from tha
Annica."

She gave him a bewildered look. "How can you believe I would allow Constance's death to go unavenged?"

He looked into her unguarded eyes and saw the depth of commitment and loyalty—qualities that had drawn him to her. Slowly, he began to understand. Annica could never be loyal to him if she were disloyal to her friends. Her commitment was more than loyalty—it was rooted in honor. It was something he'd searched for without knowing he was doing so, what he needed to believe still existed in the world. He'd be willing to die for a fraction of this measure of Annica's devotion, but he'd done nothing to deserve it. He had tricked her, trapped her and refused to say the words that would set her mind at ease. *He had not been loyal to Annica!*

He placed one finger under her chin and lifted her face to his. "Annica, I—"

The coach jerked to a halt at the front steps of Clarendon Place, interrupting his confession. He would tell her everything later. For the moment, he had to keep her safe. He hopped down, tossed a sovereign to the driver and lifted Annica out.

"You know I will simply leave again," she warned him.

A feeling of loss built in his chest. How could he ever live without his sprite—his Lady Reckless—at his side? He had to keep her safe until he could finish his duty to the crown. Richard Lovelace had written to Lucasta, "I could not love thee, dear, so much, Lov'd I not honour more." For the first time, that little paradox made perfect sense to him.

He carried her up the steps and, before he could kick it, the door was opened by a breathless Chauncy, evidently alerted by a diligent footman. A stone-faced Hodgeson stood behind him.

"Milord!" Chauncy gasped. "Is her ladyship taken ill?"

"No, Chauncy," he answered, "but that will be ou
story."

"Milord?" the valet asked. He and Hodgeson followec
them up the stairs.

Tristan placed Annica on her feet in the center of he
bedchamber and stood back to regard her with a challenge
"Consider yourself confined until further notice."

"You jest!" she gasped.

"Do I look as if I jest?" He set his features in his mos
intimidating expression—the one that had been known to
send sailors scurrying and to make pashas tremble. In fact
Mary retreated to one corner, looking as if her knees were
knocking.

"You are out of your mind!" Annica accused. "You
cannot think for a moment that I will countenance such a
tactic?"

"I have business to be about, and I will not have you in
the middle of it, nor can I allow you to interfere. I hope to
conclude it by tomorrow night, but until I am finished, you
will give me no reason to worry."

Chauncy's gaze swept Annica's form. "Oh, milady
What have you done?"

Hodgeson moved to Annica's side, as if to shield her from
unseemly curiosity. "She has, on occasion…that is, she—'

"Will not be going abroad like this again. Where do you
buy them, Annica?" Tristan gestured at her trousers.

"Do you seriously think I will aid you in punishing me
Auberville? Do not make me laugh."

Tristan's jaw tightened. "Chauncy, send to every tailo
in London with instructions not to fill any orders for Lad
Auberville. Mary, find the rest of her trousers and bur
them."

Hodgeson raised his eyes heavenward as if to say he ha
done that before, but he remained silent as Mary went t

Annica's wardrobe and began to search for the offending garments.

"Am I a prisoner, Lord Tristan?" Annica asked.

"I made you promises and I mean to keep them, if you will let me. Tomorrow, when this is over, I shall tell you everything. But I do not have time now. You must defer to me in this—for your own safety. For Constance. Do you understand?"

"I understand quite well." Her voice was quiet, but Tristan knew better than to think she was agreeing.

He turned to the others. "Chauncy, either you or Hodgeson will look after Lady Auberville at all times. She is in grave danger. Can I count on you?"

"Yes, milord," Chauncy nodded.

"Yes," Hodgeson agreed reluctantly.

Annica stood quite still, her arms folded across her chest and a defiant jut to her chin. He suspected she was hatching some plan for revenge. "These tactics will not work, Tristan. If you think you can bully me into submission, you are mistaken."

"I do not want to bully you, Annica, but I cannot reason with you. You leave me no other option."

"You could trust me, Auberville."

He feared from the terrible calm in her evergreen eyes that, despite any promise to the contrary, she'd leave him the first chance she got. He'd better clean up this nasty affair as quickly as possible.

Chapter Twenty

Annica hurried downstairs to join the group in the library. Chauncy was hard on her heels, as if to emphasize that she was not even safe in her own home. That particular point did not need reinforcing. A quelling glance at the piratical valet stopped him short before he could follow her into the library. She pointed to a spot across the foyer from the library and then closed the double doors firmly in his face.

"Oh, 'Nica!" Sarah exclaimed. She rose from the sofa in front of the little tea table and hurried to her. "Thank God you are safe! We were so worried when we heard."

"Heard what?"

Grace frowned and pressed her fingertips to her temples. "That Roger Wilkes was found dead last night, Annica. You met with him. Did you...did you do it?"

"We know you would only do such a thing in self-defense, 'Nica," Charity said earnestly.

Her mind reeled and her limbs went numb. Yet another murder! "Wilkes is dead?"

"Last night, his throat slit—just like Mr. Bouldin and Constance. That is why we came. We needed to be certain you were safe." Sarah reached out and touched Annica's hand.

"Tristan saw me following Wilkes in Whitefriars. He waylaid me, escorted me home and set the servants to watching me. He says it is for my own good."

"Thank heavens!" Grace and Charity exclaimed as one.

"But Wilkes was well enough last night when he left the Bear and Bull," Annica added hurriedly.

Charity sagged, relief flooding her features. "Then it had nothing to do with you. Or Auberville. Thank heavens."

"What did he say?" Sarah pressed.

Annica took a deep breath and relayed the details of her conversation. "Wilkes seemed to think the man responsible for the murders was watching him. That's what made him run without taking the money," she explained. "He was terrified."

"And you were going to follow him!" Grace shook her head in disbelief. "The other man must have seen you and Wilkes together and knew you were onto him."

Sarah must have sensed her reluctance to discuss the matter, for she changed the subject. "Well, at least we are on the right track in looking at the regimental roster. Was Mr. Renquist not looking into—"

"Renquist! Drat! I haven't spoken to him. I sent him after the man who frightened Mr. Wilkes. Pray God he does not turn up dead, too!"

"What shall we do?" Charity asked, her blue eyes wide.

"You have an appointment with Madame Marie, do you not?"

"Yes." Charity glanced toward the mantel clock. "In fact, I am supposed to be there in twenty minutes."

"Tell Madame that I will be needing another pair of trousers later this afternoon. Ask her to send word to Mr. Renquist that I must meet him there at five o'clock." Annica went to Tristan's desk, scribbled a few lines on a sheet of paper, folded it and slipped it in an envelope. She wrote a

name on the front and handed it to Charity. "Ask Madam
to see that this is delivered at once."

Charity looked at the name and winced. "'Nica—"

"We shall get to the bottom of this one way or another
Naughty Alice has helped us before."

Alone in the library after the door had closed, Annica
stood and crossed to a window. In the side courtyard
Chauncy was talking to a disreputable-looking man. When
the stranger turned to say something to the valet, Annica
heart gave a painful flutter. Scar-face—Mr. X, the foreign
looking man who had met Wilkes when she had followed
him—was entreating Chauncy earnestly, using broad ges
tures and an angry tone. She could not hear the exact word
through the glass panes, but she deduced the accent to b
Arabic. Mr. X was linked to Clarendon Place! Was *Chaunc*
in league with Morgan and Wilkes?

Curiosity drove her to Tristan's desk. The narrow middl
drawer was locked as always. This time, with the weight o
so much evidence behind her, she did not even hesitate. Sh
seized her husband's letter opener and forced it into the gap
She did not have time for finesse, so she picked and prie
until the lock gave with a sharp crack and a splintering o
wood. Auberville would be very angry when he saw th
damage she had done.

She rummaged through the contents of the drawe
quickly. When she found every note she had ever writte
him tied together with a red ribbon, she thought she coul
feel her heart breaking. Would he feel betrayed when h
discovered that she had snooped where she had no business
Turning back to her search, she found a sterling pen, a bo
of nibs, ink, sealing wax and ribbon, a seal with the Au
berville crest and a black-bordered folder bulging with of
ficial-looking papers.

She sank into his high-backed leather chair and opene

ie folder. His discharge papers from the Royal Navy. Some trange letters that made no sense at all—in code?—to, from nd about people named Omar, The Turk, Mustafa el-Daibul nd The Sheikh. And three lists: regimental, battalion and ompany. Allowing the rest to drop to the floor, she ran her nger down the shortest list.

They were all here! All of them! Taylor, Harris, Faringdale, Wilkes, Morgan, Chauncy and…Tristan Sinclair, ord Auberville! Ice formed around her heart.

Dear heavens! A case *could* be made that Tristan was the illain! The evidence was circumstantial, but it was no wonder that her friends had cautioned her. There he was—in lack and white—in villainous company. He had served in orthern Africa. He knew pashas and emirs. He had connections. He could inspire obedience from men. He was nown to be dangerous.

But murder? Could Tristan have murdered those women, nd Roger Wilkes, too? Could he have slit Harry Bouldin's hroat? And Constance's? Never.

Annica's sense of injustice became inflamed. She knew 'ristan—knew that he could not have done those things. ut the circumstances looked grim. His reputation, his secrecy… Someone, likely Morgan or Chauncy, was trying to nake it look as if Tristan was the villain by putting papers 1 his desk for the police to find! She folded the roster and ushed it into the bodice of her gown.

This, then, was what had engaged Tristan's attention ight and day—the effort to clear his name and find the true illain. Oh! If only he'd told her, trusted her, she could have elped him. Anxious to find any evidence in his favor, she egan to shuffle through the letters. Desperation made her lumsy, and she dropped the sheaf of papers. When she athered them from the floor, one name leaped off a page t her. Chauncy.

"Chauncy, bring me word of the time of our next meet-

ing. Sheikh…'' And it was dated scarcely a week ago. Sh
recognized the handwriting from the sample Constance ha
brought her. Geoffrey Morgan!

"Chauncy…'' she mused aloud, remembering Mary
comment about him being an old "freebooter.'' Then A
was the villain!

"Did you find what you are looking for?''

Annica's head snapped up to find the valet standing
the doorway, an angry stain creeping up his cheeks. Sh
dropped the papers into the drawer and closed it. Affectin
an air of confidence, she stood and faced the foe straig
on. "Yes. I did. Bring me tea, Chauncy. I must write
letter.''

"I am afraid I must escort you back to your room, m
lady.''

"Yes, of course. After I have written the letter.''

"If it please your ladyship, you may write the letter
your room. Now that you have seen those papers, I cann
allow you to leave. I will instruct Mary to bring your tea
your room.''

"I am going nowhere with you, Chauncy. Leave,'' sh
demanded in a steely voice, dipping her pen in the inkwel

"I deeply regret that I cannot do that, milady.''

Annica's heart raced. She had to escape this very minut
If she allowed him to take her back to her room, he wou.
dispose of her posthaste. No, she would not go quietly.

"Accustom yourself to the fact that I am going nowhe
with you, Mr. Chauncy. If you intend to remove me fro
here, you will need help. Go find it. I shall wait.'' Sh
glanced down at the sheet of paper. She only had a mome
to leave Tristan a warning. "Beware of Chauncy,'' sh
scrawled.

Across the room, the valet assumed an expression of dee
regret. "Perhaps you should know that I shall restrain yo
physically, if necessary.''

She had never been mishandled by a servant in her entire life. When Chauncy started for her, she was shocked, but she knew she was overmatched. She slipped her warning to Tristan under a corner of the blotter, snatched the pen tray from the desk and threw it at Chauncy's head, missing by inches. He came on without the slightest hesitation. She hurled the humidor next, then a leather-bound book from a small stack on the corner of the desk.

Nearer to panic than she cared to admit, Annica seized two more books from the stack and fired them in rapid succession. The second book met its target. Dazed, Chauncy staggered to his knees and rubbed a spot on his forehead. She used the opportunity to retrieve the letter opener and slip around him toward the door.

"Your ladyship!" The valet reached one hand out as if to grab hold of her skirts.

"Lay one hand on me, Chauncy, *just one,* and I will see you on the gallows! God help me if I won't!" she bluffed.

She threw the library doors open and sprinted for the front door. Her luck held; the foyer was empty.

Heart pounding, she lifted her skirts and ran for all she was worth. The wind in her face was like a rude slap, reminding her that she might never be able to return.

"Silence!" Tristan roared. Everyone was talking at once. He rubbed his temples and winced. The worst had happened. Annica had escaped. And now he could not keep her safe.

When the library grew still enough to hear dust settle, he gestured to his valet. "One at a time. Chauncy, you first."

The man peered balefully from behind the slab of raw meat covering his blackened eye. "She was going through your desk, milord. I did not know what she had seen, so I told her I would have to accompany her to her room. Most regretfully, milord, I went to take her arm, but she flew into

a rage and began to throw things. I was hit, and she ran pa
me.''

"Mary?" Tristan asked.

"I am sorry, m'lord. I do not know a thing about this."

Hodgeson was more agitated than Tristan had ever see
him. He took pity on the man. "Anything to add, Hodge
son?"

The aging servant shifted his weight from side to side
wringing his hands. "Milord, Lady Annica is not a coward
I have never seen her shy away from a fight. Indeed, th
Sayles family used to have some famous rows, and my lad
Annica was always in the middle of it, holding her own
She was raised on strife and contention. One might say sh
learned to thrive upon it."

"Have you any notion why she fled, Hodgeson?"

"Begging your lordship's pardon, but milady woul
never suffer oppression. 'Tis a principle with her. I wante
to warn you last night, but you, ah…you were in a bit of
temper. I very much feared that something like this woul
happen."

Tristan fought to hide his impatience. "Yes, well, wher
do you think she went?"

"Home, milord?"

"You mean to the Sayles home? 'Tis worth checking,
suppose. Thank you, Hodgeson. If you have any more ideas
do not hesitate to tell me. You may go now."

Hodgeson, Chauncy and Mary left together, clearly re
lieved to escape the ominous atmosphere in the library.

Tristan turned his attention to the chaos around him. Hi
first order of business was to find Annica. To that end, h
checked the file that Annica had "liberated" from hi
drawer and put back with scarcely a sheet out of place. H
riffled through the papers, to see if there was a clue as t
what she'd been seeking. All the documents seemed to b
in order, and nothing appeared to be absent. On second in

pection, he discovered that his company roster was missing. What possible interest could she have in a list of those he had served with in the Mediterranean? He scanned the names and paused. Bloody hell! Why hadn't he seen it before?

On his way to the door, his foot caught the edge of *Mansfield Park*. When he bent to retrieve it, a scrap of paper fell to the floor. He put the book aside and unfolded the note.

"Stop hiding behind your hirelings. I'll kill them all just like I killed this one. Show yourself, coward, or escape while you can." Dark, rust-colored blotches stained the paper.

What the hell was going on? He fanned the pages of the book to see if any explanation would fall out. None. Anxiety made his every nerve jangle.

Whose blood was on this note? Not Constance's—the stains were nearly black with age. How had Annica come into possession of such a communication? Surely it could not have been intended for her.

Or had it? Had her prying into the disappearance of a maid and the death of her friend drawn her into the white slavery scheme by their association with Wilkes? Damnation! Tristan had confiscated her only defense—her little pocket pistol. His heart grew cold at the thought.

The edge of a folded sheet of paper peeked from beneath his blotter. He slid it out and read the hurried script—Annica's handwriting! What was she thinking?

Fear, once so foreign and now so familiar, replaced anger and hurt. The possibility that his wife might be yet another casualty of the traitor known as "The Turk" made his pulse race.

He went to a locked cupboard hidden behind one bookshelf and removed a pair of matched pocket pistols. After checking to make certain they were loaded, he slipped them in his coat pockets. His coach was still waiting.

If Annica had become entangled in this miserable affa[i]r it would be his fault, and he would never forgive himsel[f.]

Dressed in the new trousers the modiste had provide[d,] Annica sat on a short stool in Marie's tiny office at her sh[op] off Piccadilly, watching Francis Renquist pace in circle[s.] She wished she could concentrate on his account of follow-ing the man who had frightened Wilkes the previous nig[ht,] but her mind kept wandering back to Tristan. Had he di[s]-covered her note yet? Would Chauncy try to silence hi[m] too?

"When I got a good look at him, Lady Annica, I realize[d] I'd never seen him before. He made some interesting sto[ps] before he got onto me. A bawdy house, another taver[n,] White's. He wasn't wandering, he was looking for someon[e.] I lost him at the Surrey docks," Renquist was saying.

"Where?" she asked, coming back to the conversatio[n.] "A bawdy house? Was it Naughty Alice's?"

Renquist nodded.

"And White's? The gentlemen's club?"

Renquist nodded again. "I saw him through the windo[w] having a word with another man. When he left he heade[d] for the docks. He was hell-bent-for-leather by the time w[e] crossed the Thames."

"Is that where you lost him?"

"The fog was thick on the wharves. I wish I'd have bee[n] able to stay with him. He might have led us to where the[y] hold the women. I could not pick up his track. It was as [if] he'd turned to smoke." Renquist sat across from her an[d] met her eyes. "I came back to the Bear and Bull. I hope[d] you had waited for me there. I do not like the idea of yo[u] being on the streets alone, even dressed as a man. Tho[se] clothes cannot stand up under scrutiny. This has to sto[p,] Lady Annica."

Annica rested her elbows on her knees and buried h[er]

ce in her hands. "I know. Auberville discovered me. He
ok me home and forbade me to leave the house."

"Yet he relented."

"He never relents. I fled," she admitted. Several hot tears
illed over her lower lashes. She was closer to despair than
e'd ever been.

Renquist removed a clean hankie from his vest pocket
d placed it in her outstretched hand. She blotted her eyes
d blew her nose.

"Why did you leave?" he asked.

"Honor requires me to avenge the deaths of Mr. Bouldin
d Constance, and to put an end to the white slavery plot.
orst of all, Mr. Renquist, I fear Tristan has something to
 with this whole affair. He is connected in some way."

Renquist squatted by Annica's stool and took her hands
 his. Somewhere in their common adversity, a line had
en crossed and they found themselves on equal footing.
f I find out…I need to know if there are things you'd
ther not know."

Annica fought to focus through her tears. She and Au-
rville had married so quickly that there was still so much
e did not know about him. Could he be capable of such
rfidy? She knew he was hiding something, but what?

Mr. Renquist's implication frightened her. "You suspect
at Tristan is behind all this. I am painfully aware that the
idence points to him, but there may be another explana-
n, and—"

"Take care, m'lady. That's all I'm saying."

Chapter Twenty-One

The silence in the Crawford library dragged out as the pa ties regarded each other with suspicion. Tristan had track them there after inquiries at Grace's home revealed that t ladies were meeting for the rout there. He did not blink he studied Charity, Grace, and Sarah by turns.

Sarah was the first to speak. "So, it was you who se for us, Lord Auberville. But why?"

"Did you think it was Annica summoning you?" I noted the subtle glances each of the women passed to t others. Such a veiled maneuver would have been envied conference rooms the world over. But he did not have tir for subtlety. "Shall we jump right to the point? Which you is hiding Annica?"

All three women blinked in quickly masked surprise his opening gambit. He could tell that they hadn't expect him to be so direct.

Charity lifted her chin a fraction of an inch, as if to s that she was ready to do battle. "I do not know where s is at the moment, Auberville. I saw her last this afterno at Clarendon Place."

"Did she say anything of her plans?"

"Only that she intended to get to the bottom of the m

ers of Mr. Bouldin, Constance and Mr. Wilkes," Grace
admitted.

Tristan's mind reeled. Annica could not have the faintest
notion of the danger she was in. And who was Mr. Bouldin?
One thing at a time. "Why?"

Grace glanced at the other women before lifting one
shoulder in an elegant shrug. "My dear man…" She gave
him a sad smile. "We—the Wednesday League—have often
noted how rarely women obtain justice when they wait for
a man to acquire it for them."

Justice. There was that word again. "So you blithely took
on a murder investigation?" Tristan's left eye began to
twitch just above his scar.

"Yes," Grace answered simply.

"Did you stop to consider—" He choked.

"The risks?" Grace finished. "Yes. But then Constance
was murdered and we could not stop."

Sarah left her chair and went to stand behind the sofa
where Grace and Charity were seated. The ladies bent their
heads together in a quick, whispered consultation. Apparently they reached an agreement, appointing Grace spokes-
woman.

"Roger Wilkes was our primary suspect for the murders
of Constance and Mr. Bouldin, but we concluded that, since
Wilkes was murdered in the same manner, the real culprit
must have murdered them all."

"And who, pray tell, is Mr. Bouldin?" Tristan asked, his
head beginning to throb.

Grace bit her lip and looked disconcerted by having said
more than she intended.

Tristan knew he'd have to disclose a little information to
gain their trust. He deeply regretted not having done so with
his wife when she had questioned him in the dormer room.
No government secrets were worth Annica's safety—risk of
betrayal be damned! "The man behind this caused the fail-

ure of an important mission in northern Africa several yea
ago. I suspect he has kidnapped and murdered over thre
dozen women, and now, it would appear, he means to k
my wife. If you will not help me, I'd advise you to stay o
of my way. You can only delay me in finding Annica, ar
under the circumstances, a delay could be fatal." He let tl
thought take root.

Grace turned to him and sighed. "Auberville, I hav
vouched for your character. We really have no choice b
to trust you. Annica's life is at stake and there is no tin
to waste. But first I must have your assurance that what v
are about to tell you will never leave this room."

"You know me to be discreet, Grace. Do you need mo
reassurance than your own experience?"

She took a deep breath, looking for all the world lil
someone about to plunge into murky depths. "Mr. Bould
was a Bow Street Runner. He did our more unpleasant tasl
for us. When we put him onto Roger Wilkes, he was mu
dered."

Tristan let that pass for now. He took the crude note fro
his vest pocket and held it up for the ladies to see. "Wou
this have anything to do with Mr. Bouldin's death?"

"It was pinned to his jacket," Charity admitted.

Auberville raked his fingers through his hair. He cou
scarcely believe that these women had become involved
an international incident without realizing it. "Then tl
message was meant for your group. How long ago w
that?"

"Three or four weeks ago. I recall that it was a good te
days to two weeks before your marriage," Sarah said.

He had a quick flash of Annica hurrying down a lane
Whitefriars, of her being accosted by a footpad and near
killed. Coincidence? And before that, the coaching accider
and the riot in St. James's Street... He had thought the
was something odd in the way Annica had been singled o

by the ruffians. Good Lord! His wife had been stalked for nearly two months! "How long did Mr. Bouldin work for your group?"

Sarah frowned. "Before I joined. Three or four years, Grace?" she asked, turning to the older woman.

Grace threw up her hands in defeat. "Three."

"Three *years?*"

Charity cringed. "Before that, we managed on our own."

"Before that?" What had this group of demure Regency ladies been doing? Tristan sank into Henry Crawford's over-tuffed chair. He'd better know it all. "You ladies exact revenge?"

"*Justice,*" Sarah corrected him. "We obtain justice for wrongs done women."

Charity shrugged. "I suppose there is an element of revenge in there, too. Annica always says that revenge is a sort of wild justice. Actually, I believe Francis Bacon said it first."

Tristan rubbed his right temple to ease the nagging headache. "May I assume, then, that your quest for vengeance—pardon me, *justice*—on behalf of Lady Sarah led you to Roger Wilkes and his friends?"

"We discovered Roger Wilkes's identity last. We had already disposed of Taylor, Harris and Farmingdale."

Another sharp pain pierced Tristan's left temple. "I will not take umbrage to what has gone before, ladies, but I'd like to know why your group did not come to me when there were three dead bodies strewn about."

"The issue became clouded when women began disappearing. Not to put too fine a point upon it, Auberville, but you are a man," Sarah informed him. "We've never felt a man would sanction, let alone understand, our activities, and most of our cases required a sensitivity to female concerns. Aside from that, when our investigation led us in a different direction, it began to appear as if…"

"As if I might be the villain?" he asked.

Sarah had the good grace to blush. "Annica swore it wa not possible, that she could not love you were you capabl of such things, but we…the rest of us, that is, thought th evidence rather compelling. Especially when you vouche for Wilkes the night of Constance's murder."

His mind seized on one thing only. Annica had told he friends that she loved him. Her whispered admission of lov the night of Constance's murder had been sincere, and nc a reaction to the pleasure he'd given her!

"Lord Auberville?" Sarah Hunter asked.

He focused on the group again, knowing he'd have to pu their suspicions to rest if he was to gain the information h would need to save his wife. "I am not your enemy Through my affiliation with the Royal Navy and because c the connections I made in the Foreign Office, I was aske to initiate an investigation into the disappearances of wome in a white slavery scheme. That must be when our path crossed."

"Ah. The Foreign Office! That would explain the cor nection." Sarah nodded. "We thought you were connecte through the Royal Navy, in league with the other villains.'

"What a great relief." Charity heaved a huge sigl "Does 'Nica know you are working for the Foreign O fice?"

Yet another cause for regret! "I do not believe I hav told her," he admitted. "Do you have any idea where sh might be?"

Sarah cleared her throat. "She was going to Madame Ma rie's to meet Mr. Renquist. After that, she was going to se a fallen sister named Naughty Alice. 'Twas in her brothel– his, actually—that Farmingdale's business venture came t light."

So *that* was how Annica knew the bawdy house. "Wh is Renquist?" Tristan asked.

"Mr. Bouldin's partner. He is investigating—*gads!*" Sarah got to her feet and whirled toward the door. "He was supposed to follow you, but if the culprit is not you or Wilkes, milord, it is Geoffrey Morgan! Oh! I trusted him! I believed in him! Someone fetch me a pistol!"

Tristan seized her arm and turned her back around. "Softly, Lady Sarah. Allow me to handle this. Do not discuss this with anyone. *Anyone.* Send to me if you have news of any sort. And swear you will not take matters into your own hands."

"We cannot do that, Lord Auberville," Charity said. "You cannot interfere with the business of the Wednesday League."

"And you must not interfere with the business of His Majesty's Foreign Office," Tristan parried. "If you will not give me your word, I will be forced to have you detained at Newgate for treason."

Charity and Grace looked subdued, but Sarah came forward, a challenge in her soft violet eyes. "We shall give you twenty-four hours, Auberville. If Annica has not contacted one of us by then, we shall be forced to take matters into our own hands—treason be damned."

Tristan was right. Francis Renquist was right. She should not be in this part of town alone. Night had fallen and, even though she was now safely enclosed in the kitchen of the bawdy house, she could not help the shiver of misgiving that traveled up her spine and raised gooseflesh on her arms. Why did she have such a silly feeling now, when none of her midnight forays had inspired such deep foreboding?

The door from the corridor swung open and Naughty Alice entered. She did not recognize Annica at once, and sauntered toward where she stood by the fire. "'Ere now, gent. 'Tain't no time to be shy. If ye come to see me, then come see me." She crooked one finger at Annica and began to unfasten her low chemise, a flirtatious smile hovering on her lips.

Annica held up her hand. She swept her hat off and le her hair fall down her back. "I could not wait for you to come to me. I had to see you."

Alice's expression was one of horror when she recognized Annica. She glanced over her shoulder toward the corridor "Get outta here, milady!"

Annica shook her head. "Not until you tell me all you know. I cannot wait any longer, Alice. Roger Wilkes wa: murdered last night."

"I know that, milady! So why have ye come abroad' Have ye no sense at all?"

"The matter is urgent, Alice. It warrants such a risk. must have answers tonight. Did you find the names I need?'

"Get outta here! I ain't got time for this now."

"A moment ago you had time to attend a man." Annic: reached into her jacket pocket and came up with a gol sovereign. She held it out to the bawd. "Pretend I am man. You must allot at least a quarter of an hour for each client. I have ten minutes more."

"Can ye not see I'm tryin' to save ye grief? Do not ques tion me, milady. There's not time for it. Get ye gone be fore—"

"Alice?" a masculine voice called. "Where the hell are you, woman?"

An uneasy shiver ran up her spine at the sound of tha voice, but she had no time to puzzle it when Alice grasped her by her coat sleeve and dragged her to the kitchen door

Alice turned to the corridor, panic etched deeply on he face. "Go! For the love of God, *go!*"

"I'll wait—" she began, incredulous at Alice's actions.

"Get out of here. Run! Go somewhere safe! Hurry."

"But—"

"Bad pennies have a way of turnin' up!" Alice gave her firm push with those words.

Annica found herself standing outside while she was still ying to frame a reply. The door closed in her face with a olid thump. Angry at the peremptory dismissal, she was oised to return when she realized that Alice was terrified, ot annoyed.

Annica gathered her hair to the top of her head and pulled er hat on. Fog swirled around her as she entered the street, nd she felt in her pocket for the letter opener she'd taken om Tristan's desk. She tightened her fingers around the ndle, feeling better as her footsteps echoed on the cobestones.

She thought she heard a scuff and scratch behind her, and er heartbeat quickened. She was being silly.

When she came to a cross street, she stepped to the side nd pressed her back to a brick wall, waiting to see if anye was following. Several minutes—more like a lifetime Annica—passed. Nothing. She heaved a sigh of relief. aughty Alice's fancies had made more of an impression her than she'd suspected. She began walking again, headg for the safety of Madame Marie's.

The sound of a boot scrape behind her came too late to ve her from anything but the quick realization that she as in deep trouble. Iron-hard arms closed around her chest, ueezing the breath from her lungs. A dark laugh expelled ul breath across her neck just before a sack was dropped er her head. She fought, but her assailant was ready. ghts exploded inside her brain, and she had one last moent of rational thought before everything went dark.

I'm sorry, Tristan.

Armed with the information from the Wednesday League, ristan laid a trap for Francis Renquist. Since the Bow

Street Runner was supposed to be following him, that w;
an easy task. Tristan led the chase, followed by Renqui;
who was in turn followed by The Sheikh. Thus Renqui
became both predator and prey. Once nabbed, he could (
naught but confess.

Tristan pushed the man into his waiting coach and sh
the door. "Recent events have run the ladies afoul of n
investigation into a white slavery ring. They have decide
to trust me. I suggest you do the same."

"That would depend upon her ladyship, Auberville
Francis Renquist lifted his chin and fixed Tristan with ;
unreadable expression, making it clear that his loyalty l;
with Annica.

"My wife can tell you nothing, Renquist. She is missin
No one has heard from her since she questioned a bawd I
the name of Naughty Alice. Do you begin to understand n
urgency?"

The runner nodded. "You know who's behind th
then?"

A dark, frightening fury rose from somewhere deep
Tristan's gut—an anger he hadn't felt since Tunis. "We'
suspected for nearly a month, but we cannot locate the cur

"Who is it, and where is he?" The runner looked rea
to do battle.

"Richard Farmingdale. As to where—God only know
Each time Wilkes looked to be leading us to him, someo
got in the way—you, Annica…"

"'Twas you who knocked me unconscious?" Renqu
asked.

"That was our first hint that others were investigating t
missing women," Tristan admitted. "We never suspect
Annica's group had become involved in the white slave
plot."

"You know everything," Renquist sighed. He looked
most relieved.

"I pray that is the case," Tristan said. "Except for one
ing—do you know where to find my wife?"

"If she has not been seen since she met Alice, I'd con-
lude as you have—the bastard's got her. And that being
e case, she is at the Surrey docks."

Cold seeped into Annica from the rough floor beneath her
heek. A tremendous pain throbbed in the back of her head.
otal darkness enveloped her. Slowly, painfully, she pushed
erself into a sitting position and willed her hand upward,
) find a large knot and dried blood at the base of her skull.
he winced and let her hand drop.

She remained very still for a few moments, both to quell
e aching in her head and to gain her bearings. Silence
dicated night. Lapping sounds invaded her consciousness,
llowed by a slight rocking. She was aboard a ship. Still-
ess after the gentle rocking meant the ship was moored or
ocked. Voices grew louder, as if coming nearer. A door
pened and closed.

She crawled on her hands and knees toward the thin line
f light, praying she would not bump into anything or put
er hand in something vile. A rough voice, that of a man
nnica assumed to be the captain, was explaining a sailing
chedule.

"We have clearance. I sent the night watch to fetch the
st of the crew. We will leave when they've returned. We'll
ake Tunis in record time."

Tunis? *Tunis!* The city where Tristan had served in the
iplomatic Corps?

"Damn delays. The crew should have been on board,
aptain Abrams. And sending the night watch to collect
em means that no one is standing guard. If there's a prob-
m, el-Daibul will have your hide."

Annica caught her breath. She recognized that voice! It
elonged to the man who had talked to Wilkes in the garden.

And the name el-Daibul was familiar, too—one of thos
contained in Tristan's papers. She pressed her cheek to th
floor and squinted through the crack at the bottom of th
door. The wood panel was too thick and the gap too narro
to afford more than a glimpse of three pairs of shoes in th
other room.

"I should never have got involved in this," the captai
said. "If I did not need the money to make the payment
you could go whistle for a ship." Disgust was thick in h
voice.

"There are other captains, Abrams. I'll just look in c
Auberville's wife."

With a sigh, Abrams said, "The woman—that's wh
worries me. Someone is bound to come looking for her. W
must leave tonight. I'm not spending the rest of my life :
Newgate just because you want to put this woman out c
the way."

Annica shuddered. If the plan was to "put her out of th
way," how did they propose to do that?

"I'd as soon kill her for all the grief she's caused me,
the familiar voice was saying. "But Mustafa el-Daib
wants her first. He always coveted what Auberville had."

Auberville. Annica's heart twisted. Just hearing his nam
brought a lump to her throat. Lord! Had it been worth i
Was justice more important than her life? More importa
than her marriage and her husband's trust?

She hugged herself against the sudden cold. Nause
churned in her belly and her head felt as if it would explo
with pain. She could not credit the treachery and betray
of these acts to the most likely suspects. Geoffrey Morga
had won her friendship when all he'd asked in payment f
a debt was the benefit of a doubt, and the voice in the garde
had not been his. Roger Wilkes was not intelligent enoug
to conceive of, let alone execute, such a scheme. Mr. X wa
clearly no more than a messenger. Chauncy's demeanor i

licated that he was too accustomed to obeying orders to be comfortable giving them. Who, then, could be behind this treachery? Dear Lord—she, who was seldom wrong, had been nothing *but* wrong since this whole affair began!

Metal scraped as a bar was slid back, and the wedge of light exploded and blinded her. Annica's heart beat faster and her mouth went dry. The only man she could think of who was capable of such villainy was…surely not!

"Farmingdale?" She blinked, trying to adjust her eyes to the harsh lantern light. But she had seen him board a ship bound for Jamaica with her very own eyes!

"Surprised, Lady Annica?" he asked, a nasty grin splitting his face. "Did you really think you had seen the last of me?"

Annica rubbed the back of her head, glad that she'd had a chance to collect herself before he opened the door. This was what Naughty Alice had meant about "bad pennies" turning up. "Not really, Mr. Farmingdale!"

"I went over the side before we left the Thames. Had unfinished business, you see. There was still money to be made. Slaving pays good wages, Lady Annica. I'm surprised Auberville didn't explain that to you."

"I cannot believe this," she muttered.

"Loose ends, Lady Annica, loose ends. Let this be a lesson to you. Never leave loose ends." Farmingdale shook his head. "You've been deuced hard to kill, but I've got you this time."

"So you were behind my accidents? What a pity you are such a blunderer," she taunted.

"'Twasn't my fault. Auberville had developed an instinct where you are concerned. But I've got you now, Lady Annica. You won't escape this time."

"I hope you have been very careful. Auberville will be coming for me soon."

Farmingdale laughed, a hollow sound. "You'd like to

think so, wouldn't you? But you are out of luck, Lady Ruin Auberville will not find you.''

"Will he not?" she asked.

"We'll be underway within two hours, and you shall far no better in my hands than I did in yours. The wheel ha turned, milady, and now I'm on top."

"The top of a dung heap is not very high, Mr. Farming dale,'' she said, without much hope that he would appreciat her wit. She was right. He delivered a stinging blow to he left cheek, sending her staggering against the bulkhead.

"You are mad to taunt me,'' he snarled. "Ah, but tha only makes my victory sweeter. You shall see how varie and amusing my tastes are, my dear. By the time we arrive you may even be relieved to meet Mustafa el-Daibul. H knows how to treat a woman—you may depend upon that.'

A lump formed in Annica's throat. She could only gues what Richard Farmingdale was threatening, and she'd rathe jump overboard. "Is Mustafa el-Daibul The Turk?" sh asked, knowing that was the name of the ringleader.

Farmingdale laughed. "Not bloody likely, Lady Annica El-Daibul is not half clever enough to pull this off. But am amazed that you have not figured it out. Auberville i The Turk, you little twit! He wanted you removed. Aye, h just handed you over like so much dirty wash."

Annica lifted her chin proudly. "Do not even try to pas that one off, Farmingdale. Tristan would never have dea ings with the likes of you and Wilkes."

"His fine sensibilities will be of no use to you now, Lad Annica." Farmingdale sneered. "You are mine now, and will have you well broke in before we arrive in Tunis. E Daibul will revel in adding to your education. Men like hi expect their doxies to do tricks. I shall like seeing *you* d tricks, Lady Auberville."

Her skin crawled as Farmingdale reached out to touch

ock of her hair. Her throat closed and she gagged at the hought of him doing the things Tristan had done.

She slapped at his hand and shrank away in revulsion, needing to hold on just a little longer. Tristan would be earching for her. She knew that with absolute certainty.

"Accustom yourself to the notion that I am now your master. Not Auberville," Farmingdale was saying, his breath foul on her cheek. "Look up. See who is in charge now."

Annica lifted her head in a slow arc. When her gaze met his, he stepped back a pace as she froze him with a glare. She doubted this ploy would work once they were under sail. Farmingdale had some very wicked things planned. Unwavering, unblinking, she followed his retreat from the room with a stone-cold glare, groping in her pocket for Tristan's letter opener. Gone! The knowledge that Farmingdale had touched her, searched her while she was unconscious, threatened her sanity.

When the door closed, she pounded her wadded blanket with her doubled fists. The voices in the other room faded and a door closed somewhere. A cold calm begin to fill her. She shook her head and dashed the tears away from her cheeks with the back of her hand. A long black hairpin slipped from her hair and fell to the floor with a muffled *ing*. She stared at it in the dim light filtering beneath the door for a long minute before picking it up and crawling oward the locked door.

"'Tis you! You are The Turk! I know you are. You won't defeat me. You won't!"

Chapter Twenty-Two

Renquist joined the hushed group behind a warehouse "The dock master gave clearance for two ships to sail wit the tide. The *Mary Jane* and the *Dolphin*. He vouches fo the captain of the *Mary Jane*, but he knows little of th *Dolphin*," he whispered.

Tristan released the neck of a longshoreman and allowe him to slip to his knees.

"I swear I never seen 'er, sir. I only seen one bloke car ryin' a drunk over 'is shoulder. I swear before God!" th man babbled while he rubbed his neck.

"Where?" Tristan asked.

"Down toward the end." The man scrambled to his fee and backed away.

"What ship did he belong to?"

"I never seen 'im before." The sailor glanced right an left, ready to bolt.

Renquist threw him a coin. "Keep your mouth shut, mar Take my advice and lose yourself until tomorrow. A pir will ease that raw throat."

Tristan turned to fasten his gaze on The Sheikh and al lowed himself a grim smile when his friend recoiled. Th darkness was controlling him again—the bleakness, th

oneness. "I'll lay odds the drunk was Annica, uncon-
ious. So, Renquist, what are the captains' names?"

"The *Mary Jane* is captained by Henry Tilman. The *Dol-
.in*'s captain is Frederick Abrams."

The Sheikh closed his eyes and muttered under his breath.
Christ…Freddie."

Tristan pondered for a moment. "Abrams was in our unit.
ere's a link. Where else would The Turk go but to an old
mrade? I'll dispatch a messenger to Kilgrew, then catch
 to you." His voice was tightly controlled. "Stall Abrams.
o not alarm him, but do not let the *Dolphin* sail. Offer
m immunity. Find out if Farmingdale is aboard. If all else
ils, shoot him."

The Sheikh nodded and hurried north on the pier, Ron
ist not far behind.

Clink, click…the tumblers fell into place. Annica with-
ew her hairpin and gave the knob a cautious twist. It
oved! She closed her eyes for a second and said a silent
ayer, thanking God and asking for strength.

The smallest push of her index finger swung the door
tward on its hinges. The adjoining cabin was empty, and
c tiptoed to the far doorway to give the knob an experi-
ental turn. Unlocked.

The companionway, too, was dark and empty. A faint
ght filtered downward from the hatch. Feathery gray ten-
ils drifted across the opening to the main deck. Fog! She
ayed it was very thick.

She crept down the narrow passageway and climbed the
ep ladderlike steps to the deck. Ahead, just thirty feet to
r left, a gangplank disappeared over the edge to a dock
low.

The rise and fall of masculine voices from the quarter-
ck—one in particular—came clearly through the fog. She
ew the voice this time. Geoffrey Morgan.

Her stomach twisted. Matters just kept growing worse
this quagmire of treachery and deceit. She turned her co
collar up and crept from the shelter of the overhangin
hatchway to hide behind the mainmast on her way to th
gangway.

"...surprised to find you in these circumstance
Abrams," Morgan was saying.

"I needed the money, Geoff."

Annica peeked around the mast to see Morgan nod. "A
berville is rabid. I would not want to be the one to cro
him. Would you, Abrams?"

"Jesus, no! His wife is safe enough, Morgan. I wor
vouch for her once we're underway. Farmingdale has it
for her."

Annica frowned. Tristan? Involved with the captain? N
This was wrong. Tristan had nothing to do with this schem

Morgan spoke again, a firm, almost lethal tone in h
voice. "Where is Farmingdale, Abrams?"

"He said he had some last minute scores to settle. H
should be back momentarily."

Sarah! He is going to hurt Sarah. Annica thought
panic. *He is going to get even with her just as he inten
to get even with me!*

She slipped to her knees and crawled behind a row
barrels standing between her and freedom. The conversati
was lost as she made her way ever closer to the gangwa
There would have to be a diversion if she was going to ma
her escape.

And there, mounting the gangway in answer to her u
spoken prayer, was Tristan, exuding determination, streng
and purpose. He did not call for permission to board, b
took the deck as if it belonged to him. His attention w
focused on the group on the quarterdeck, and their attenti
was on him.

Abrams froze in place. If ever she had seen naked fear, e saw it now—etched clearly on the captain's face.

"Abrams," Tristan said in a voice cold enough to freeze icksilver, "where is my wife?"

"She's below, Lord Auberville." The captain rubbed his lms on his pant legs, the gesture betraying his nervous- ss.

"And where is that traitorous bastard, Farmingdale?"

"At your service!" a voice answered from the gangway. chard Farmingdale stepped aboard, a cocked pistol in his nd.

Annica's heart began to race. Her plans for escape dis- lved in an instant.

Mounting to the quarterdeck, Richard Farmingdale ined the barrel of the pistol on Tristan's heart. "Good of u to accommodate me, Auberville. I was afraid I'd have go looking for you. What good is revenge if no one ows you've got it?"

"Revenge, Farmingdale? What wrong have I done you? n I not the one with cause for revenge?"

"So, you know about the Algerian affair, eh? I thought u might be onto me." The man gave a high-pitched giggle d his finger on the trigger began to twitch. "But no, Au- rville. I had a profitable scheme going here—providing Daibul with a certain, er, valuable commodity. Then Lady nica got onto our little diversion with Sarah Hunter and k it up like one of her ridiculous causes. She stumbled o my scheme."

"Let her go, Farmingdale. You can accomplish nothing holding her." Tristan brought up both his hands in a sture of reconciliation. "If you release her, I may let you e."

Farmingdale's grip on the pistol tightened. "Good try, berville. But I promised her to el-Daibul. That will even score for her interference. Punish you, too."

Annica saw Geoffrey Morgan take a cautious step clos
to Farmingdale. Was he going to join him, or attack? In t
second of time that Farmingdale's attention shifted, Trist
removed a pistol from his waistband and thumbed the ha
mer back. Geoffrey Morgan, too, reached for something
his waistband.

Fear and urgency surged from her chest in the form of
cry when Farmingdale's pistol came back around in li
with Tristan's heart. "Tristan! Look out!"

"Annica!" He turned toward the sound of her voice.

Her heart skipped a beat. "Here," she called.

Farmingdale whirled in her direction and squeezed t
trigger, and Tristan lunged for him.

The sound of a shot reverberated in the heavy air. H
step faltered; her feet seemed to be mired in quicksand. A
other shot followed fast on the first, then a third, and s
she could not move. A ball whizzed past her right ear.

Tristan leaped from the quarterdeck, a smoking pistol
his right hand. Another shot rang out, but he didn't lo
back or break stride on his way to her. Weak with reli
she sank to her knees on the deck. She slumped forward
rest her forehead on the wooden planking.

"No!" Tristan howled, and a moment later he was kne
ing beside her, gripping her shoulders and lifting her up
look into her eyes. His hands slipped up and down her ar
as if to reassure himself that she was all in one piece "N
God, Annica!" he muttered. "I thought you'd been sh
How could I ever have lived without you...."

She gazed up into his eyes. They were filled with pa
and tenderness as his finger traced the bruise on her chec
"Tristan..." was all she could manage to whisper. S
could not catch her breath from wanting him so.

His expression changed with the sound of her voice. H
features took on the soft, vulnerable look of a much young
man. The scar beneath his left eye all but disappeared in t

ow smile that curved his lips—lips that bent to cherish
rs.

She nearly swooned with the sweetness of it. She whis-
red his name against his lips, and he groaned. His hold
ghtened around her so that she could scarcely breathe. The
eling was so exquisitely intimate that tears came to her
es.

"Annica," he moaned, and with that single word she
arveled that the Wednesday League could ever have
ought him guilty.

The pounding of running feet on the wharf, coupled with
outing voices growing nearer, penetrated her confusion.
constable's whistle sounded a shrill alarm. Tristan stood
d dragged her up with him.

"Go, Annica! Run! A coach is waiting behind the ware-
use. Don't look back!"

"Come with me," she begged.

"Damn it, Annica! I cannot protect your reputation if you
not go! Trust me!"

Trust him? Yes—with her whole heart and soul. With
erything she was or ever would be.

Leave him? *Never! Oh, never!*

Looking down at Richard Farmingdale, Tristan felt
guely cheated. Never mind that death had not been easy
painless. Farmingdale should have been drawn and quar-
ed—the old punishment for treason. He should have an-
ered individually for each man and woman whose death
had caused. It was little enough comfort to note the two
gged holes oozing dark blood and stained with gunpow-
r. One hole, considerably lower than the other, was es-
cially satisfying. Had Farmingdale had the colossal bad
ck to survive, he'd never have raped another woman. He
s no longer equipped for the job.

Annica had been right, Tristan realized. Some crimes re-

quired justice. When the courts failed and the cause w
grave enough, those with courage must accept the challeng
Revenge? Justice? Did it matter what it was named?

He turned to Geoffrey Morgan, known in some circles
The Sheikh. "Good shot, Geoff. My aim was just a lit
off. Thanks for correcting the error."

"My pleasure," the man said.

"Somehow, it doesn't seem enough."

"For Constance?"

"And Sarah, and the Algerian fiasco."

"A trial could have been a very messy thing," Gec
mused.

"Embarrassing for the women and their families," Tr
tan agreed, "not to mention dredging up the Algerian aff
again."

"Kilgrew could never have allowed that to come out
Geoff nodded. "Better this way, really." Prodding at Fa
mingdale's inert body with the toe of his boot, he aske
"What next?"

Tristan glanced over his shoulder toward the figure of I
wife, small and inconspicuous, sitting on a wooden cra
The workman's cap was pulled low over her face and t
youth's clothes concealed her womanly curves. In the ga
ering fog and darkness of night, he prayed she would
unnoticed.

Renquist and Lord Kilgrew were on the wharf, huddl
with a group of officials in a hushed conference. "Looks
if Kilgrew is about to wrap this up with his usual dispat
All will return to ordinary in no time," he said.

"I yearn to be ordinary, Auberville," Geoff sighed. "I
you really think it's possible?"

Tristan grinned. "Not for you, Geoff. But you could p
tend."

"I wouldn't be so smug, Auberville." Morgan inclin

head in Annica's direction. "What with Lady Annica in
ur life, yours isn't likely to approach 'ordinary' again."

Lord Kilgrew joined them and squatted by Farmingdale's
dy. He shook his head when he saw the nature of the fatal
unds, but did not question them. He felt for a pulse, bent
head to Farmingdale's chest to listen for a heartbeat, then
ttled back on his haunches to look up at them.

"Good work," he said. "Nice and tidy. Well, not tidy,
rhaps, but certainly thorough."

"Not thorough enough for my taste," Tristan said.
There's still el-Daibul."

"Nothing we can do about that, lad. Foreign country, and
that. We shall have to leave him to his own country-
en."

Geoff scoffed. "Do you see him punishing himself?"

"Mmm," Kilgrew murmured noncommittally. "Next
ne, perhaps." He glanced around. "All the villains appre
nded?"

Tristan made a subtle move to block Annica from the
an's view. "All of them, sir. The few that are left had no
ea what was happening. There'd be no point in prosecut-
g."

Kilgrew pondered this statement for a long moment. "I
all leave that to you, Auberville."

Geoff gestured widely at the empty wharf. "I think we've
en the last of them."

"Then we can safely close the matter?"

"Yes."

"Good…good," Kilgrew pronounced as he got to his
et. "The municipals will finish cleaning up here. Come to
office in the morning and we'll wrap up the reports."

Morgan took Kilgrew's arm and led him toward the gang-
y. "I'm relieved to have this over, sir. Hope you don't
ve anything else at the moment. I'd like leave to take care

of some personal business...." His voice became muffl
by distance and fog.

Alone on the deck, Tristan went to Annica's hiding pla
He helped her to her feet and regarded her somberly. "We
sprite. Now you know."

Wisps of night-dark hair escaped her cap and curl
around her neck and cheeks. Her face was flushed and t
bruise on her cheek made her look fragile, awakening b
need to protect her. Full, rose-pink lips trembled slight
indicating nervousness or uncertainty. "Yes," she wh
pered. "Now I know."

"And what will you do with that knowledge?"

"I could never utter a word, Tristan. That would be tre
son. Disloyalty, at the very least. I shudder to think of t
damage this could do if it ever became known."

She knew and she understood. She was loyal and stea
fast. And, even when he had ordered her to go, she h
stayed. She would never desert him—never leave him—a
he knew that now with unshakable certainty.

He took a step to close the distance between them, swe
ing with the desire to make love to her. He couldn't wait
draw her into his arms, feel her warmth and smell the cle
fresh scent of the forest on her, tell her how much he need
her. She stopped him with one dainty hand, palm agair
his chest.

"But you must know the worst. When we go home, y
will find that I...I violated your privacy. I pried your de
drawer open. I was desperate, you see. I had just se
Chauncy meet with a man I thought was connected to N
Wilkes. I thought Chauncy might be...but now he is ju
your valet and, well, suffice it to say that you have or
seen the worst of me. I promise there is a better side."

"Annica—"

"And the awful truth is that I cannot promise it will nev
happen again. If there is a worthy cause that needs a cha

on, I shall likely become a part of it. If there is a woman ho is wronged, or a law that is unjust—''

He laughed—a low chortle that started deep in his chest d bubbled upward in a release of all his long-repressed ars.

She hugged him fiercely. ''God help me, Tristan,'' she ept. ''I love you more than life, but I cannot change who am.''

''You *are* my life, Annica, and I would not want you if u were anyone else.''

He lifted her in his arms and carried her down the gang- ay. He'd wanted to make love to her in a coach since the y he'd carried her from the riot on St. James's Street. Oh, s. They would take the long way home

* * * * *

Princes...Princesses...
London Castles...New York Mansions...
To live the life of a royal!

In 2002, Harlequin Books lets you escape to a
world of royalty with these royally themed titles:

Temptation:
January 2002—*A Prince of a Guy* (#861)
February 2002—*A Noble Pursuit* (#865)

American Romance:
The Carradignes: American Royalty (Editorially linked series)
March 2002—*The Improperly Pregnant Princess* (#913)
April 2002—*The Unlawfully Wedded Princess* (#917)
May 2002—*The Simply Scandalous Princess* (#921)
November 2002—*The Inconveniently Engaged Prince* (#945)

Intrigue:
The Carradignes: A Royal Mystery (Editorially linked series)
June 2002—*The Duke's Covert Mission* (#666)

Chicago Confidential
September 2002—*Prince Under Cover* (#678)

The Crown Affair
October 2002—*Royal Target* (#682)
November 2002—*Royal Ransom* (#686)
December 2002—*Royal Pursuit* (#690)

Harlequin Romance:
June 2002—*His Majesty's Marriage* (#3703)
July 2002—*The Prince's Proposal* (#3709)

Harlequin Presents:
August 2002—*Society Weddings* (#2268)
September 2002—*The Prince's Pleasure* (#2274)

Duets:
September 2002—*Once Upon a Tiara/Henry Ever After* (#83)
October 2002—*Natalia's Story/Andrea's Story* (#85)

 **Celebrate a year of royalty with
Harlequin Books!**

Available at your favorite retail outlet.

HARLEQUIN®
Makes any time special ®

Visit us at www.eHarlequin.com

HSROY02

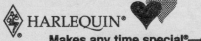

Escape to a land long ago and
far away when you read these thrilling
love stories from Harlequin Historicals

On Sale September 2002

A WARRIOR'S LADY
by Margaret Moore
(England, 1200s)

*A forced marriage between a brave knight and
beautiful heiress blossoms into true love!*

A ROGUE'S HEART
by Debra Lee Brown
(Scotland, 1213)

*Will a carefree rogue sweep a headstrong young lady
off her feet with his tempting business offer?*

On Sale October 2002

MY LADY'S HONOR
by Julia Justiss
(Regency England)

*In the game of disguise a resourceful young
woman falls in love with a dashing aristocrat!*

THE BLANCHLAND SECRET
by Nicola Cornick
(England, 1800s)

*Will a lady's companion risk her reputation by
accepting the help of a well-known rake?*

HH**H** **Harlequin Historicals®**
Historical Romantic Adventure!